THE WITCH'S KEY

BOOK 1

SARRA CANNON

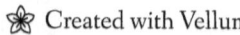

For our YouTube quarantine crew.
Thank you for being a part of this magical experience.
You brought my writing back to life.

THE ONLY LIFE I'D EVER KNOWN

They buried my parents on a Friday, and by Saturday afternoon, I was on my way to live with an uncle I barely knew in a town I'd never heard of before in my life.

Well, technically he was my great-uncle.

Martin Thorne.

I'd only met him a handful of times when he'd come to visit my dad on official "family business", as they liked to call it. Back then, the family business just meant that the grownups would close the door and speak in hushed tones.

In a way, I wished they'd never opened that door and told me what it was they really did for a living. I didn't want to know the truth anymore. Not after what happened to my parents.

And after they were gone, I definitely hadn't wanted to go live with a family member who'd been a Keeper for most of his life.

But where else could I have gone?

My Great-Uncle Martin was all I'd had left when my parents died.

To be honest, he'd always creeped me out. In the eyes of a young child, there was something terrifying about his tall, thin frame and pale, almost-translucent skin. He'd once put a bony hand on my arm, and I'd recoiled at the blue veins pulsing underneath the surface.

In my mind, I'd always thought of him as '*the dying man*', because there had always been something ancient about him.

But in the end, it was my parents who had died first, and it was Great-Uncle Martin who had saved my life.

I'd spent the entire summer with him now, and as the time passed and I had some distance between myself and the death of my parents, he'd become one of the only reasons I had to keep going.

And still, even time hadn't taken away the pain of it all. I missed them so much, even now, it sometimes felt like my chest would cave in on my heart, crushing it beneath the weight of my grief.

"Lenora?"

A light knock on the door woke me from a terrible dream that seemed to slip away the moment my eyes opened.

I groaned and rolled over in the small twin bed that had been mine now for the past three months. A bird cawed outside my window, and I glanced over just in time to see a black raven spread its wings and fly away.

A raven? Was that just a coincidence?

The thought came and went in an instant, because I suddenly remembered why Martin was waking me up so early when he usually let me sleep in as long as I wanted.

I pulled the covers over my head. Couldn't I just skip my

senior year? Take classes online? Avoid all normal human interaction forever?

Another knock, and this time the door opened just a crack.

"Lenora, have you seen the time? Breakfast is ready for you downstairs."

With a sigh, I sat up and turned toward my soft-spoken Great-Uncle Martin.

I'd been living with him now for an entire summer. It turned out he wasn't actually creepy at all. He was more like a sweet teddy bear, and I couldn't even fathom the thought of leaving the comfort of his calming presence to enter the world of regular teenagers.

Talk about creepy.

"I can't do it," I said, shaking my head. "There's just no way."

Martin's eyes sparkled with compassion. "May I come in?"

"Of course."

He always asked before he came into my room, which I appreciated. I was the intruder in his home, and yet he acted like I'd always belonged here.

"I understand how difficult this is," he said. "Try to see it as a chance for a fresh start. I may not agree with it, either, but attending Newcastle High School is part of the conditions the Council placed on allowing you to stay with me."

"Which I totally don't understand," I said, a tiny spark of anger igniting in my chest. "Why does the Council suddenly care so much about my high school education? And why do they get to place conditions on me living with a member of my own family? It's not like they cared about any of this when my parents were alive. I've never had to go to a normal school before. Why now?"

"You know as well as I do that the Council doesn't need to give reasons for their proclamations or their rules," he said. "But from what I understand, they want you to get a taste of normal life before you make a decision about whether to take the test to become a Slayer on your birthday."

I groaned.

Just the thought of the Council's test made my stomach churn.

I used to want nothing more than to be just like my parents, but now, I wasn't so sure. I'd watched them die, and I would never forget that night for as long as I lived.

I'd always believed they were invincible. That we were an unstoppable team, and that I would someday be just as powerful as they were.

But that night, they hadn't even had a chance. I still wasn't sure what happened the night they died. The attack had come out of nowhere, and I'd just watched it happen. I couldn't move or cast. I'd just watched.

It was my fault they were dead, and when I really thought about it, I didn't see any way I could follow in their footsteps and become a Slayer. I wasn't strong enough. I wasn't worthy of that title.

And yet, being a witch was the only life I'd ever known. Could I even fit in with normal people after that?

I sighed and threw the covers off my legs, revealing the same pair of black leggings I'd been wearing all summer. Turns out when you're grieving, no one cares if you change clothes.

"Okay, I'll go, but I don't have to be happy about it," I said.

Uncle Martin smiled. "No teenager ever is. Now, get dressed and meet me in the kitchen. I made your favorite pancakes."

I smiled despite my generally crappy mood, and turned to my closet.

What did normal, regular humans wear to their first day of school? And what vibe did I want to give on day one?

Did I even want to try to make friends?

Or did I want to send a clear, *'leave-me-alone-or-I'll-put-a-curse-on-you'* kind of message? I could be the mysterious, loner orphan, or I could try to fit in, whatever that meant.

I'd grown up traveling the world with my parents and being homeschooled in things like alchemy along with basic math. I'd never had friends my own age before, as lame as that sounded. Was there really any point in trying to make some with just a year left, anyway?

After standing in front of a closet full of clothes I barely even recognized anymore, I finally went for what I felt would be a safe in-between. Black jeans, graphic tee with the Umbrella Corp logo, and a pair of black boots.

I parted my long, brown hair down the middle and twisted each side into a fat messy bun, then threw on some black eyeliner and my favorite moonstone ring.

Finally satisfied, I made my way down the long, empty hallway to the even longer grand staircase, and down to the large, chef's kitchen in the back of the house. I still wasn't comfortable living in such a giant old house full of strange, witchy relics, but at least I wasn't getting lost as much anymore.

Uncle Martin said this house was my legacy. The Thorne legacy. He told me it would be mine when he passed away someday, since we were the last of our name now, but every time I thought about living in this big, empty house all by myself and growing old alone the way he had, I got the itch to run away forever.

Or burn it to the ground.

But that was just me.

Besides, I wasn't quite ready to lose the rest of my family just yet. As scared as I'd originally been to move in with him, Martin had saved my life. If it hadn't been for him, I don't think I would have made it through the summer.

I grabbed an apple off the counter and stuffed it in my bag before sitting down to a large stack of pancakes.

"Took you long enough," he said with a wink. "But you look beautiful, as always."

I smiled. "A slight upgrade from sweats and leggings, huh?"

He lifted his hands in defense. "I never said a word, did I?"

"No," I said, lowering my head in recognition of his politeness. "But you could have."

"There's one more thing that outfit needs, though."

He motioned toward a drawer across the room, and it floated open at the flick of his wrist. A small box tied with a red ribbon made its way through the air and into his hand before he set it down in front of my stack of peanut butter, chocolate chip pancakes.

I narrowed my eyes at him.

"What's this?" I asked.

His ancient grey eyes sparkled. "Open it."

I pulled a knee to my chest, resting my black boot on the chair. I wasn't great at receiving presents. We'd never really been much for gifts growing up in my house. Mom's idea of a birthday treat was letting me be the one to stake the vampire.

"It's not going to bite, I promise," Martin said. "Come on."

I tugged on the ribbon, and my mouth fell open slightly as I opened the box. Inside, a familiar silver locket lay on top of red velvet. I opened it to find the familiar photos of my mother's parents had now been replaced with pictures of my own mom and dad.

"I thought the Council took this," I said, my voice hitching slightly as I ran a finger across the pentacle engraved on the front of the locket.

He'd chosen the perfect photos of them to put inside, their smiling faces trapped forever in a memory of a time that would never come again, no matter how much I wished for it.

"I petitioned to have it returned to you once the evidence was no longer needed," he said. "I had to call in a few favors, but that locket belongs to you, Lenny. Your mother would have wanted you to have it."

"Thank you," I said, standing and throwing my arms around him.

How could I explain to him what this meant to me?

"Here. I'll help you put it on." He turned his head to the side, but I didn't miss the way he cleared his throat.

I'd never seen Martin cry. Not even at my parents' funeral.

He'd been my rock, and I suddenly realized just how much I'd come to love him over the past few months.

I hadn't even wanted to come here at first, and now, I didn't want to so much as walk out the door.

"There's one more thing, of course, if you're ready for it," he said as he slipped the locket around my neck and fastened it.

I gasped as a silver key slid down the chain to rest next to my mother's locket.

I nearly laughed with joy.

"Does this mean what I think it means?" I asked, twirling around and grasping the key with both hands.

Martin nodded and smiled. "The Council made their ruling just yesterday," he said, his smile fading with a hint of sorrow. "It wasn't your fault, dear girl. Of course it wasn't."

I swallowed back the guilt that seemed to get stuck in my throat and focused, instead, on the really good news.

I had my key back.

I was free to use my magic again.

I wasn't sure I wanted to become a Slayer and move up in the ranks of the coven, but I would always be a witch. And a witch needed her key.

"This doesn't give you carte blanche to go casting whatever you want," Martin said, and then added under his breath, "So much like your mother."

"What does that mean?" I asked, unable to take my eyes off the locket and key. What had started as a bad day was really looking up.

"It means I want you to be very careful at school today," he said, his tone suddenly even more serious than normal. "Don't let anyone see the key, and don't tell anyone who you really are."

I looked up and smiled. "I think I can handle high school," I said. "I might not like pretending to be normal, but I don't think anything dangerous is going to happen in English class. Besides, how many dangerous people can there really be in a town like Newcastle? You said yourself it was boring here most of the time."

I expected my comment to make him smile, but instead, he looked concerned. I hadn't expected Martin to be the overprotective type, but maybe after what happened to my parents, he was feeling scared today, too.

"Is there something I should know about?" I asked. "Are there people like me at school here?"

Martin raised an eyebrow and took a deep breath, slowly shaking his head. "I don't believe there's anyone quite like you in the entire world, child. But no, there's nothing you should know about. I simply want you to be careful," he said. "Go straight to school and come straight home afterward, and you'll be fine. Are you sure you don't want me to drive you to school?"

I imagined the looks we'd get pulling up in Martin's antique black car. Not really the first impression I wanted to make today.

"I'm sure," I said, wondering what he really thought could happen to me in the three blocks between here and the high school. It would take me less than ten minutes to walk there, and we lived on a relatively busy street.

I would be fine.

"If you insist," he said. "Just come home as soon as you're finished. I have plans for us this afternoon."

What? This was the first I'd heard of any plans.

"Like what?" I asked.

"You'll see when you get home," he said. "For now, you'd better eat your breakfast. You don't want to be late for your first day."

"Thank you, Uncle," I said, standing on tip-toes to kiss his pale cheek.

I turned and ran out the door. There was no time for pancakes if I wanted to try out my key before school.

"Lenora, where are you going?" Martin called after me, but I was already halfway back up the stairs to my room.

I sat down in front of the large, mahogany cabinet I'd been given when I was just five years old and crossed my legs underneath me. I took a deep breath and placed a fingertip on the silver key, making sure my intentions were clear as a bell.

I was out of practice after a few months, but apparently using a spell cabinet was like riding a bike. Once you learned how to do it, you never really forgot.

The cabinet doors swung open before me, and I giggled with excitement at the sight of all my herbs and potions and gemstones. My collection of tarot cards. It was like seeing old friends again.

I clasped my hands together.

So, what spell should I cast first?

DO YOU ALWAYS ASK SO MANY QUESTIONS?

Twenty minutes later as I stood in front of the doors to Newcastle High, I felt nearly invisible. Just like I wanted.

Everyone who walked by smiled and greeted friends they'd probably had since preschool, but no one seemed to notice me at all.

My spell had worked.

I'd used just enough amaranth to help me blend in, but not enough to make me completely invisible. Hopefully, this would make high school a lot more tolerable.

I would show up, do whatever I needed to do to survive it, keep my head down, and that would be that. It was just one year, after all.

I took a deep breath and told my feet to start walking, but I couldn't seem to force them forward. Literally every single muscle in my body rebelled against the idea of high school.

"It's not as bad as it looks," a bubbly voice said out of nowhere.

At first, I assumed she was talking to someone else, but then this small, energetic girl was suddenly there, smiling up at me like we were old friends.

She was pretty with high, sculpted cheekbones and bright blue eyes that were definitely focused on me.

"At least, it's usually not all terrible," she said. "You're new here, right? I mean, of course you are, because I've been going to this same school with these same people since I was about five years old, and I would have known if you'd been here before. It's not like we get a lot of new people here in Newcastle, despite the name. I hadn't even heard we were getting a new student this year. My name's Peyton, by the way. What's yours?"

The petite blonde hadn't even taken a single breath during that entire monologue. I had to wait for my brain to catch up with her mouth.

"Um, I'm Lenny," I said, glancing around and wondering why in the world she was talking to me.

Was my spell wearing off already? Or was this girl somehow immune?

"Lenny?" she asked. "That's a strange name. I don't think I've ever known anyone named Lenny before. Is that like a family name or something? Or maybe it's a nickname. It's got to be a nickname, right? But for what? Lenn—"

"It's short for Lenora," I said.

I looked around and realized that somehow we'd ended up inside the front entrance of the school. I didn't even remember moving.

"Lenora is such a pretty name, but I like Lenny, too," she said. "So, where are you from, anyway? You don't seem like the type of person who grew up in a small nowhere town like this."

"I'm from all around, I guess."

"Oh, military family," she said, nodding. "I bet it's hard to travel around so much. Or maybe it's harder to stay in one place after you've seen the whole world. Here, I'll show you where to check in and get your schedule and everything. It's not a very big school, so you'll find your way around pretty easily. I'll help you find your classes, if you want. I'm sure it's scary going to a brand new school, but Newcastle is a pretty cool place most of the time. Did your parents retire and move here for a new job or something?"

"Do you always ask so many questions?"

I wasn't ready to tell anyone about my parents just yet, and to be honest, I was surprised she hadn't already heard about a new girl moving in with the creepy old guy in the big, spooky house. It seems like that would have been prime gossip info in a town like this.

Of course, despite the fact that Martin always seemed to be coming and going, I had hardly left the house all summer.

"I'm sorry," she said with a laugh. "I'm talking too much. First day of school excitement. I'll slow down."

There wasn't a drop of awkwardness about her. There was just true, genuine happiness, like a beam of sunshine. I'd never met anyone like her before.

I instantly liked her, which was really strange for me, because I rarely liked anyone.

So much for my determination not to make friends or interact in any way today. Maybe I could do like Martin said and try to just be a normal high school girl for a little while. Just the thought of it made my stomach flip with nervousness.

Me? Normal?

If my parents were still alive, we'd most likely be in Europe somewhere fighting vampires in an ancient castle, but it seemed life had other plans for me right now.

As I looked around at the huge crowd of students, all I could think was that I'd have been more comfortable with the vampires.

"It's okay," I said. "If you hadn't said hello, I might have just turned around and gone back home."

She smiled again, and I couldn't help but smile back. Her energy was contagious.

"Nah," she said. "You look like the kind of person who is stronger than she thinks. You'd have come in eventually. Anyway, this is the office. Let's find out who you have for homeroom."

"Don't you have somewhere else you need to be first?" I asked. "Why are you helping me?"

"We all have to stick together right now, especially with everything that's going on," she said, her eyes looking downward.

"What's going on?" I asked, a strange pit in my stomach.

First, Martin telling me to be extra careful, and now this. What was going on in this town?

"It's just terrible, isn't it?" she asked, all the joy draining from her voice. "I can't even bring myself to talk about those girls. Nothing like that has ever happened in Newcastle before. No one really knows how to deal with it."

I wanted to ask her more, but she quickly shifted her energy and the smile returned.

"Let's talk about something else," she said. "It's our first day, after all. Besides, it's really not that bad around here. It can even be fun. I promise. Come on, let's get your schedule, and then I'll take you to your homeroom."

I followed her into the office and luckily, Peyton did all the talking while I just leaned against the wall and pretended not to be there. For the most part, my spell seemed to be working. Everyone else looked straight past me, as if I wasn't there at all.

Peyton was different, though, and I was determined to find out why.

As soon as I figured out where my locker was.

"Here we go," Peyton said as she handed me a slip of paper with my class list on it. "We're in a lot of the same classes. That's lucky, huh?"

"Yeah," I said, following her through the crowd. This day definitely wasn't going like I thought it would.

We made it to a group of lockers at the end of the hallway.

"This is you," she said. "That envelope I gave you should have your combination in it. I didn't look, I promise."

I started to put in my combination, but before I was finished, a chill ran down my back that was so strong, my entire body shivered.

I stopped breathing for a moment, my hand stopping completely as I focused on that feeling. It was the last thing I had expected to feel here today in a town like this.

Martin had said everyone in this town was human. Normal.

Mostly, he'd said. They were mostly human.

"Do you need help?" Peyton asked, taking the slip of paper with the combination on it. "Here, I can show you how to do it. I remember the first time I..."

I tuned her voice out for a moment and slowly turned around, searching every single face in the hallway. My heart raced, and I hardly allowed myself to take a breath as I scanned the room.

That feeling had come from someone here. Someone close.

And then, suddenly, there he was.

He was tall. Over six feet, if I had to guess.

His dark hair was just long enough to fall across his forehead, but not so long that it covered his dark, serious eyes. His tanned skin practically glowed with the health of immortality, even under these crappy, fluorescent lights.

He was strong, too, judging by the muscles that strained against the sleeves of his grey t-shirt.

But most importantly, there was a certain energy about him that I'd come to recognize over the years as...other. This guy, whoever he was, was not human.

And he was staring straight at me.

SO INCREDIBLY NORMAL

Dark eyes held me to the spot, and it was as though everyone else in the hallway disappeared entirely.

He saw me, but it was more than that.

He knew who I was. Or at least what I was.

Which put me at a distinct disadvantage, because even though I could tell from the magical energy radiating from him that he wasn't entirely human, I wasn't good enough at this to tell exactly what he was.

And that made him dangerous.

The bell rang, and in the blink of an eye, he was gone.

"Earth to Lenny," Peyton said with a laugh. She touched my arm, and I seemed to break free from whatever spell had held me there. "He's really cute, right? He's new here, too, kind of. He doesn't say much in class, and as far as I know, he hasn't even dated anyone yet, which is not for a lack of interest, if you know what I mean."

"Who is he?" I asked, fumbling with my locker combination again until it finally popped open.

"His name is Kai Richards. Despite his height and apparent athletic ability, he isn't on a single sports team, and he's really good at math. That's pretty much all I know about him. Well, that and almost every girl in school wants to date him, so get in line."

Kai Richards. Not much to go on, but at least it was a start.

I would have to remember to ask Martin about him. A guy with that kind of supernatural energy didn't just move to town without Martin noticing. So, why hadn't he mentioned Kai to me earlier?

I didn't like having a big question mark over his head. After what happened to my parents, I wanted to know as much information as possible about the people close to me. Especially the non-human ones I might have to sit next to in class.

Besides, now I had a project. Something to keep my mind occupied throughout the day.

"We'd better get going," Peyton said. "We have to be in the next hall before the second bell rings. And we both have Mr. Wallace for homeroom. He's not exactly known for being the most lenient teacher around here, even if it is your first day. You don't want to paint a target on your back right away, either."

She was right. I really didn't want to draw anyone's attention today, if I could help it.

Somehow, I'd already gotten the attention of two people, despite my attempt to blend in at all costs. As far as I was concerned, two was enough for one day.

I definitely didn't want to get on the wrong side of any of my teachers.

For the most part, I managed to get through the first day

without any major mistakes or embarrassments. Other than Peyton and Kai, most people ignored me, which meant I at least had some magical ability left after a summer of being out of practice.

I understood why the spell hadn't worked on Kai, but I still didn't understand why my spell hadn't worked on Peyton. As far as I could tell, she was purely human. She just seemed to be immune to this particular spell, which made me immediately want to test a different one on her.

I would have to think of something else to do tomorrow just to see if she was immune to everything, or just that one spell in particular.

I was already thinking about different herbs to mix together when I got home as I stepped out of the main building. I nearly ran right into Peyton and another girl I was pretty sure I had a few classes with. I couldn't remember her name, though.

"There you are," Peyton said. "I was just talking about you."

How someone could be so bubbly and energetic at the end of a full day of boring classes was beyond me.

"This is my friend Brandy," she said. "Brandy, this is Lenny. She's really cool and well-traveled, and you're going to love her."

"Hey," Brandy said, lifting her chin toward me. Her makeup was immaculate, making her dark skin look lit from within. Her jet-black hair hung in tight curls around her face, and there was a smile in her dark eyes. "Peyton hasn't been able to shut up about you all day. I can't believe I didn't see you around today. She said we had a couple classes together, but I didn't even notice you at all. I'm sorry. I must have been in my own little world."

I smiled. Magic was so much fun when it worked.

"It's no problem," I said. "I blend in."

"Pretty girls like you don't just blend in," Peyton said, rolling her eyes.

I gave her a look. I'd never thought of myself as a pretty girl. In fact, I was incredibly plain, which is part of what made it easy for me to fade into the crowd, even when I wasn't using magic to make it happen.

But her compliment made me feel good.

"Well, thank you, but I'm honestly just glad I made it through the day without too much trouble," I said. "What you did for me this morning was really nice. I appreciate it."

"It was my pleasure," Peyton said, a slight gleam in her eye. "But if you really want to repay me, you'll agree to come with us to Sir Bean this afternoon and hang."

I raised a questioning eyebrow.

"Excuse me? Did you just say Sir Bean?"

Brandy laughed. "It's the local coffee shop and bakery here," she said. "A lot of us hang out there after school to do homework and just, well, avoid going home for as long as possible."

A strange warmth spread through my stomach. Had I really just been asked to hang out with friends after school?

It was the kind of thing that seemed so incredibly normal. So human.

And to think I'd been dreading this day for months. What would Uncle Martin say when he found out I'd made actual friends?

Then again, he was expecting me home right after school. I still had no idea what his plans were for this afternoon, and we'd never discussed any rules about hanging out with friends or staying out late.

I'd never even imagined it would be an issue.

"It sounds fun, but I really should get home. My uncle will be wondering where I am if I don't show up, and it's my first time out of the house, uh, in a while."

Okay, that sounded really lame, but it had literally been months since I'd even stepped off my uncle's property.

"So, call him," Peyton said with a shrug.

I laughed at the thought of Martin having a phone. That wasn't exactly how he communicated with the outside world. Not that I had a phone, either.

Crap. How out of touch was I that I didn't even have my own cell phone? I had to be the only person in school, which was going to look a bit fishy if I did manage to keep these new friends.

I would have to talk to Martin about buying me a phone. I'd never needed one before, but if I was supposed to be blending in and trying out a so-called normal life, I was going to need all the trappings of a modern-day teenager.

Maybe that meant I could also talk him into buying me a new car.

"I must have left my phone at home today," I said. "Maybe I'll come with you tomorrow, if you're going."

"Nope. Not good enough," Peyton said. "I haven't had nearly enough time to grill you about all the places you've lived, what kind of music you like to listen to, why you moved here to Newcastle. I have a million questions."

"Probably more than a million, knowing Peyton," Brandy added.

"Besides," Peyton paused for dramatic effect. "There's a certain tall, dark, handsome, and aloof someone who just happens to work at Sir Bean. But if you don't want to go, that's fine."

My breath caught in my throat.

"Kai works there?" I asked, trying to sound casual and failing miserably.

Peyton's face broke out in a huge smile, and she bumped Brandy with her elbow. "Told you she had a major crush on him."

"It's not a crush," I said quickly, defending myself.

"Oh?" Peyton asked. "You just nearly drooled all over yourself this morning when you saw him, but it's no big deal. It's definitely not a crush."

My cheeks warmed. Okay, so he was a good looking guy who had nearly taken my breath away the first time I saw him, but this wasn't a crush. I just wanted to know what he was.

Still, how was I supposed to explain that to someone like Peyton?

I don't like the guy, I'm just trying to figure out if he's a demon or a werewolf.

Come to think of it, it was probably better if they did think I had a crush on the guy. That would at least make my interest in him logical.

"You know what? Maybe I left my phone in my locker," I said. "I'll be right back. You want me to just meet you there?"

"Of course not. We'll wait for you," Brandy said, carefully reapplying her already-perfect lip gloss.

They started talking about chemistry homework as they

took a seat on one of the benches outside the main entrance. I jogged inside to find a quiet place to contact my uncle.

It was amazing how fast the school had emptied out. I passed a single teacher on the way to the bathroom, but other than that, the entire place was deserted.

In the girl's bathroom, I double-checked the stalls to make sure no one was hiding out in there, and then I placed a hand on the door.

"*Cincinno,*" I whispered.

Warmth spread out from my palm as a single flash of golden light sealed the door closed. I couldn't exactly afford for someone to walk in here and find me talking to my uncle in a mirror, now could I? Talk about an interesting first day at school.

I took a deep breath, leaned forward toward the first mirror above the sink, and exhaled. As my warm breath fogged the mirror, I drew our family sigil and whispered, "*Martin vocatio.*"

It only took a few seconds for his image to appear before me.

He looked frantic, and I immediately felt guilty for scaring him.

"What's wrong?" he asked. "Did something happen? Where are you?"

"I'm fine. Nothing has happened," I said, surprised again that he was so concerned. He was normally so calm. "I'm sorry. I didn't think you'd be worried about me. I just wanted to ask you if I could go out with some friends after school."

He let out a long breath, his shoulders relaxing as he placed a hand on his chest. "You scared me to death. I was expecting you home any minute."

"I know, but I actually managed to meet a few new friends today, and they want me to go to a coffee shop called The Bean or something? I want to go, but I wanted to make sure it was okay with you first," I said. "Apparently, most of these people have cell phones, but all I had was a mirror."

He laughed. "Getting your use out of having that key back, I see. Of course you can go to the coffee shop with your friends," he said. "We'll see about ordering some cell phones when you get home tonight. I've avoided modern technology long enough."

"Thanks," I said. "What about our plans?"

"That can wait, child. We'll do it another day."

I considered telling him about Kai, but for some reason, I wanted to keep that information to myself for now.

It was possible Martin already knew this guy's family or what they were, but for now, I was honestly just enjoying the mystery of it. It gave me something to think about other than the fact that I was stuck in this town instead of out hunting with my parents.

"Now, please, clean the family sigil off that disgusting mirror before you go," he said. "I don't want some poor freshman conjuring an old man in the mirror by accident tomorrow."

"I will. See you in a bit," I said.

I threw some hot water on the mirror and wiped it off with a paper towel, hoping that was good enough. Good timing, too, because someone was pulling on the outside door like their life depended on it.

"*Solvo*," I whispered as I placed my palm on the door, and it immediately flew open, nearly knocking the girl on the other side onto her butt.

I winced. "Sorry, I think the door was stuck."

She gave me a nasty look as she rushed past me, but I didn't care.

I was having one hell of a day, and it was the most fun I'd had in a really long time.

THERE ARE NO COINCIDENCES

Sir Bean was a short walk away from the high school. It was smack dab between a dry cleaner and a nail salon in a small strip mall, and it seemed to be the only place that had any real business this afternoon.

I stood there for several minutes just staring at the logo on the sign out front.

A knight in full armor riding a coffee bean, his sword stretched out in front of him.

"What?" Peyton asked, staring up at the sign with me.

"I don't understand," I said. "It's a knight riding a bean."

She laughed and put her arm around me. It was such a foreign feeling, I almost pulled away, but it was actually nice. Her instant trust was comforting.

"It's a play on our mascot, you know," she said. "The Newcastle Knights. Get it?"

"I mean, I get it, but it's weird, right? It's a knight, riding a coffee bean. Beans don't even have legs. Where could he possibly be going? What's he fighting for?"

"He fights for coffee beans everywhere!" Brandy said, putting her hand up like a sword.

I laughed so fully, I hardly recognized my own voice. Even though it was fun, it was also slightly terrifying.

What if I actually liked being a normal person? What would I do with my life?

It was a sobering thought, but I was determined not to bring down the vibe of the afternoon.

"Well, let's see if the coffee's any good," I said.

"It's amazing," Peyton said. "But the coffee's got nothing on the cupcakes. They're to die for. Trust me. I've tried every single flavor they have. Twice."

"Ah, everything makes so much sense to me now. You're high on sugar," I said.

Peyton laughed and bumped my arm, the same way she'd done with Brandy earlier. Why did that make me feel like I belonged? It was such a simple gesture, but it carried so much meaning for me.

"Nailed it," Brandy said. "Did you know she actually carries a giant pencil case full of candy in her bag? It's an addiction."

Peyton herded us toward a small table in the back. "It's busy today," she said. "But I guess that's really no surprise, since it is the first day back to school. Everyone has to gossip about what happened over the summer and make cool videos for TikTok."

"What's TikTok?" I asked.

Brandy and Peyton both looked at me like I'd grown five heads, and I tried to think of a way to play it off like I'd just been joking. But no, I had no idea what TikTok was, which apparently was some kind of sin.

Before they could start grilling me about my lack of knowledge, though, a girl with her brown hair in a high ponytail and a Sir Bean apron on came pushing through the crowd, waving madly at us.

"You made it," she said, sitting down to catch her breath. "I can't let the manager see me taking a break on such a busy day, but I've been keeping an eye out for you. What took you so long? All the tables were almost gone."

"Olive, this is Lenny," Peyton said. "She's our new friend. Lenny, this is Olive, our cupcake goddess. We've all been friends since we were kids."

"Cupcake goddess? That sounds promising," I said. "Nice to meet you, Olive."

Olive's cheeks reddened slightly, and she looked down, obviously embarrassed. "You guys are too sweet. I don't make them myself, anyway. My mom is really the mastermind behind the amazing cupcake flavors, and she hardly ever lets me into the kitchen when she's baking," she said. "Speaking of which, we have some new ones in the cafe today, if anyone wants to try something. I should take your order, anyway, before Melvin gets angry."

"Ooh, what's new?" Peyton asked. "Something I've never tried before? Because I was looking forward to the s'mores cupcakes again today, but you know me. I can't resist new flavors."

"Neapolitan, chocolate peanut butter pretzel, and maple bacon are the new ones today, but the bacon ones are almost sold out."

Peyton jumped on the chance to try the last of the bacon cupcakes, but I couldn't resist ordering the chocolate peanut butter ones.

What can I say? I have a thing for that flavor combination.

"Get me a caramel latte, pretty please," Brandy said.

"No cupcake for you?" I asked.

"She refuses to eat gluten. It's a tragedy," Peyton said. She fished two twenty-dollar bills from her backpack and stuffed them in Olive's hand. "Get us all caramel lattes. And keep the change."

"You don't have to pay for mine," I said. "I have a few bucks in my bag."

"Peyton's parents are loaded," Brandy said with a wink. "Abuse it."

I laughed. I was pretty sure Uncle Martin was loaded, too, but we'd never really talked about money before. A lot of the things we purchased in our family used a different kind of currency.

"Thanks. I'll get it next time."

A strange thrill went through my body. I was already assuming there would be a next time. It was such a strange feeling, and I was scared to actually trust it.

Maybe I'd stepped out of Martin's house and into some kind of alternate reality.

Olive turned and froze, gasping as she placed a hand to her mouth.

In fact, most of the people in the cafe grew quiet for a moment and looked toward a guy with shoulder-length blond hair who'd just walked in.

The silence was brief as everyone tried to pretend they hadn't noticed the guy, but there had definitely been a shift in the energy of the place.

"What just happened?" I whispered. "Who is that?"

Peyton leaned in, and we all huddled close together.

"That's Troy Valentine. His sister, Marcia, went missing about three weeks ago. She's the most recent girl to disappear," Peyton said in a hushed voice.

"You mentioned something about that earlier today," I said, a chill going through me. "How many girls have gone missing? And what happened to them?"

"No one knows," Olive said, sitting back down and leaning in. "One day, they were going about their normal lives, and the next, they were gone without a trace. Four girls total so far in the past six months. All of them students at Newcastle High. All of them are still missing."

Holy what?

My mouth went dry, and I dug my nails into the palm of my hand. Four girls missing without a trace? In a town that had almost no history of crime or violence.

Why hadn't Martin mentioned this to me? Was this why he'd been so strange this morning?

What were the chances four missing girls was some kind of coincidence?

I wasn't an expert Slayer or anything like my parents, and I certainly wasn't trained as a Keeper like Martin, but I didn't need to be to answer that question.

There was no way this was a coincidence.

And if I had to guess, I'd say there was some kind of supernatural being behind their disappearance. Kidnapping four girls wasn't usually something humans did, even if that's what the news had to say.

Nine times out of ten, if there was a serial killer or mass murderer out there, he or she was far from human, no matter what they looked like on the outside.

Just then, as if on cue, Kai stepped out to take over at the cash register. It was the first time I'd seen him since that morning, but the moment my eyes landed on him, he turned his head toward me.

Just like earlier, our eyes locked across the crowd. It was as if he could feel my presence, the same way I could feel his. And just like before, his gaze nearly knocked the breath from my lungs.

I wiped my sweaty palms against my jeans.

"I have to get back to work. I'll be back with your orders in a sec," Olive said, disappearing into the crowded cafe.

I pulled my gaze from Kai's and leaned toward the other girls. "Hey, so just out of curiosity, when did you say Kai started school here?"

"Sometime toward the end of the school year last year, I think," Peyton said. "Just before summer, maybe?"

"No, it was earlier than that," Brandy said. "He started just after the new year. I remember, because it snowed that first week back, and he stopped to help me get my car back on the road after I slid on some ice. I think that still might be the only time he's actually talked to me, but that was definitely last winter. January or February at the latest. Why?"

"Just curious," I said.

I'd already started counting backwards, though, and the results made me feel sick to my stomach.

Four missing girls in the past six months, and a handsome new guy who just happened to come to town about six months ago.

And who just happened to be something other than human?

I didn't like the way that was adding up.

Something my parents always taught me is that there are

no coincidences. Everything happens for a reason, and if you see a pattern start to emerge, pay attention to it. It might save your life.

In this case, maybe it could save four lives.

I knew what Uncle Martin and the Council would say. Stay out of it. If this was really a matter for us to be concerned with, the Council would have already sent someone to deal with it.

Or maybe they already had sent someone. It was none of my business as a young witch.

But like my parents, I'd never really been good at following the rules.

I needed to find out just who Kai Richards was, and I needed to do it fast.

As the others at my table talked, I watched.

If anyone was paying attention, they would just think I was your average awkward teen with a major crush, staring at the object of her desire. At worst, they would think I was a stalker.

I could live with that, as long as no one suspected what I was really up to.

Basically, I needed his DNA, which sounded a lot more disgusting than it was.

Since I'd never even spoken to him before, and since he was obviously keeping an eye on me, I needed to be sneaky about it.

So, I watched his every move from the corner of my eye.

I did my best to be discreet about it, but I nearly jumped out of my seat the minute I saw him step into a back room and take a sip of a drink with a white straw.

"You okay?" Brandy asked.

"I have to run to the bathroom," I said. "Be right back."

I started toward the front of the cafe, and Peyton called out after me. "The bathroom's the other way."

"I'll find it," I called back, waving my hand over my head.

With any luck, they'd go back to their discussion about Peyton's epic birthday party plans coming up, and they'd forget all about me for a minute.

Thanks to my spell from this morning, most people took no notice of me at all. I was just a blur in the crowd. Kai, of course, seemed to notice me just fine, but he was back on the registers now, and the cafe was swamped.

In fact, there were so many people inside, it was probably some kind of fire code violation. Wall-to-wall teenagers hopped up on sugar and first-day-of-school nerves.

Slowly, I inched my way closer to the door marked "employees only" and watched the patterns of anyone who came in and out of that door.

From what I could tell, there wasn't an actual kitchen in this cafe. There was just a back store room where employees could go to take a break or grab things to restock the main room, like straws, napkins, flavorings for the coffee, and stuff like that.

Besides the manager, who Olive had called Melvin, there were four other employees working. Olive and one other girl were making coffees and packaging cupcake orders. They were also managing orders coming from the tables. Kai was obviously on the register for now, and there was a younger guy bussing tables and restocking the napkin stations.

The manager and the young guy were the two who went into the back room the most, so I kept an eye on both of them from my hiding spot at the end of the bakery counter. I waited for a moment when the kid had just started to empty the trash and the manager was dealing with a couple of very obviously upset girls complaining about the quality of their iced coffees.

I bent down as if I needed to tie my shoes and whispered, "*Tacitus.*"

Casting a spell on my boots was likely overkill, but hey, I'd been denied the use of my magic for the past three months. Now that I had my key back, I was going to use it.

The simple spell made my boots silent, so between that and the spell I'd cast on myself this morning, I was able to very quickly and easily slip through the employees-only door, grab a napkin, and lift Kai's straw from his drink. With what I'd like to think of as ninja-like skills, I slid the wrapped straw into my bag and got the heck out of there.

No one suspected a thing, and I made my way back to my table with a smile on my face. Inside, though, my heart was racing.

"That must have been some bathroom break," Brandy said. "You were gone for twenty minutes."

"No, seriously?" I asked. It hadn't seemed that long.

"Okay, maybe ten, but still," she said. "You missed all the good talk about the party. I know you're new, but trust me when I say that Peyton's parties are epic."

I did my best to get into the conversation, but all I could think about was getting home and casting a spell on that straw.

By nightfall, I hoped to know exactly what kind of magical being this Kai Richards was.

I COULDN'T SEEM TO HELP MYSELF

"L enny, is that you?" Martin appeared in the grand
foyer an instant after I walked through the door.

"No, it's one of the other people who live here," I
said with a smile. "I brought you a present."

I presented him with a regal gold and navy box that
sported the Sir Bean logo, but it was the cupcake inside that I
knew he would love.

"It's lemon meringue. Your favorite," I said. "Apparently,
one of my new friends is a cupcake goddess. Or at least her
mother is. Have you ever tried one?"

"Can't say that I have," Martin said. "Come with me to the
kitchen, and we can eat dinner and talk about your day. I've
been dying to hear how things went. Better than anticipated, I
presume?"

"Much better."

I stared longingly at the stairs leading up to my room. I
desperately wanted to get up there and cast that spell, but I
owed Martin a conversation. Plus, I was starving.

The cupcake at Sir Bean had been delicious, but the sugar content must have been through the roof, because it was making my head feel swimmy.

We made a couple sandwiches and cut up some fresh fruit before sitting down at the ancient walnut table in the kitchen. There was a formal dining room in this house that probably rivaled the Queen's, but we never used it. It was way too cozy in the kitchen, which is where you could find us most of the time when we were together.

We talked about my day, my use of the mirror, and our plans to order cell phones.

"So, just out of curiosity, have you ever known a normal human who was immune to one of your spells?" I asked.

Uncle Martin shook his head. "Can't say that I have. Why do you ask?"

I explained about Peyton and the invisibility spell.

"I mean, obviously I didn't make myself entirely invisible. I just made it so that people wouldn't notice me unless I was speaking to them," I said. "But she just walked right up to me and started talking. It didn't work on her at all."

"Interesting, indeed," he said, scratching his chin with an index finger. "Are you quite sure she's human?"

I shrugged. "I didn't sense anything different about her. I'm not perfect at identification yet, but I can usually sense when someone isn't fully human."

The corners of Martin's lips twitched a bit, and I leaned toward him, my chin in my hands.

"And what's that about?" I asked. "You're trying your hardest not to laugh at me, aren't you?"

He did a very good job of controlling himself, but I could still tell.

"You're talented, just like your father was at your age," he said. "But you still have so much to learn. There are mystical beings you've never even heard of in this world. There are those who can cloak their magic so completely you would never know it until the moment they crept up behind you and put a dagger of ice in your heart. I wouldn't expect there to be a lot of that sort at the local high school, but it's possible this girl has a touch of magical blood in her lineage that made her immune to that one spell. If she was worth worrying about, I would have heard her name before. She's likely harmless."

Harmless. Sure, when it came to Peyton, I believed him.

But what about Kai?

And what about the missing girls?

I desperately wanted to ask him about both subjects, but if he told me to leave it alone, I'd have to listen to him. In this case, I figured it was better to do my own investigating and ask for permission later.

"Thank you for dinner. I'd better get upstairs and start on my homework," I said.

"Homework on the first day?" he asked. "Barbaric. Besides, we haven't had a chance to split this cupcake yet."

"Oh, I had one already. That one's all for you," I said. "Good night, Uncle."

"Good night, dear one. I'll see you in the morning."

I rushed up to my room faster than anyone who was simply looking forward to homework. I had a much more important project to work on.

I fished the straw out of my bag. It was still wrapped in the napkin, so hopefully any DNA Kai had transferred to the actual straw was still there. This was my first reconnaissance mission, and I didn't want to screw it up.

I disappeared into my large closet and rifled through some of my father's books. It took longer than expected to find the book on identifying magical creatures, but I finally found the spell I was looking for.

Over the past few years, my parents had taught me a lot, mostly by showing me what they were working on. I was smart, and I caught on pretty quickly. But Martin was right. There was still so much I didn't know.

I'd seen my parents use this particular magical spell a few times in the past to verify a creature's identity, so I was hopeful I would be able to replicate it on my own.

I sat down on the floor in front of my spell cabinet and took a deep, centering breath. When I felt ready, I lifted my finger to the silver key I wore next to my mother's locket. With clear intention, the spell cabinet doors swung open, revealing all of my tools.

Like any good witch, I'd been collecting magical items since I was about five years old. When he or she is ready, every witch in our coven is gifted with a spell cabinet by the Witch's Council, and it's up to her to decide what she wants to fill it with.

Within reason, of course.

Certain types of magic were forbidden until you'd unlocked the next key.

Over the years, I'd chosen to fill mine with various herbs, salts, gemstones, and spell components we'd found on our travels. I also had a section at the top that housed my favorite deck of tarot cards, a small cauldron, a mortar and pestle, and a sage smudge.

Naturally.

I pulled the miniature cauldron down from the top shelf, along with the mortar and pestle and a handful of herbs.

It took me a while to locate my vial of melted snow from the Arctic, but I finally found it hiding in the back behind a dragon's fang.

I took all the tools to my desk in the corner and unwrapped the straw I'd stolen from Sir Bean.

This better work.

I read the spell's instructions about fifteen more times before I started mixing it all together. When the base ingredients were all in place, I used a small pair of embroidery scissors with a skull on them to cut off the top of the straw, right where Kai's lips would have touched it.

"*Cognosco.*"

My hand trembled as I let the straw fall into the mixture below.

Excitement bubbled inside me as the spell did its work. The white smoke that poured from the cauldron looked exactly like it was supposed to. Now, I just had to wait a few minutes for the spell to identify Kai's origins.

When that happened, the smoke would change colors. Red for vampire. Orange for were. Pink for fae. And so on.

I had a list of smoke colors and their corresponding creature here in the spell book, so it was only a matter of time.

Only, time was ticking and the smoke hadn't changed colors.

I tapped my foot against the wood floor. When I'd watched my parents do this, the smoke had changed much faster.

After ten minutes, I started losing hope. The smoke was dissipating. Soon, there would be nothing left. I read through the spell again and shook my head. I'd done everything right. I hadn't missed an ingredient or said the wrong word. It should have worked.

Disappointment fell over me like a shadow as the white smoke went out entirely, leaving nothing but a pile of ash inside the cauldron.

Either I'd been completely wrong about Kai and he was human, after all, or he'd somehow managed to cloak his identity. This, of course, just made me even more determined than ever to figure out what he was.

I pulled down all of my father's old books, searching through them for clues until I could hardly keep my eyes open.

When my alarm went off the next day, I woke to find myself surrounded by a giant pile of leather-bound books. As I attempted to crawl out from under them, I nearly knocked my old laptop to the floor.

I'd hardly slept at all the night before. Instead, I'd tossed and turned, dreaming about the night my parents died and all the things I wished I'd done differently.

I'd learned months ago that the best way to get through nights like that was to just stay awake. So, a few hours earlier, I'd pulled out the laptop, connected to Martin's base-level Wi-Fi, and done a little research on the missing girls.

There wasn't a lot to learn, though. It was always possible the police were holding back on what they knew, but according to the local press, there were no leads and no real clues to follow.

The girls' families had all just woken up one day to find them gone. No note. No evidence of a struggle. Nothing missing or out of place. They'd just disappeared.

At first, there had been some speculation that the girls had just run away from home. That's what people always said when teen girls went missing. But after the third teen disappeared, people started to take it more seriously.

At this point, it seemed like everyone in town was just waiting for them to find the bodies.

I shuddered at the thought of it.

I wanted to believe all four of those girls would be found alive, and if there was anything I could do to help, I at least wanted to try.

Which is why I didn't say a word about it to Martin. Instead, I planned to do some extra research at school today and see what I could find out from my new friends. There had to be some clues the police were either overlooking or that they thought weren't important. Things I would recognize that they would think were trivial or unrelated.

I had to at least try.

Still, in the back of my mind, part of me was saying I should leave it alone. Let the Council deal with it. Stop being so impulsive and headstrong.

I was still convinced it was my actions that had gotten my parents into trouble a few months ago. Maybe I needed to leave the hard work to the Slayers who were qualified to deal with it.

Why did I always have to jump head-first into everything dangerous?

I couldn't seem to help myself.

"Leaving early today?" Martin asked, just catching me as I walked out the door. "You haven't even had breakfast."

"I'll grab something at school," I said. "I'm going to do some work in the library before the first bell. I might be late again today, too. I'll try to make it home for dinner."

"Well, that's quite the change from yesterday," he said

with a smile. "It's good to see you enjoying yourself, but perhaps you can carve some time out for me this weekend. There's something I want to show you."

"What is it?" I asked.

"Don't worry about it now," Martin said, waving his hand. "Have a nice day."

"Bye," I said.

Martin had some kind of surprise for me. I was sure of it.

I stepped out the front door with a smile on my face, but it was immediately wiped away by the sight of the dark-eyed guy standing on the sidewalk directly outside the gate of my uncle's house.

Kai Richards not only knew what I was. He apparently also knew where I lived.

"We need to talk," he said.

NOT YOUR ENEMY

I did the stupid thing and looked behind me, just to be absolutely sure Kai was talking to me, which of course he was. There was literally nothing behind me but the door to the house.

What in the world was he doing here? Did he know what I'd done?

My hands immediately went clammy, and I started to sweat.

"I don't want to be late for school," I said.

"This won't take long." His voice was deeper than I'd anticipated. "I'll walk with you."

By this point, my heart was pounding about a thousand beats a second, and I wondered if I was going to pass out.

How could he possibly know? What powers did this guy have, exactly?

I nearly tripped over my own feet as I joined him on the sidewalk. He towered over my five-foot-four-inch frame, and I wondered if this guy had superhuman strength to go along with his size.

As the daughter of two natural-born Slayers, I had exceptional speed and some innate magical talent, but I wasn't gifted with strength the way some others were.

Maybe I should start bringing some kind of weapon with me to school. Or would that get me kicked out? Yeah, probably not a great idea for the principal to find a silver dagger in my backpack.

Of course, until I figured out what he was, I wouldn't know what type of weapon would hurt him, anyway.

"I'm guessing you just want to introduce yourself," I said, stalling as we walked toward the school. "Just part of the Newcastle High welcome committee, right? They always send the sweetest, most non-intimidating students to make sure us newbies feel safe. Well, it's super nice to meet you. I'm Lenny, by the way. Not that you asked."

He didn't look amused.

"You already know what I want to talk about," he said. "You're messing with things you don't understand, and it's going to stop."

Well, now that just made me want to dig deeper. He obviously didn't have me quite as pegged as he thought he did. Telling me to stop was nothing but more temptation.

"Or maybe you want me to stop because I understand more about what's going on than you want me to," I said, stopping to look him in the eye. I had to look up quite a bit to get there, but hopefully I managed to look somewhat menacing, despite the height difference.

Okay, well, apparently that was amusing to him.

He smiled. Or maybe smirked was a better word for it.

"You're what? Seventeen? A witch with her first key who thinks she can take on the world? I've seen your kind before. You need to stay out of this before you get yourself killed."

I lifted my chin in defiance.

"And who exactly do you think you are? We're in the same grade at school, so that makes you what? Eighteen, maybe? Unless you flunked a few grade levels trying to understand the basics of how to be a decent human being," I said. "Oh, but wait, you're not human, are you? I may not be skilled enough yet to know what the heck you are, but I can guarantee you I didn't grow up in a small town like this, and I know a lot more than you think."

His eyes narrowed in on my face, which was probably turning pink right about now.

"You stole my straw yesterday, didn't you?"

He took a step closer, causing me to take a step back toward the wrought iron fence behind me.

"I knew something was up when it went missing, but I underestimated you. I never dreamed you were sneaky enough to get it without me seeing."

I wasn't sure whether to take that as an insult or a compliment, but when he took another step toward me, I lost the ability to care.

"You obviously didn't find the information you wanted from it," he said. "Can't you see you're in over your head. Even from day one."

He was standing so close, I couldn't breathe. He was right about me, and I didn't want him to be.

How was it that he could see me so clearly, and I couldn't see the truth about him at all?

"Who are you?" I whispered.

He put a hand on the fence behind me and leaned down, so close I couldn't see anything beyond those dark eyes of his. They seemed to be looking inside me.

"I'm not your enemy," he said, something sincere in his voice making my mouth go dry. "Don't make me change my mind on that. You've had enough trouble this year. I'm sure the Council would like to keep it that way."

His words knocked what was left of my breath from my lungs. It was like he'd physically punched me in the stomach.

He knew about me. About my parents.

"How do you know about the Council?" I asked. "About my parents? If you were a member of my coven, I'd know about it."

"Word gets around the community when something like that happens," he said.

For the first time since I'd laid eyes on him, he had a human expression on his face.

Sorrow.

Empathy.

Had I misjudged him?

"I'm sorry for what you went through, Lenora. I don't want anything else to happen to you here," he said. "Just stay out of it. Don't keep digging into my past or trying to find answers about me or what's happening in this town. Leave it alone, and I'll do my best to make sure you're left alone, too."

His eyes locked on mine for a long moment before he pushed off the gate and started walking toward the school, leaving me standing there with my mouth open and my heart racing.

"Wait," I shouted, somehow managing to find enough strength in my legs to follow him.

He stopped, but he didn't turn around.

"You know my name. My past. Apparently, you know everything about me, and yet you won't even tell me the most basic thing about who you are or how you know all of these things?" I said. "Not exactly fair play, is it? You can't expect me to just turn away from that and pretend there's nothing going on here. What do you know about those missing girls, Kai? Did you do something to them?"

His entire body tensed. Before I could even blink, he'd grabbed my arm and pulled me tight against him. One second, he was at least six feet away, and the next, he was almost on top of me.

And I thought I was fast.

"How did you do that?" I asked, breathless.

"I'm not going to warn you again. Let this go," he said, loosening his grip on me.

His dark eyes met mine, and I could see just how much this meant to him. He was serious about it, but there was something more reflected in his gaze. At first I'd mistaken it for anger, but I could see now I was wrong.

He was scared.

But of what?

Before I could say another word to him, I blinked and he was gone again, mixing in with the crowd of students already entering the school.

I was still just standing there in a daze when Peyton found me a few minutes later.

"Everything okay?" she asked. "You look like you've already had a rough morning, and it's not even eight yet. Did you have bad dreams last night, too? Because I'm telling you, I had some really weird ones last night. Something about a cat in the woods. It was crazy, and strangely compelling when you think about it."

"How is a cat in the woods compelling?" I asked, not exactly wanting to offer up information about how my day was going so far.

"Because it was a tiger or something. I was trying so hard to find it. I mean, it was just a dream, but my whole body hurts this morning, like I was running in my sleep," she said with a yawn. "I'll be fine, though. I just downed a double-espresso at home before I got here. With any luck, that'll kick in any minute."

Brandy joined us as soon as we hit the main entrance to the school, but she gave me a strange look.

"What?" I asked. "Do I have something on my face?"

"Nothing you want to talk about this morning?" she asked.

What now?

Was everyone just determined to grill me about my business today? These people barely knew me.

"Not that I can think of, why?"

Her jaw dropped open, and she smacked my arm.

"You've got to be kidding me," she said. "I saw you talking to Kai on the way in this morning. He was practically all over you. I have never, and I mean never, seen him get close to anyone like that. Since when are you guys a thing?"

Peyton screamed and grabbed my arm. Apparently, that espresso just kicked in.

"What? You talked to Kai this morning and you weren't even going to mention it to us?" she asked. She pushed me over to a corner, and they both blocked me in completely. "Tell us what happened."

"Don't leave anything out, either," Brandy said. "This guy has been a mystery since he first got here. We need details."

"Ooh, what's happening here?" Olive asked, her eyes twinkling as she approached.

I felt like some kind of caged animal.

"Lenny's dating Kai," Peyton said. "We're trying to get her to spill the beans about it."

"Oh, come on," I said, my cheeks warming. "We're not dating."

My mind was spinning, trying to come up with any kind of story that would make sense. I didn't exactly want rumors flying about me dating Kai Richards. The guy was angry enough as it was.

"Well, you were definitely talking to each other, and getting up close and personal from what I saw," Brandy said.

"As of yesterday when we left Sir Bean, you had never so much as talked to him. What happened last night that you aren't telling us about?" Peyton asked. Her eyes narrowed, but then she broke out in a huge smile. "I'm so excited for you. I mean, I knew you were pretty, but I had no idea you were such a siren. No one has been able to get his attention in six months, and you bag him in a day."

I groaned.

"I haven't bagged anyone," I said. "We just ran into each other on the way to school this morning, and I introduced myself. While we were walking, I tripped and snagged my backpack on the fence. He helped me untangle it. It was totally innocent, and completely embarrassing. He probably thinks I'm such a clutz at this point and will never talk to me again."

"Oh," Brandy said with a pout. "Well, dang. I thought maybe you guys had made a connection or something."

"I wish," I said with a laugh that I was sure came off sounding too fake.

"At least now he knows who you are," Peyton said. "That's a step forward, right? Now you have an excuse to talk to him again if you see him in the halls. To say thank you."

She was sweet to try to be encouraging about it, but Kai had made it clear he wanted nothing to do with me. He probably wanted me gone from the school, to be honest. But I wasn't going anywhere, and now that I'd had a few minutes to recover from our encounter, I was more determined than ever to figure out what was going on in this town.

We Thornes didn't intimidate easily.

But it was obvious I was going to need more information about him if I was going to get to the bottom of all of this. I needed a plan, but the bell rang, I had to settle for homeroom, instead.

"Hey, before I forget, you're all invited to my house next Monday after school," Peyton said. "We can go swimming, veg out by the pool, watch some TV, and just hang out for a while. My parents won't be home until Tuesday morning. They're at another one of their business conferences in the city, so I've got the house all to myself. What do you say?"

"You already know I can't resist your impromptu pool parties," Brandy said. "I'll be there."

"I have a few things to do with mom that afternoon," Olive said. "But I'll have her swing me by your house as soon as we're done. I don't have to work Monday, thank God."

"Lenny, what about you?"

I smiled. "I'm there," I said. "I don't actually own a bathing suit, though. I can just put my feet in or something."

I wondered if Martin knew a place in town where I could buy a bathing suit. I hadn't been shopping at all since I got to Newcastle.

Peyton laughed. "You can have one of mine," she said, linking her arm in mine as we walked toward homeroom. "I have a couple I've never worn. This year is going to be so much fun. I'm so glad you came to school here, Lenny."

"Me, too," I said.

And I realized that even though Kai had pretty much scared me half to death this morning and there were some weird things going on in this town, I was more grateful than ever to be surrounded by new friends.

Maybe this really was the fresh start I'd needed all along.

A PLACE OF LEGEND

That afternoon, I turned down a second invitation from Peyton to join her and the others at Sir Bean.

It wasn't that I didn't want to hang out with my new friends again, but rather that I wanted to avoid running into Kai. He'd rattled me this morning more than I realized, and I'd spent most of the day replaying our conversation in my head.

He was hellbent on getting me to back off, but why?

It was hard to imagine someone who didn't even know the first thing about me was trying to keep me safe. So, the alternative was that he didn't want me poking in his business because he had something important to hide.

He was involved in the disappearances in one way or another. I was sure of it.

As much as I didn't want Martin telling me to stay out of it, I had decided to ask him what he knew about Kai. After our encounter this morning, I didn't want to be stupid about this.

I had basically been threatened, and I wanted the most

powerful person in my life to know about it. Just in case I went missing, too.

When I got home, though, I couldn't find Martin anywhere.

His two cars were both still parked in the garage, though, so he had to be around here.

I checked his study on the first floor and then the kitchen. Those were his two favorite places in the house, as far as I knew, but there was no sign of him.

Upstairs was nothing more than a bunch of empty bedrooms and bathrooms, besides mine, but I didn't find him in any of those empty rooms, either.

I was about to give up entirely when I heard voices echoing downstairs.

I followed the noise, assuming Martin had visitors in the kitchen. Only, the voices were coming from his study.

Strange. I'd just checked down here a few minutes ago.

I didn't mean to sneak up on him, but the tension in his voice got my imagination running wild. Martin was usually so calm and controlled.

"I will not bring her into this unless I absolutely have to," he said. "I won't subject her to such speculation."

"Lenny has a right to know," a familiar voice said.

"That's my decision to make. Not yours," Martin said sternly.

"I have a right to know what?" I asked.

Martin turned toward me, his eyes growing wide for a moment. "How long have you been standing there, child?"

My stomach twisted into knots. I didn't like the thought of anyone keeping secrets from me. Least of all the one person I trusted to look out for me.

"Long enough to hear you say you weren't going to tell me something, but not long enough to know what it is you're hiding," I said. "Is that Gianna?"

I stepped forward to get a better look, and I realized he'd been talking to the mirror on the wall near the door. I recognized my mother's best friend on the other side of it, but before I could say hello, Martin swiped his hand across the glass and shook his head. Gianna's image disappeared instantly.

"That was not meant for your ears," he said. "I thought you were going out with friends after school today."

I stared at him. Did he really think it would be that easy? That he could just dismiss me like that and expect me not to push?

"Well, I didn't," I said, crossing my arms. "I came home, instead. I looked for you, but you weren't in here just a few minutes ago. Where were you?"

"Nonsense," he said, walking past me so that I had to follow him down the hallway. "I was here in my study speaking with Gianna. You must not have seen me."

I shook my head. That wasn't possible.

There was no way I'd missed a six foot tall man speaking into a mirror.

I wanted to call him out on his lie, but I paused when he opened the door to the garage. I'd been expecting him to go to the kitchen and put on a pot of coffee or something.

"Where are you going now?" I asked.

"We," he said. "Where are we going."

I followed him toward the black 1937 Cadillac he loved and adored. "Okay, where are we going, then?"

"Someplace I would have introduced you to many years

ago if I'd had the chance," he said, opening the passenger-side
door and motioning for me to sit. "Get in."

"What were you talking to Gianna about?" I asked.
"You're keeping some kind of secret from me now?"

Martin's eyes met mine.

"I am keeping many secrets from you, Lenora. If you say
you trust me, you have to trust me completely," he said. "That
means believing that I have your best interests at heart and will
tell you what you need to know when I feel you must know it.
Now, get in the car. I want to show you something."

He walked around to the driver's side, as if his words
hadn't been that big of a deal. As if keeping secrets from the
people you loved was normal.

"I don't want to go," I said. "Not unless you tell me what
you were talking about in there. Was it something about these
missing girls in town?"

Martin stopped before getting into the car, his head
towering over the top of the vehicle.

"What do you know about that?" he asked.

I sighed. "If we keep this up, we're just going to trade questions all day," I said. "I don't want to do that."

Martin nodded. "Good. No more questions," he said.
"Get in."

I groaned. Okay, that had seriously backfired on me.

I didn't really want to get in the car, but I'd been curious
about Martin's surprise since he'd first mentioned wanting to
show me something. Besides, I had a feeling Martin wasn't
going to budge on answering my questions, anyway.

So, the only question to ask myself was did I trust him?

He waited patiently in the driver's seat as I thought about
my answer.

It didn't take that long, though, for me to decide that yes, I did trust Martin. He'd been there for me this summer in a way no one else had, and I knew he loved me just as much as he'd always loved my father.

My father trusted Martin with his life, and I would do the same.

I opened the car door and got inside.

Neither of us spoke, but Martin let his emotions show for a moment with a slight grin that lifted his lips on the corners.

He drove us through Newcastle and out toward the edge of town. Blackbird Lake was pretty small, as far as lakes go, and it was surrounded by trees and cabins on all sides.

I'd heard my dad talk about it a lot, but even though I'd lived here in Newcastle for a few months, I'd never made it out here before now.

My dad had spent a lot of his childhood out here, because just like me, he'd moved in with Uncle Martin after the death of his own parents. Dad had only been eight when his parents died, though, which broke my heart.

Losing my parents at the age of seventeen wasn't exactly how I had hoped things would go down for me, but I was so grateful I had as much time with them as I did.

A chill went through me as we drove out of town and into the thick expanse of woods that surrounded the lake area. It was like driving into a different dimension. The roads were bumpier out here, and there was hardly any sign of the sun through the canopy of trees above us.

I smiled as we passed an old gas station and bait shop called Old John's. My dad had described its blue roof and giant plastic fish statue a hundred times, and being here now to see it with my own eyes was like recapturing a piece of him I'd almost forgotten.

"You're taking me to the training ground?" I asked, not taking my eyes off the trees.

Martin didn't answer, but I didn't need him to. I'd been so preoccupied with my grief and the idea of having to go to high school like a normal person that I'd completely forgotten about the training grounds out here.

I sat up straighter, watching with anticipation as we zipped through the curves and turns out here in the woods. We only passed a handful of cars, despite the warm, sunny weather. It was probably a totally different scene a week or two ago before school started back, but now, it was like a private little oasis in the middle of nowhere.

About ten minutes after we passed the bait shop, Martin slowed the Cadillac and turned down an overgrown path. I winced as we bumped along the drive, wondering if a car this old could really handle a road like this.

Martin seemed unconcerned, though, as he took us deeper into the trees.

When he finally stopped, I jumped out, anxious to see this place for myself. I ran forward and scanned the tall pine trees for the mark, smiling when I finally saw one.

A circle of thorns with crossed daggers and a rose in the center was branded into the tree in front of me about six feet up.

The Thorne family sigil.

It was hard to believe I was really here. In my mind, this had been a place of legend.

"Your father learned nearly everything he knew out here,"

Uncle Martin said, crossing behind me to walk deeper into the woods.

I followed him back, taking it all in as we walked.

"It still doesn't seem real that he's gone," I said, trying to place him here as a boy. "I always imagined that if I ever got to come out here, it would have been with him."

Martin stood in a clearing about fifteen feet away, staring at it with the strangest expression, as though he were seeing something play out in front of him. His jaw tightened and his eyes glistened, and I realized for the first time just how hard it must have been for him to lose my father.

He'd raised him as his own son, in many ways, and I'd been so wrapped up in my own despair that I hadn't even imagined someone strong like Martin might need comforting, too.

"I miss him," I said, joining Martin in the clearing.

I slipped my hand into his, and he squeezed it for a long moment before clearing his throat.

"I didn't bring you here to reminisce," he said finally. "I brought you here to train. Your parents taught you well, but by the time your father was seventeen, he knew five times what you know now. It's time I brought you up to speed, so that if you decide to take that test and join the ranks of Slayers, you'll be able to hold your own. Now, let's get started."

Thirty minutes later, sweat beaded on my forehead as I stood in the center of the clearing in the woods.

"Grab another handful of dirt," Martin said. "Try again."

I groaned and did as he asked, taking another clump of damp earth in my hand.

When we first started, I had assumed I would show Martin just how much I knew and how far I'd come in the years since my parents had first started taking me along on some of their assignments.

Instead, I'd gotten my butt kicked.

I was used to daggers and spells. I had never tried to take something as basic as dirt and shape it with the power of my mind.

"Earth is an extremely powerful element," he said. "It's often overlooked, because it isn't as flashy as fire, but it's grounding. Its power goes deep inside and takes root. Focus on the dirt in your palm. Pour your power into it until it hums."

I closed my eyes and focused on the feel of the cool, damp earth on my skin. I imagined my own energy flowing down my arm and into the dirt, surrounding it in glowing light.

Of course, there was no real light, but it was one of the best ways I could come up with to visualize what Martin was telling me to do.

The first few tries, nothing had happened.

This time, though, a gentle vibration buzzed through my hand and up my arm.

I smiled and opened my eyes. "I feel it," I said.

"Don't lose it," Martin warned. "Feed it slowly. Pour yourself into it until it feels like it's connected to you. Like it's an extension of you."

I let my instincts take over. I imagined the energy flow gradually increasing, bit by bit until my entire arm and shoulder buzzed with it.

"Good," Martin said. "Now, close your eyes. Imagine a shape or object in your mind. Something simple."

I pictured the first thing that came to mind. A small block, like a child's toy.

"I've got it," I said.

"Now, mold the earth into that shape," Martin said.

"What incantation do I use?" I asked, opening my eyes for a moment.

He shook his head. "No incantation," he said. "This type of manipulation spell doesn't need it. It only needs your clear intent. All you need to do is focus, but do it loosely. Hold on too tight, and you will break the connection."

I closed my eyes again and focused on the hum of the earth in my hands. I pictured it rearranging itself into a solid, stable cube of earth.

I poured my imagination and my power into it, and I could feel the edge of the break Martin was talking about. If I pushed any harder, my connection to the power inside the dirt would break and become useless.

Instead of pushing harder, then, I relaxed into it. I took several deep breaths and formed a clear picture of the object in my mind.

The vibrations against my skin increased, almost tickling me in a way, and I opened my eyes to see a block of dirt in my palm, perfectly formed.

"Wonderful start," Martin said.

I smiled, pride soaring through me. But then, I frowned.

"What good is something this basic going to be against a vampire or a powerful demon someday?" I asked. "Am I supposed to just hit him in the head with a cube-shaped clump of dirt? Somehow, I don't think that's going to save my life in a bind."

"Everyone starts with the basics," Martin said, leading me back toward the car as the sun set.

I could just make out the purple and crimson hues through the trees.

"Magic is incremental. Transmutation is an enormously powerful form of magic," he said. "This is transmutation in its most basic form, but this is how you learn. One tiny step at a time. No witch can harness the full power of any magical discipline when they are just starting out. This is the purpose of the witch's key. You cannot draw so much magic that it burns you out or kills you, the way many witches did before the Council was formed. Instead, your magical capacity increases at the rate of your knowledge and skill."

I wrapped my hand around the key hanging against my chest. It was nothing I hadn't heard before, but I had never liked the idea that someone else had control of my fate and power as a witch. I could only move up to the next key if I passed the Council's test.

"But what if I don't want to be a part of the coven or answer to the Council?" I asked. "Would I still have access to my own power? Or am I bound to this key forever?"

Martin suppressed a smile and his eyes darted toward me.

"Dangerous questions for such a young witch," he said.

"Nothing my parents didn't ask themselves," I said.

Martin stopped walking and turned toward me, his brow furrowed. "What do you mean?"

"I used to hear them talk about the keys and the Council sometimes," I said. "They questioned the idea of being held back until they had permission to access higher levels of magic. They talked about ways to lift the restrictions, things like that."

"Hmm," Martin said, resuming his walk toward the car.

It was hard to study his expressions in the growing darkness, but this seemed to be news to him. For some reason, it made me feel unsettled. Scared.

When we made it back to the Cadillac, he turned to me before starting it up again.

"I want you to promise me something, Lenny."

I nodded. "Of course. Anything," I said.

"Promise me you will never question the use of keys again," he said. "You will never openly express any doubts about the coven or the Witch's Council to anyone outside of this family. Do you understand me?"

My eyes widened, and fear grew inside me like vines slithering across my insides.

"Why?" I asked. "Do you think—"

"Do you promise?" he asked, cutting me off.

I swallowed.

"Yes," I whispered.

He relaxed, his shoulders falling back against the seat.

"Good," he said. "Let's not discuss this further. Now, what would you like for dinner?"

We talked about more mundane things on the drive home, but I couldn't get the thought of Martin's words out of my mind.

Did the Witch's Council have something to do with the death of my parents? Had they done something wrong by questioning the keys or wanting more power?

I tossed and turned all night that night just thinking about it, waking only once to find a raven perched on the edge of the roof outside my window, its dark eyes blending in with the shadows.

FRIENDS FOR A LIFETIME

The rest of the week passed quickly enough. I got to hang out with my new friends almost every day at Sir Bean after school. It was fun, and I felt like I belonged in a way I never had before with people my own age.

That first week of school, I put my whole heart into experiencing life as a normal teenager. I even got a cell phone.

At first, the only number I had programmed in was Uncle Martin's, but gradually, I started adding the numbers of my new friends. Friday afternoon at Sir Bean, Peyton snagged my journal and wrote her number at the top of the first empty page.

"So you can text me over the weekend," she said, smiling. "And don't forget about coming to my house to swim on Monday, too."

I had grabbed my journal back as quickly as I could. I certainly didn't want her reading about what I'd learned at the training grounds or my doubts about Kai's true identity.

I still hadn't figured that one out.

We hadn't talked since that day he'd been waiting for me in front of the house. He must have decided I'd sufficiently backed down from my investigation, which is exactly what I'd done.

I hadn't had any time to look into the cases of the missing girls or even to question Uncle Martin about Kai or his family. Instead, I'd been focused on school work and my new training in the woods.

Martin took me out there over the weekend and drilled me nonstop until I'd nearly passed out from exhaustion. It was fun to play around with my magic again, though, and I was definitely learning a lot.

I hadn't brought up the issue of the keys or my questions about the Council, though. Martin had seemed pretty serious about me never mentioning it again, and to be honest, I was terrified to find out the answer.

The Witch's Council ruled our coven. To lose faith in them after everything else I'd lost would destroy me.

Besides, Martin seemed to trust them. He'd worked as a Keeper in the coven for decades. Maybe even a century or longer. So, if I trusted Martin, I would also have to trust that he would only put his faith in an organization that deserved it.

On Monday, Peyton gave me a ride to her house after school, which was on the other side of Newcastle. The rich side, according to Brandy, and as soon as we drove up to the gate that surrounded Peyton's house, I decided rich was an understatement.

This was generational wealth.

I wouldn't have even thought anyone in a small town like Newcastle had this kind of money.

Actually, the only houses I'd ever seen like this were

estates in Europe owned by centuries-old vampires. Just who were Peyton's parents, anyway?

"Wow, your house is beautiful," I said.

Peyton scrunched her nose as she pulled her Audi sports car through the gate. "It's impressive, but it's not exactly the homiest place in the world," she said. "My parents are rarely ever here, which means I'm alone a lot. I prefer going over to Brandy's house. It's not as big, but their house really feels like home, you know?"

"Not really," I said. I'd never had a house that felt like a true home. Home had been wherever my parents' job took them.

"Brandy hates it, though. She says she wants to be rich like me someday, and she's determined to become a model and make millions someday," Peyton said. "Did you know she has six older brothers?"

"Brandy does?" I asked, my eyes wide.

"Yep. All of them handsome and all of them overprotective of their pretty younger sister," Peyton said with a laugh. "They've all graduated and moved on to college or new jobs now, but when they were all home, that house was filled with laughter. It still is, because her parents are the coolest ever, but I know she misses her brothers."

"And you don't have any brothers or sisters?" I asked.

She parked in a huge garage that housed five other cars. I tried not to gape.

"Sadly, no," she said. "Which is not for lack of trying on my parents' part. They wanted a house full of kids, but it just didn't work out. I'm actually adopted, but I don't talk about it much."

"Oh, wow. I had no idea," I said.

That got my imagination going, though. If she really was descended from some line of magical beings I couldn't identify, maybe she had no idea about it. Were her parents vampires? Why the heck didn't Uncle Martin tell me there was so much supernatural activity in Newcastle?

It was almost like he'd specifically tried to hide it from me.

"It's not really a big deal, but there are times I wonder who my real parents are," she said, a sad expression darkening her features for just a moment. "But I know how lucky I am to have been adopted into this family, and I love my parents. I just wish I could see them more."

"What kind of business are they in?" I asked. "You said they were off at some conference today?"

"For the past three days, actually."

She opened a door through the garage and led me through an elaborate mudroom to the kitchen, which was immaculate and gigantic. White marble countertops. A walk-in refrigerator. Copper pots hanging above the island. This was a real chef's kitchen, but I suddenly understood the sadness in her voice when she talked about her parents being gone all the time.

This felt more like a showroom than the cozy kitchen Martin and I shared.

I was starting to understand what she meant by a place that felt like home. This wasn't it.

"They're interior designers," Peyton said. "I'm sorry to sound bummed out about it. I actually never tell anyone I'm adopted, but for some reason, I feel like I can trust you. That's not weird, is it? I mean, I know we just met."

I wanted to hug her. She was just so genuine and sweet. I

loved that she felt like she could trust me so easily. I felt the same way about her.

"It's not weird at all," I said. "I haven't had a lot of chances to make friends in my life. It means a lot that you trust me."

She smiled. "Okay, enough sappy talk. Come on, let's go find you a bathing suit."

When Peyton had said she had a spare bathing suit I could use, what she apparently meant was that she had a Nordstrom's in her closet. She led me into a bedroom as big as the kitchen, through a private bathroom that rivaled the only spa I'd ever been inside, and into a closet twice the size of my bedroom at Martin's house.

The whole room smelled of lavender.

She opened one of the hundreds of drawers to reveal no less than a dozen bathing suits with tags still attached.

"Pick one," she said. "I could never wear them all, and we seem to be roughly the same size. Sometimes, I think this is how my parents apologize for being gone all the time. Like all they ever really wanted was a doll to dress up."

She gasped and put a hand over her mouth.

"I don't know why I just said that. That's a terrible thing to say."

When she looked up at me, there were tears in her eyes.

I couldn't help myself. I threw my arms around her as she cried.

"I'm so sorry," she said. "I don't know what's gotten into me. I guess I'm just feeling extra sad about them missing most of my first week of school my senior year. I was trying to stay so positive, but sometimes there just comes a point where you can't hold it in anymore. Do you ever feel that way about your parents?"

I tensed and pulled away as she wiped her eyes.

"My parents died earlier this year," I said. "It's not something I like to talk about, either."

"Oh my gosh, Lenny. I had no idea," she said, taking my hand. "Now, I feel like a real jerk."

"It's okay," I said. "You didn't know."

She shook her head and sniffed. "I should have. You mentioned living with your uncle the other day. I just didn't put it together."

"Let's just go downstairs and hang out for a while," I said, holding back tears of my own. "This has actually been really good for me. Having friends, I mean. It's helping me feel like there's hope for a life after what happened. It means more than I can tell you."

She wiped at her cheeks again and put on her best Peyton smile, instantly warming the entire room with the joy behind it.

"No matter how dark things feel sometimes, there's always something to be grateful for, isn't there?" she said. "Right now, I'm feeling extremely grateful for good friends. Get dressed. I'll meet you down there."

I CHOSE a black bathing suit—one of the only ones that wasn't a teeny tiny bikini, thank you very much—and headed back down to the kitchen. By the time I got down there, Brandy was leaning against the counter in her bathing suit, popping open a sparkling water.

Olive and her mom had just arrived, too.

"Mom, this is the new girl I was telling you about."

"So nice to meet you, Lenny." Olive's mom was a tall, thin woman with the kind of energy that seemed to fill up the entire kitchen. Her dark blonde hair was cut in an asymmetrical bob that framed her face. She gave me a warm smile and patted me on the back. "I've heard nothing but good things about you. Welcome to Newcastle."

"Thank you, Mrs.--"

I could not for the life of me remember Olive's last name, but her mom waved away the thought.

"Just call me Ms. Julie," she said.

She placed a white baker's box on the marble counter and gave Peyton a wink.

"Is that what I think it is?" Peyton asked.

"My new flavor just for you to test out," Ms. Julie said. "But wait until everyone's gone. I don't want anyone else influencing your opinion. Text me later. I'm just dying to find out what you think."

"I will. Can't wait." Peyton hugged Olive's mom like they must have known each other for a long time.

And I guess they had. Peyton had said they'd all gone to school together since kindergarten.

As I watched them, I wondered what that must feel like. To have had the same friends for a lifetime, really. A part of me definitely wanted that, even though I'd never really thought about it until now.

My parents had each other, sure, but they hadn't been close to anyone else but me. They hadn't even talked to Uncle Martin all that often. We were like a closed family unit, and even though it had seemed lovely at the time, I suddenly realized there was so much I missed out on as a kid.

"I'll be back to pick you up in a couple hours," Ms. Julie said. "You girls have fun. Be safe."

"Thank you," Olive said, sticking her tongue out at her mom's back once she'd turned.

"What was that for?" Peyton asked.

"She's going to hang out with her new boyfriend again," Olive said. "I'm so sick of him. He gives me the creeps."

"It's his eyes, I think," Brandy said, leaning against the counter. "Like he's always high on something."

"Is he?" Peyton asked.

"Maybe," Olive said with a shrug. "Let's not talk about him. Anything but him. I just want to have some fun."

"Fun we can do," Peyton said, smiling as she started to run. "Race you to the pool."

She ran straight through the open sliding doors along the back of the house and jumped in. Laughing, we all followed her in and had the best afternoon I'd ever shared with girls my age in my life.

Later, Peyton gave me a ride home, and her eyes grew wide when she saw the house.

"Wait. You live here?" she said, equal parts wonder and fear in her eyes. "Everyone says this is a haunted house. I didn't even think anyone lived here anymore."

"I moved in with my great-uncle after my parents died. He, uh, keeps to himself a lot," I said. "But it's definitely not haunted."

Looking at it from this perspective, though, I could see why people would say that.

It was a dark house in all respects. A massive Victorian painted a dark grey with back trim and a black roof. Even the windows looked dark with Martin's thick curtains covering them and no light showing through from inside.

A familiar raven perched on the front porch near the door.

Maybe I needed to talk to Martin about installing some outside lights to make the place look more inhabited. Especially if I ever wanted to convince people to come visit me.

"So, I'll see you tomorrow," I said, opening the car door to get out.

Peyton touched my arm, and a flicker of warm energy flowed through me. I smiled. Definitely not fully human, but what?

It was going to be fun to find out. Especially if she didn't even know about it, herself.

"Hey," she said. "Thanks again for listening to me earlier. It was really nice to get that off my chest, instead of holding it all in for a change. It means a lot."

"That's what friends are for, right?" I said, smiling.

"Definitely," she said. "See ya tomorrow."

I waved goodbye as she turned around in our driveway and headed back toward her house.

I'd never felt so close to someone who wasn't family before, and even though I really liked Brandy and Olive, too, there was just something about Peyton that felt so warm and true.

It was as if we were kindred spirits. Destined to be friends.

As I walked back into the house, I felt this warmth deep inside. It felt like hope and comfort for the first time in a really long time.

Like everything was going to be okay, despite Kai's warning or the missing girls.

Somehow, it would all work out for the best.

But the next morning, as I strolled up, actually excited for another day at school, I noticed the scared looks on everyone's faces as I passed. People were huddled together, whispering and holding hands. Some people were even crying.

I found Brandy and Olive holding each other near the picnic tables out front, and I rushed up, my heart racing.

"What's wrong?" I asked, a black hole of fear opening in the pit of my stomach.

"It's Peyton," Brandy said, her dark skin stained with tears.

"She's gone missing."

CROSSING A LINE

This couldn't be happening.

"We just saw her yesterday afternoon," I said. "She dropped me off at my house last night. That was just a few hours ago. It's not possible that she's gone. She's probably just late for school."

My entire body was shaking.

Peyton was the first real friend I'd ever made, and even though I'd only known her a few days, I already felt so close to her. She couldn't be gone.

This whole thing had to be some kind of misunderstanding.

"It's true," Brandy said. "Her mom called me early this morning asking if Peyton had decided to sleep over at our place. She's done that a few times when her parents were out of town, but I haven't seen Peyton since I left her house yesterday afternoon."

"Me, either," Olive said. "She texted mom about the

cupcake at like eight or nine last night. The cops think that was the last time anyone heard from her."

"Lenny, you were probably the last person to see her before she disappeared," Brandy said. "Did she say anything about where she was going after she dropped you off?"

It felt like someone had just dropped a massive weight on my chest.

"No. She just said she was going home," I said. "Maybe she just went to visit someone else? Does she have a boyfriend?"

No one in my new group of friends seemed to have a boyfriend, but I was grasping at straws, wanting to make sense of this.

"Not anymore," Brandy said. "She'd been dating Maddox Penn for two years, but they broke up over the summer."

"Maybe she went to his house," I said. There had to be a logical explanation.

"There's more to it than that," Brandy said, wiping her face with a tissue. "Believe me, I want this not to be real more than you do. I've known Peyton my whole life, Lenny. She's my best friend. But they know she's been taken. She's not just visiting a friend or something. I can't say anything else, because the police told me not to talk about it, but they're going to want to question you, too, Lenny. They might already be talking to your uncle."

My mouth went dry, and I had to sit down on the picnic table's bench for a second.

The police knew for sure Peyton had been taken?

My mind had already put it all together, but I just didn't want to believe it. The four other missing girls, and now this. It couldn't be a coincidence.

Whoever took those other girls had Peyton, too.

But why?

After the confrontation with Kai, I had taken a step back from figuring out what happened to those girls. Besides, I knew my uncle Martin wouldn't want me messing in this stuff. This was potentially Council business, and if not, it was human business.

I shouldn't get involved.

But now, the only friend I'd ever made was gone.

I had to find her.

I closed my eyes and let my head fall into my hands.

Find her? How the heck was I going to do that? I knew nothing about this town or most of the people in it. I didn't know anything about the other girls who had gone missing or why the police knew for sure Peyton was gone, too.

I didn't have the first clue about where to start.

Except, I did have one clue.

A chill went through me, and I looked up slowly.

I had an encounter with a supernatural mystery dude just last week who very forcefully told me to mind my own business. He'd practically threatened me if I didn't stay out of it.

Which meant he knew a lot more than I did.

I stood up and scanned the crowd of students gathered outside the main entrance to the school. He had to be here somewhere. Besides, he was super tall, so it should have been easy to find him.

"I don't know how I'm going to focus at school today," Brandy said. "I think I'm just going to call my mom to come get me. Do you both want to come over to my place and wait for news?"

"I'll call my mom, too," Olive said. "She's just as upset about this as I am. Peyton's parents must be a wreck, too. They worshipped her. They're never going to forgive themselves for being out of town."

"Geez, you're talking about her like she's never coming back," I said. "She's been gone a few hours. We're going to find her."

Brandy's lower lip quivered, and tears started falling down her cheeks again in a steady stream.

"You're right. We can't give up hope," she said. "But you don't know what it's been like this year. Every time a girl has gone missing, we've put up posters all over town, started a Facebook page, searched the woods, held candlelight vigils. We've kept the hope alive. But then, six months goes by without a single clue or sign of them, and it's hard to believe they're ever coming back. We've done this four times now, and none of those girls have ever come home."

"Listen, it's going to be different this time," I said, touching Brandy's arm. "This time it's Peyton. We can't let this happen. We'll find her."

Brandy nodded, but I could tell she didn't have much hope.

And she was right. I hadn't been here when those other girls disappeared. I hadn't been a part of those vigils and the search for them.

It couldn't have been easy to go through that over and over again with no results. Eventually, it had to feel hopeless.

Which is why we all needed to do everything we could to help bring Peyton home.

Brandy and Olive both stepped aside to make phone calls. I thought about calling Martin, but I hadn't decided exactly what to do yet. I really hoped the cops weren't headed to his house to ask if they could talk to me. Martin hated the human police. He wasn't likely to be super cooperative.

At the same time, though, maybe hearing about my friend's disappearance would make him want to get involved.

Maybe I should have asked him about the missing girls, already. Technically, Uncle Martin was a retired Keeper, but if the Council was planning to get involved in searching for the demon or vampire or whoever took those girls, they would have told Martin.

The Council wasn't going to send a Slayer into his town without him knowing about it.

But it was totally possible Martin would keep me out of the loop.

Still, I found it hard to believe the Council would have sent me to this town and insisted I go to this school full time if they knew about these girls and had plans to get involved somehow. Maybe this particular situation just hadn't made it onto their radar yet.

With the Council, it was all about balance. As long as members of the magical community didn't go too far and tip the scales too noticeably in a negative direction, the Council mostly left them alone.

But something like this? Where did they draw the line?

That was part of the business my parents never really let me get involved in. I would go with them on some of their jobs when things were simple, but they didn't let me in on any of their behind-the-scenes information like conversations with their Keeper or the research they did on their targets.

For example, I might know that a demon had crossed the line, and I would be allowed to go with them when they captured him or banished him, but I didn't always know exactly what he had done to get their attention.

I had an idea, of course, but sometimes the details were kept private.

Still, whoever was taking girls in Newcastle had to be crossing a line here. Four missing girls was bad enough, but five in little more than six months?

That was serial killer mania. If the national news media got wind of this, it would be a PR nightmare for the entire community. Part of the reason the Council existed was to keep a balance between the supernatural community and the human community.

Too much activity, and humans would know we all exist.

There were certain divisions inside the Council that dealt with different aspects of trying to keep the magical community secret from humans. Slayers were the most severe. If a Keeper decided a Slayer needed to be called in, it was bad news for whoever had done something wrong.

At that point, it usually meant banishment, eternal imprisonment, or death. Period.

I would say five missing girls called for the attention of a Slayer.

Talking to Martin about it was the smart thing to do, but I wasn't sure I could handle it if he told me to leave it alone. There was no way I'd be able to sit back and wait for the police to find her. Obviously, they were getting nowhere with the other girls.

I had to do something, and right now, the only thing I could think of was finding Kai. He knew more than I did about this whole situation.

The other day, he'd said he wasn't my enemy. He'd even

acted like he wanted to protect me from getting hurt. I didn't want to believe he had anything to do with those girls going missing, but I was still convinced he knew a lot more about this situation than he was letting on.

And it couldn't have just been a coincidence that he showed up in Newcastle right before the first girl went missing.

I needed to find him, and I needed to confront him.

Even if he didn't do this, I was willing to bet money he knew something about the person, or creature, who did.

Before, I'd looked at this as a tragic event that didn't really affect me in any way. But now, it was personal. I was going to find Peyton, and I was going to bring her home.

I dared anyone—even Kai—to try and stop me.

FOUND YOU

I needed a plan.

The school wasn't dismissing anyone without parental permission today, which made sense. The last thing they needed was more missing teenagers in this town.

I considered calling Martin to get permission, but he'd been acting so overprotective lately, I was afraid he'd lock me away in my room. There was no way he was going to let me skip school to investigate Peyton's disappearance.

I didn't want to break his trust, but I needed to find answers. If he told me one more time to just trust him and not to ask questions, I was going to lose it.

While I worked through it all in my mind, I listened to the conversations happening around me in homeroom.

Mostly, it was just a regurgitation of the newspaper articles I'd read, but every once in a while, I caught a snippet of something I hadn't heard before.

For example, all of the girls were home alone when they went missing. Some people were also saying that every girl had been a regular at Sir Bean during the weekdays after school. Several people thought the owner, Melvin, might have something to do with it.

"I heard he has some kind of police record from before he moved to town," the guy behind me said. "I was going to ask Kai about it, since he works there, but he's not here today."

My ears perked up at that little tidbit.

Kai was absent today? I wanted to know why.

When they called Olive's name over the loudspeaker to go home, I slipped into the hallway with her.

"Did you get ahold of your uncle?" she asked.

"No, but I really can't stay here," I said. "Do you think your mom could vouch for me?"

Olive looked nervous. "I don't know if that's such a great idea. They're being really strict about who goes home with who, and if mom checks you out and you disappear, too—"

"I'm not going to disappear, Olive. I just need to get home, and Martin wasn't answering the phone. He's old. He's probably taking a nap or maybe he has his phone turned off," I said. "I'll be fine. I promise I won't go anywhere else. I'll walk straight home."

She sighed and bit her fingernail. "I'll ask, but I can't promise she'll say yes," Olive said. "My mom's been really stressed lately. I don't know if it's about the girls going missing or the huge success of the cupcake business, but she's super high strung. I never know from one day to the next how she's going to be, but today, she's probably going to be devastated."

We walked together to the office, and Olive's mom pulled her daughter into a big hug. "I'm so glad you're safe," she said. She'd obviously been crying. "This is such a tragedy. I don't know what we're going to do. If anything happens to our sweet Peyton, I just..."

Her voice trailed off, and she held her daughter tighter.

"Are you ready to go, sweetheart?"

Ms. Julie held her daughter's face in her hands, then hugged her again.

This was getting awkward with me just standing here watching. I cleared my throat.

Olive seemed to take the hint.

"Mom, you remember Lenny from yesterday, right?"

"Of course," she said.

She pulled me into a hug, too, and I stiffened. I wasn't used to this kind of affection. Not even from my own mom. I pulled away as quickly as I could.

"How are you holding up, Lenny?" she asked. "You couldn't have known Peyton very long, but she gets into your heart fast, doesn't she? Plus, I can't imagine how difficult it must be to start a brand new school, make a new friend, and then have her disappear suddenly. I promise you, Newcastle wasn't always like this. It's always been a very safe place to live, until recently."

She shook her head, and I thought she was about to cry again, but she managed to get it under control.

"I'm not handling it well at all," I said, laying it on thick. "I don't see how I can stay here all day and listen to everyone talk about this. Do you think you could sign me out, too? I don't live far from here, and I just want to go home and lay down for a while."

"Oh, honey, I don't know," she said. "Have you talked to your parents?"

I swallowed. I hadn't realized how often people assumed you had parents to talk to.

"No, I live with my uncle," I said, leaving it at that for now. "I couldn't reach him, but I know he won't mind if I come home. He's there now, actually. I just couldn't get him to answer the phone. I promise, I'll just walk straight home from here."

"Nonsense," she said. "I couldn't have you walking home by yourself, even if it's close. I'll check you out and drive you there myself."

My shoulders relaxed in relief. "Thank you."

I needed to learn to forge some documents from my uncle to get me out of situations like this in the future, but for now, this would do. Thank goodness for new friends and their overly nice mothers.

A few minutes later, we all loaded into Ms. Julie's Ford Explorer. It smelled like cupcakes.

"Where do you live, Lenny?" she asked.

I directed her toward the house, and she frowned. "100 Moonlight Drive? But that's..."

She didn't complete her thought, but I already knew what she was going to say.

That's the abandoned house. Or that's the house with the creepy dude.

"Yeah, I know it looks dark, but my uncle's just elderly," I said.

Martin would probably kill me if he heard me say that.

The truth was, he was well over a hundred years old, so elderly was in fact an understatement. Slayers and Keepers, once initiated, had expanded life expectancy. We weren't exactly immortal, but we lived a lot longer than your average human.

I hadn't been initiated yet, though. I couldn't make that move and get my next key until I'd taken the Council's initiation test at eighteen. I still had eight months to decide if I was going to take it or not.

"I didn't realize anyone still lived there," she said, clearing her throat and glancing at Olive in the passenger seat. They shared a look that sent a wave of warm embarrassment up the back of my neck.

We didn't talk the rest of the way to the house, but since Martin lived just a few blocks away from the school, it only took us a few minutes to get there. Ms. Julie parked on the street in front of the house, right where Peyton had stopped the night before.

"I can't believe she was just dropping me off right here a few hours ago," I said. "Whoever took her must have done it late last night. What time did she text you?"

"What?" Ms. Julie asked. She obviously hadn't been listening to me.

"Peyton. What time did she text you about the cupcake last night? What did she think of the new flavor?"

Ms. Julie nodded, tears in her eyes again.

"It was about nine when she finally texted me," she said. "She said it was my best recipe yet. I just can't believe she's gone."

"Me, either," I said, glad to at least have an idea of the timeline we were dealing with here. "Thanks again for dropping me off."

Olive handed me a slip of paper with her number on it. "Text me if you want to come over later," she said. "I think we might hang out at Brandy's for a while this afternoon and wait for news."

"Thank you. I'll message you later if I get a chance."

I got out of the car and headed inside as quietly as I could. To be honest, I was relieved there hadn't been a police car outside the house when we pulled up.

It was probably only a matter of time before the police found out I was possibly the last person to see Peyton before she disappeared. That meant it was also only a matter of time before I had to talk to Uncle Martin about what was going on.

But there was something I wanted to do first.

I silenced the soles of my boots again as I entered the house and ran up to my bedroom. At this time of day, Martin was likely to be working in his study on the other side of the house.

I shut the door of my room and took a second to catch my breath before walking over to the small cauldron I'd left on my desk the other night.

I quickly gathered all the herbs and components I needed for the location tracking spell, including my father's magical compass, cleaned out the cauldron, and took a deep breath.

First, just to try it, I took a note Peyton had given me the first day of school with her phone number on it. There was likely some trace of her DNA still on the paper.

I mixed everything together and took a deep breath before dropping the paper into the mixture and whispering, "*Invenio*."

As suspected, though, nothing happened.

Supernatural kidnappings 101. Cloak your target's location. But I had to at least try it, right?

Now, I just had to hope Kai hadn't cloaked his.

I lifted up the piece of straw I'd used in my spell the other night and shook my head.

There wasn't a lot left of the top quarter, and it hadn't even worked right in the first place, but this was my best shot at getting information today.

I dropped the tip of the straw into the spell mixture.

"*Invenio*," I said again as I held the compass in my other hand and waited.

I needed this to work. I needed something to prove that I could do this without my parents here to help. That I could still make a difference in the world.

I needed this to work so that I could help find Peyton before it was too late.

"Please," I whispered, tapping my toes inside my boot.

I stared at the needle on the compass, silently begging it to move.

Come on.

It jerked a couple of times, went still, and then started spinning around in circles so fast, I couldn't follow it with my eyes.

My stomach knotted as I watched. Was it supposed to do this? I couldn't remember.

I held my breath, waiting and praying.

Then, finally, the needle stopped with an abrupt click. It was clearly pointing east, and a smile slowly crossed my face.

"Found you," I whispered before grabbing my bag and heading back out to begin my official investigation into the disappearance of my first real friend.

SO MANY QUESTIONS

L uckily, Martin hadn't heard me come in, and as far as
I could tell, he hadn't heard me leave, either. I would
likely have some major explaining to do if he found
out I'd skipped school, but for now, I had my mind on more
important things.

I kept my eye on the compass in my hand as I followed its
directions.

A magical compass guided by a location spell worked
much like a modern-day GPS system. It would lead you to
where you wanted to go, turn by turn. That way, you didn't
end up trying to swim across a lake to reach your destination.

What it didn't tell you was how far away your target was
from your current location. I didn't have a car, or even a bike,
so I really hoped Kai was somewhere close and that he hadn't
just used whatever crazy superspeed powers he seemed to
have to teleport to school from Mars or something.

If he was even a couple miles away, it was going to take me
forever to get to him.

Especially in this heat.

It was still pretty early in the morning by the time I started walking, but it was probably eighty-five degrees already. By noon, it would be over ninety.

I walked faster, turning west on Broad Street and then making a right turn onto Sanders. About ten minutes later, I was walking down East Hathaway when the needle on the compass started spinning again.

At first, I worried maybe it had broken from the spell, but then, just like before, it suddenly clicked into place.

The needle now pointed directly to my left, and when I turned my body in that direction, I realized I was standing right in front of a small blue house with a well-maintained lawn and a bed of pansies out front. Frilly lace curtains framed a bay window in front of the house, and a pink butterfly wind-catcher attached to a pole in the yard waved in the breeze.

There was even a small garden gnome in front wearing a pink dress and yellow hat.

I raised an eyebrow.

Kai lived here?

Maybe he lived with his grandmother or something. This was definitely not what I was expecting.

I walked up the sidewalk, my heart beating faster with each step. Would he even open the door? He was not going to be happy to see me, and I hadn't even really thought about what I would do once I actually found him.

What was my plan?

Seriously, I'd just walked for twenty minutes and hadn't thought through a plan? What kind of natural-born Slayer was I?

I took a deep breath and stepped onto the porch of the blue

house, but before I could knock, the white door swung open.

Kai towered in the doorway, shaking his head.

"You just couldn't leave it alone, could you?"

"Peyton is gone," I said. "Did you take her?"

I suddenly realized that deep down, I already knew he didn't. If I'd really believed he was capable of that, I never would have come here alone. I might be naive, but I wasn't stupid.

He studied my face, and I forced myself to meet his eyes without fear.

"Why did you come here?" he asked. "I thought I was clear about my feelings on this. Besides, you know Peyton isn't here."

"I need your help," I said. "You can't really expect me to stay out of it after this, can you? Besides, if you don't invite me in, I'm just going to stand on your front porch for the rest of the day singing show tunes. That might get some of your neighbors asking questions you don't want to answer."

He barely held back a smile before bowing his head and opening the door in a grand, sweeping gesture. "Mi casa es su casa," he said. "Come on in."

My jaw tensed as I crossed the threshold of his house. I never really thought of myself as a stupid person, but yeah, this was probably really dumb. No one knew where I was right now, and if I'd misjudged him, I would be the sixth missing girl in this town.

I also hated the fact that my heart was racing for an entirely different reason than fear. There was something about being this close to him again, alone, that sent my nerves into overdrive.

Why did the one guy I needed help from at school have to

be so incredibly good looking? It was distracting.

"Don't worry. I'm not going to hurt you," he said. "I already told you I would do everything I could to make sure no one hurts you."

"And why is that, exactly? You don't even know me," I said.

"I know enough," he said, and the way he stared at me, like he had so many secrets, just made my stomach flip.

"Seriously, what is your deal?" I asked. "I don't have time for this mysterious stranger act. People are missing. Their lives are in danger. Spill it. I need to know what you know."

He laughed, and it was such a pure sound, it resonated somewhere deep within me. It was so beautiful, it was unsettling.

This guy was not at all who I'd thought he was.

"Here, have a seat," he said. "I've been waiting for you to get here, so we could get started."

He gestured to a pack of Reese's Peanut Butter Cups on the table behind a can of my favorite pineapple seltzer water.

My jaw nearly fell to the floor.

I tried to say something, but I couldn't find any words for a very long, awkward moment.

Kai leaned against the doorway into the next room and hooked his thumbs in the pockets of his jeans as he watched me. Apparently, shocking the crap out of me was next-level entertainment for him.

Was this some kind of trap? Lure me in with tasty snacks and then chop my head off or something?

If it was a trap, it was a darn good one.

I never could resist chocolate and peanut butter.

"How do you know so much about me, down to my

favorite flavor combinations?" I asked. "You're freaking me out."

"Sit down, and I'll explain it."

I thought about it for a few seconds, but in the end, what choice did I really have? I hadn't come here to just yell at him and walk away. I came for answers, so if he was offering them, I had to listen.

I sat down and opened the pack of candy, just to prove to him I wasn't scared. And maybe a little bit to alleviate my extreme levels of stress.

What was it about chocolate that cured everything?

I took the opportunity to study the room around us. This was a pretty small house, but it was incredibly clean and the inside was decorated more like a little old lady lived here than a teenage dude.

"So, is your grandma home?" I asked.

He tried to hold back a smile.

"I'm staying at a friend's place for a while," he said. "She's out of town."

"I'm guessing the school doesn't know about that," I said. "And I'm guessing you're not really a senior in high school."

He sat down across from me at the small table. "Just how much does the Council know about your involvement at this point?"

I straightened.

He was supposed to be giving me answers, not grilling me with questions.

"I'm sure you already know that the Council hasn't exactly given me permission to look into this," I said. "What about your involvement? And your relationship to the Council, for that matter. Are you a Slayer?"

"Not the way you and your parents are."

"Did the Council send you here?" I asked.

"No. I don't work for the Witch's Council."

"Then how did you just happen to show up in this town right before those girls started disappearing? That can't be a coincidence," I said.

"In some ways, I knew to come here the same way I knew you'd be knocking on my door this afternoon, or that you can't resist chocolate and peanut butter when they're combined together," he said. "I have certain abilities that make it easy to predict situations."

"So, did you know Peyton was going to be kidnapped?"

Just asking the question brought tears to my eyes. I still couldn't believe she was gone.

"No. I knew someone was likely to be taken soon, but I didn't know who or when," he said. "Trust me, if I'd known, I would have done everything in my power to put a stop to it."

He lowered his eyes for a moment to his hands.

"I've actually been watching your place for the past few nights," he said.

When he looked up, our eyes met, and I could see he'd been telling the truth the other day when he said he would try to make sure no one hurt me. But why? Why did he care?

"You thought whoever's doing this was going to take me?"

"I thought there was a strong possibility," he said. "Even though most people can't see or sense it, I know that each of the girls who were taken have some magical blood in their ancestry. It's faint in most cases, but it's there. When you moved to town, I thought your strong connection to magic might make you a target, even with your uncle watching out for you."

"So, even though you've been here for six months trying to find them, you still don't know who's doing this?" I asked. "Do you know what's happened to the girls? Are they still alive? If you can see the future, how come you can't see what they're going to do next?"

"Do you always ask so many questions?" A faint smile tugged at his mouth.

"No, but I've been holding those in for a few days now," I said. "And Peyton's already been gone for more than twelve hours from what I can tell. Who knows how long he'll keep her alive."

He stood and paced the floor beside the table, as if trying to decide just how much to tell me about what he knew.

"I'm fairly certain the being taking girls in Newcastle is a demon," he said. "I haven't been able to track them, though. Believe me, if I could use my abilities to find them or see their next move, I would have done it already. It's usually only something that works with people whose intentions are pure and good, and it's not always consistent. I can't see what you're going to say next, for example, but I knew you would come here. It's hard to explain."

I let his words sink in for a moment.

"So, you can't see the intentions of evil creatures or beings, like certain demons?" I asked.

He shook his head. "No."

"Then, how did you see enough to lead you here to Newcastle six months ago?"

"Because I was tracking someone else when I came here," he said. "I didn't know I would be stepping into a situation where young girls were going to be kidnapped."

"Who were you tracking?" I asked.

"My father," he said.

I raised an eyebrow. I definitely hadn't expected him to say that. Every answer from him just led to more questions.

"Did you find him?"

Kai shook his head and stopped pacing the floor.

"I don't think I'm ready to talk about that just yet." He sat down beside me at the table. "But what I can tell you is that I'm pretty sure the girls are all still alive. For now."

I fell back against the chair, surprised and relieved. "All of them? How do you know that?"

"I've had a lot of time to research what's been happening here, and I found a connection to a series of kidnappings that have happened across the world over the past decade. Each one of these kidnappings involved five teen girls, all taken over the course of about six months."

My stomach twisted into a knot. Patterns like this were never good, and I wasn't sure I wanted to hear what had eventually happened to those other girls in the other towns.

But he was going to tell me anyway. I needed to know the truth, no matter how hard it might be to hear.

"What happened to them?" I asked.

He looked down. "In each instance, the girls were kept alive until all five were taken. Soon after, on the night of the next full moon, they were all five sacrificed together in a ritual," he said. "From what I can tell, it's the same ritual each time. I've managed to put that information together from various research and interviews I've done over the past few months, but what I haven't been able to discern is exactly what he's gaining from it. And, of course, who's behind it all. In each town, the police arrested someone for the murders and closed the book on it, but I believe all of those people were framed. The real killer is here in Newcastle."

I let this information sink in, and then I closed my eyes and counted. I had a calendar in my bedroom of the moon cycle, so I pictured it in my mind now, trying to figure out where we were in the current cycle.

My eyes snapped open, tears flooding to the surface.

"The next full moon is in three days, Kai."

My hands trembled, and I set the chocolate down. I'd just lost any appetite I had.

If he was right, we had less than three full days to find Peyton and the others before it was too late and this demon, or whatever it was, moved on to another town to repeat the horror show.

"I know," Kai said. "I was hoping there would be at least one more cycle before he took another girl, but the second I heard about Peyton, I knew we were down to just a few days."

"We can't let that happen," I said. "We have to save them and put a stop to this."

"That's exactly what I'm trying to do here," he said. "But without knowing who's behind it, I'm not sure what to do next."

I shook my head, trying to work through it. What could we do to help?

"What about the Council?" I asked. "If this is a demon who's repeating this ritual over and over, why haven't they gotten involved? Isn't this exactly the kind of thing Slayers exist to deal with?"

He stood and started pacing again. I kind of wanted to join him. The tension inside me was building to an extreme. I felt like I could have probably punched through a brick wall if I wanted to.

"It doesn't make a lot of sense to me, either," he said. "Yes, Slayers should have been called in on this, but from what I can tell, no one on the Council is even investigating this situation."

"Maybe they just aren't aware of it for some reason," I said, standing. "Maybe we need to tell them. They can send in Slayers and deal with it faster than we could on our own."

"I'm not sure we can trust the Council, Lenny," he said. "They should have sent someone to deal with this by now. I alerted them to my suspicions four months ago when I discovered the connection between this and those other rituals. I basically got the equivalent of the Council's voicemail."

I bit the inside of my lip so hard, I tasted blood.

Maybe he was right when he told me I was getting in over my head.

There were rules to this life of being a Slayer and a witch. There was an order to things. But if the Council didn't decide to interfere, what then? Were we really expected to just sit back and watch innocent people be sacrificed?

I was very not down with that idea.

But what happened to witches that defied the Council's rulings?

I shuddered. I wasn't sure I wanted to know.

This was exactly what Martin had been talking about the other day. I hadn't promised him I wouldn't break the rules, though. Just that I wouldn't speak out against the Council.

Crap. This was getting complicated fast.

But the only way Martin could help me find Peyton was if I told him everything I knew. It was a risk, but without him, I could really get myself into trouble.

"I should probably talk to my uncle Martin about this," I said. "He's been a Keeper for ages, and even though he's retired now, he would probably have something to say about why the Council isn't choosing to intervene."

Kai smiled. "And how to get around it?"

Dang. It was like he could read my mind.

And I guess maybe he could, in a way.

"I don't want to get him into any kind of trouble," I said. "But maybe he could help."

"That's entirely your call, Lenny. You need to do what you think is best, but either way, I think Martin can take care of himself."

"He's pretty old," I said, scrunching my nose. "And he's retired. He's probably a bit rusty."

"I wouldn't count him out just yet," Kai said with a knowing smile. "Keepers aren't usually skilled at combat like Slayers are, but I've heard tales about old Martin from his younger days. Back then, he was known for being a rare Keeper with Slayer tendencies. He could apparently hold his own."

I smiled at the thought of his intense training sessions. He definitely knew how to fight. "I didn't know that, but it doesn't surprise me."

Kai looked down for a second, growing quiet. When he looked up again, his voice was softer.

"I'm glad it wasn't you they took," he said. The look in his eyes said he was being genuine, though I couldn't imagine why he cared. "I'm not saying I'm glad it was Peyton. I would rather it was no one at all, but I'm especially glad it wasn't you, Lenora."

The sincerity in his tone nearly took my breath away.

There weren't a lot of people out there in the world who cared about me at all, and yet, here he was, saying these things as if we were old friends.

This guy was a pure mystery.

"Why do you care so much? We've never even met," I said. "Unless you count our super fun talk last week, which I'd rather forget."

"But we have met," he said. "You wouldn't have remembered it, because you were so young at the time, but I remember you."

"We have?" I asked, my eyes widening. "When?"

"You were probably about eight years old, and you were staying in a little village in Romania for the summer," he said. "Your parents were there investigating a vampire hive rumored to be terrorizing the area. My father had some business to discuss with them at the time, and he brought me along. I was only ten, but I remember you very clearly."

"Wait, our parents knew each other?"

Today was like bomb after bomb of new information. I wasn't sure I was taking it all in.

"They were good friends, actually," he said. "I'll tell you more about it another time. For now, though, I think you need to get home to Martin."

"Why?" Fear gripped my heart. "Did you see something? Is he in trouble?"

He closed his eyes and touched his forehead, straining at some thought or vision.

"I can't say exactly, other than he's thinking of you," he said. "He's worried."

I let my head fall back, and I groaned.

"Awesome. He's probably just found out I skipped school,"

I said, reaching for my bag. I was not looking forward to trying to explain this.

"If you want, I can drive you home," Kai said.

I raised an eyebrow. "So, you don't just travel everywhere by super-crazy-fast teleportation speed? How interesting."

He laughed again, and it was so real and pure, that I was sure I could feel it vibrate in the air around me. My arms broke out in goosebumps.

I studied him as he walked into the other room to grab his keys. He was extremely graceful. He possessed some kind of minor clairvoyance. And the air vibrated when he laughed.

What in the world was this guy?

Definitely not a witch. Or a demon. Not a vampire, either, despite his grace.

I had so many questions.

He led me out to an old VW Bug, and I couldn't hold back my laughter. This car did not suit him at all. He was this tall, dark, handsome guy cramming himself into this tiny car with a flowery headband hanging from the rearview mirror and a lucky cat bobbing on the dashboard.

When he looked over and saw my expression, he actually blushed.

"The car came with the house," he said.

"Obviously," I said.

It took just a few minutes to get back to Martin's, and I'd been quiet the whole drive, imagining a police car parked out front.

Instead, when Kai pulled up, there was a different car parked in the driveway. Not exactly a cop car, but something that was potentially much, much worse.

The raven I'd seen watching me for the past few weeks

had boldly taken a place on the front gate, watching the cars that passed by.

Suddenly, it all made sense.

"What's wrong?" he asked. "You look like you just saw a ghost."

"I have to go," I said, clawing off my seatbelt and jumping out of the car as quickly as I could. "Find me later tonight. If I'm still alive."

I muttered that last part under my breath and ran to the house, throwing open the door to find two serious sets of eyes snap toward mine.

"I can explain," I said.

A dark haired woman wearing a perfectly tailored black pencil skirt and matching jacket crossed her arms in front of her chest and focused her icy blue eyes on mine.

"Well, I certainly hope so," she said. "Or we're going to have a serious issue on our hands."

I glanced at Martin, and he shook his head. I could practically feel the disappointment rolling off of him.

But right now, it wasn't Martin I was particularly worried about.

It was Blythe Greer, the witch who had been my parents' Keeper for the past fifty years. Beautiful. Powerful. Ruthless.

She was known inside the Council for only sending messages by raven. In fact, she so rarely made personal appearances that some witches had started calling her the Grim Reaper, because if she showed up at your house, heads were about to roll.

And judging by the look on Blythe's face, my head was next.

NO LAUGHING MATTER

Blythe Greer scared the crap out of me. I'd never seen her smile. Not once the entire time I'd known her.

Even her ravens all seemed to have hard expressions when they delivered notes from her.

Seeing the ravens outside my window now suddenly made so much sense. She'd been keeping an eye on me, and now she was here to tell me to stop looking into this. I could feel it.

I'd grown to fear the sight of her, even as a child, because whenever she appeared in person, it was almost always to deliver bad news or to reprimand my parents in some way.

I needed to tread carefully here.

"I haven't done anything to interfere directly in any investigation into the missing girls," I said.

"Missing girls?" Martin asked. "How on earth did you get tangled up in that mess?"

I sighed. At least Ms. Greer hadn't been here long enough to explain everything to Martin.

"It's all anyone is talking about at school," I said. I looked

Ms. Greer directly in the eyes. "The school the Council insisted I attend, by the way."

She had literally no expression. Unless "harsh" was an expression.

"The girl who was taken today was my friend," I said.

I didn't offer anything else, because frankly, I didn't know how much the Council knew. The fact that they knew anything kind of gave me the willies, because I hadn't really done anything beyond the locating spell.

I should have guessed they'd been watching me.

"I've done nothing wrong," I said.

"Where were you just now?" Ms. Greer asked. "At school like you were supposed to be?"

I shifted my weight and adjusted the bag on my shoulder. She was going to get me into trouble with Martin now, too. Great.

"I was visiting another friend I'd made at school the past couple days."

I glanced at Uncle Martin, hoping maybe his expression would give me some clue as to what kind of trouble I was in here. Truth be told, I really hadn't done anything illegal.

Not yet, anyway.

I had used my magic a few times, but I hadn't done anything that uninitiated witches aren't sanctioned to do. Why, exactly, was Ms. Greer here in Newcastle?

"See, she was just visiting a friend," Uncle Martin said. "I told you she's done nothing wrong. A mirror spell is not a punishable offense if no one sees it. Why are you here, Ms. Greer? Let's get down to it. I'm too old to play games, especially where my ward is concerned."

I swallowed. He was protecting me, instead of yelling at me. That was a good sign, right?

Blythe Greer kept her eyes on mine for a long, silent moment. It was enough to make my hands sweat and my mouth go dry, but I at least managed to keep my knees from knocking together. Audibly, anyway.

"Put your bag down and sit," Ms. Greer said, motioning to the dusty couch in the formal sitting room no one ever used.

I glanced at Martin, and he nodded slightly.

"You may go," she said to Martin, not even bothering to look at him. "I will speak to you next."

His mouth opened for a moment, and I thought he was going to tell her to stuff it at first. After a few seconds, though, he excused himself and walked away.

Crap. Now, I really was on my own.

I did as Ms. Greer asked and set my bag down on the floor next to the couch. I dusted off a small section of the velvet surface and sat down, coughing as a cloud of dust surrounded me. Man, when was the last time anyone actually sat on this thing? 1902?

If I ever did hope to have friends who came to visit and hang out the way we'd done at Peyton's, we were going to need to make some serious changes around here.

Maybe Peyton's parents would be so grateful once I helped save her life that they'd come to our house and redecorate the entire place for free. All new furniture and paint. Give the old place a facelift.

I imagined the look on Uncle Martin's face as they tried to pull down his black chandelier, and I smiled.

"This is no laughing matter, Lenora," Ms. Greer said.

I pressed my lips together and straightened my shoulders.

I didn't want to make this any worse, but I couldn't help myself. It was a defense mechanism.

"I know why you weren't at school just now," Ms. Greer said.

I took a deep breath. Okay, so they knew where I was, but how in the heck had she gotten here so quickly? I'd only just gone to Kai's a couple of hours ago.

"I am extremely disappointed that you chose to go outside our coven for information," she said. "The situation with these young women is unfortunate, but it's not your concern. Why did you seek the help of an outsider, rather than come to me or even your uncle?"

None of my concern?

I crossed my arms in front of my chest. That was exactly why I hadn't come to her. I knew she would tell me to stay out of it.

"Does that mean the Council is sending someone else to save them?" I asked.

"The Council does not answer to you, child."

"Technically, I don't answer to the Council yet, either," I said, regretting my words the second they popped out of my mouth. "I haven't taken the test, I mean."

"You are forbidden to look into the disappearances of these human teenagers any further," Ms. Greer said. "You are not allowed to look for them, research the facts, or try to aid them in any way. This is an official order from the Council of Witches. Do you understand what that means, Lenora?"

I clenched my jaw so tight, I thought I was going to break a tooth.

There was no way I could just sit back and watch those girls die. I wouldn't do it.

"Lenora, answer me."

I bit my tongue and tried to hold it in. I even thought through an appropriate, obedient response, but I couldn't force myself to actually agree to it.

In the end, like always, my tongue had a mind of its own.

"Are you seriously telling me the Council is planning to do nothing to help these girls?" I asked, standing. "They all have magical blood. Magical ancestry, just like us. What if it was me who'd gone missing? Would I just be left to die?"

"Of course not, but it wasn't you who was taken, and none of those young women are in touch with their magical abilities in any way," she said. "They don't even know what they're capable of, and I'd be surprised if they could access any magic with how little there is in their systems, even with extensive training. Those girls are not part of our world, and they are definitely not part of our coven."

"That doesn't make them any less valuable," I said, daring to step closer to her. I was so angry, my body shook with it. "You could choose to send in a few slayers and save them right now. I know you could."

"What the Council decides and why is none of your concern, and if you have any aspirations of becoming an official part of the Slayer community, you'll do exactly as you're told and leave this alone."

"Or what?" I asked, standing my ground.

Ms. Greer's eye twitched slightly. She wasn't used to being defied in any way, but I couldn't help myself.

"Trust me when I say you don't want to find out," she said.

The threat in her eyes made me feel a bit sick to my stomach. What would they do to me if I kept going with this investigation? Would they kill me?

Surely not.

But from her expression, I honestly couldn't tell.

"At least explain to me why the Council is choosing not to get involved. It doesn't make any sense," I said. "Kai told me he has research that proves this demon has performed the exact same ritual before. Several times. How is killing this many girls okay with the Council? How is this not crossing some kind of line?"

Ms. Greer's eyes flashed red, like embers igniting deep inside her.

"The Council does not have to explain its decisions to you or to anyone," she said. "And Kai Richards is not a part of our Council. He isn't even abiding by the laws of his own sect, and his actions are eventually going to get him killed. Just like—"

She cut her words off, and tugged at the bottom of her jacket.

"I don't want to see you go down with him, Lenny, but if you continue to look into this or take any action to try to save those girls, I won't help you when the Council calls for you. I was very close to your parents, but I want to make it absolutely clear that I will not step in to save you if it comes to that."

Her words stung.

Deep down, I'd always assumed that despite her harsh ways and ruthless reputation, she was loyal to my parents. For some stupid reason, I believed that meant she would look after me the way she'd always looked out for them.

A Keeper's job, ultimately, was exactly that. To make sure their Slayers had all the information, training, and support they needed to execute the Council's orders.

As my parents' Keeper for most of their career, I felt there was mutual respect and affection in their relationship. Why had I believed that would extend to me after my parents died?

Instead, she'd been spying on me for the Council.

"Have I made myself clear, Ms. Thorne?"

I swallowed back tears and did my best to hide my emotions.

"Crystal," I said.

"Good. I don't particularly like to have to handle things in person if it can be avoided. You're lucky I was in town dealing with a different issue, but I made a stop here out of respect for your parents and their loyalty to me and to the Council," she said. "Stay out of this, Lenora, and you'll be just fine. Don't make me come down here again, though. I won't be this pleasant next time we meet."

Pleasant? Yeah, she'd been a real joy to have around for the past half hour.

According to her, I was going to have to just let my new friend and four other innocent girls be sacrificed by a demon, regardless of the fact that no one could explain why.

Such pleasant news.

Anger and frustration grew inside me, but I held it back as much as I could.

Uncle Martin reappeared from wherever he'd been in the back rooms. "Are you ready Ms. Greer? I have quite a few things I need to attend to this afternoon, if you don't mind."

"Yes," she said. "Shall we convene in the privacy of your study?"

Martin bowed his head and motioned for her to walk with him down the back hallway.

Seething, I stomped up the steps to my bedroom.

I couldn't believe Ms. Greer had been spying on me like

this. Or that she and the Council were just going to ignore these rituals.

Regardless of the fact that the girls who'd been kidnapped weren't part of our coven, this demon's murderous activities were putting the entire magical community at risk. He needed to be dealt with.

So, why weren't they doing their job?

I suddenly stopped pacing, my brain landing on a dangerous conclusion.

Maybe Blythe Greer, or someone close to the Council, was involved in this somehow. Either that, or they were protecting someone.

I needed to find out what Ms. Greer was really up to here in town.

She'd said she was here on other business, and I wanted to know what it was. What else could she be doing in a small, middle-of-nowhere town like Newcastle unless she was dealing with this demon in some way?

I needed to think fast.

Her meeting with Martin, no doubt to discuss my awful behavior, wouldn't last long. If I was going to do something, I had to do it now.

The spell book I'd used earlier was still open to the location tracking spell I'd used to find Kai, and that gave me an idea.

I flipped through a few pages to find another version of the spell that would work for these purposes without alerting Ms. Greer to my plans. Satisfied with a short spell a few pages in, I quickly gathered my materials and created a tiny bundle of enchanted herbs, no bigger than my thumb.

I dipped the herbs in honey and hid the small bundle in

my palm as I tiptoed down the steps. I did a quick search to make sure Martin and Ms. Greer weren't hanging out in the front rooms, and then I made my way outside, slipping out the back door instead of the front to avoid that pesky raven.

Carefully, keeping my eyes on that raven, I crouched on the far side of Ms. Greer's black Acura.

With trembling hands, I reached under the car and stuck the herb bundle to the metal near the front tires.

"*Persector*," I whispered.

The bundle warmed slightly as the spell took hold.

Now, all I had to do was go back up to my bedroom, grab a map of town, and wait. As soon as Blythe Greer left this house, I'd be able to see exactly where she was going.

It was a dangerous move with potentially lethal consequences.

But what about the consequences of letting someone I cared about die when there might have been something I could do about it? If I just let Peyton die, a piece of me would die with her.

If that was the truth of being a Slayer, then I couldn't take their stupid test and join them, anyway. I couldn't live that kind of life.

I'd rather turn my back on magic than turn my back on my friends.

It was hours before Ms. Greer left the house, though, and I was starting to lose my patience. What could they possibly be talking about for the entire day?

When she finally drove away, I stood, hovering over the map, dying to see where she was going, when someone knocked.

But they hadn't knocked on my door.

Surprised, I turned my eyes toward my second-story window.

Carefully, I closed the map and peered toward the window, slightly terrified that whatever demon had taken Peyton was now here to get me. Who would knock on my window after dark like this? Or ever?

With a flick of my wrist, I commanded the window to swing open.

"*Incendium,*" I said with a wobbly voice.

Kai leaned in, his eyes on the flames that engulfed my hand.

"Glad to see you're still alive," he said with a smirk. "Is this a bad time? You did tell me to find you later, remember? What happened?"

I let the spell fizzle and sighed in relief. How the heck did he get up here? And why was I so happy to see him, even after he'd just gotten me into trouble?

Maybe because he was the only one who wanted to help me save my friend.

Maybe I was willing to deal with the consequences, after all.

He climbed into my room, and the look in his dark eyes was suddenly very curious.

"What is it?" he asked. "You've got a very mischievous look about you right now."

I smiled.

"You're just the person I needed to see," I said, opening the map back up and watching as a tiny dot drove out of town. "We're going to need your car."

DANGEROUS TERRITORY

"I do not like the sound of that," Kai said, looking more nervous than I expected him to, considering the fact that he was somehow spying on my second-floor bedroom.

"Wait a second. How did you get up here?" I narrowed my eyes at him. "And just how long were you standing out there?"

I took a few steps closer to him.

"That better be the first time you've ever come up to my room in your life," I said. "How did you even know which room was mine? You better start talking before I knock you out and steal your car keys."

He threw his hand up in defense.

"I swear to you, I've never been up here before," he said. "As for how I knew it was your room, this is literally the only visible light on in the entire house."

I relaxed. He had a good point there.

"So, how did you get up here?" I asked.

"That's a story for another day," he said, and when I questioned him with my eyes, he shook his head. "Look, I need to be able to keep a few secrets today. Now, you tell me why you need my car."

I pointed to the map.

"That little dot there is the car of a woman named Blythe Greer, and—"

"Blythe Greer is here in Newcastle?" he asked.

I put a hand on my hip. How did he know so much about my business? Who was this guy?

"You seem to know an awful lot about what's going on in my life. How do you know her?"

"I don't exactly know her," he said, his eyes following the dot on the map. "I've heard the name, though. From my dad. I told you he was good friends with your parents. Why are you following her? Pretty neat tracking spell, by the way."

"Thanks," I said, pushing my thick brown hair back from my face. "She showed up here today to reprimand me for seeing you, actually."

He turned to look at me. "You got in trouble?"

"Let's just say she issued a strong warning about me staying out of this business with the missing girls," I said.

I explained to him my concerns about the Council or possibly about Ms. Greer having something to do with it. I wanted answers, and even though I knew it was dumb, I was all in at this point. No turning back.

"She slipped and admitted she'd come here to Newcastle for different business and was just doing me a favor by checking in on me," I said. "You didn't happen to see any ravens while you were out there leaping tall buildings in a single bound, did you?"

He laughed. "Not that I noticed."

"Good. Come on, we need to get going before we lose her."

"She stopped at a hotel on the edge of town," Kai said, pointing to the map. "It's possible she's doing some kind of business or meeting with someone out there, but it's more likely she's staying there for the night. It's one of the only places in town that rents rooms."

I frowned. That didn't sound very interesting. I didn't want to risk sneaking out just to end up watching Ms. Greer watch bad TV while hanging out in some run down hotel room.

"Well, we have to at least go out there and see. Maybe someone's meeting her there," I said.

"Don't you think we should think through this first?" he asked.

"I have," I said. "I want to find Peyton and the others. Ms. Greer, a representative of the Witch's Council, has suddenly appeared in my town, warning me not to get involved and basically admitting to me that the Council is doing nothing to help. There's something fishy going on, and she's my best chance right now of getting answers. What else is there to think about?"

He paced the room, making points on his fingertips.

"Well, for one, I'm ninety-nine percent sure we're looking at a powerful demon who has sacrificed many other humans before. What are we going to do if we rush in there and encounter this guy?" he asked. "Did you think about that?"

I bit my lip. "No."

"Second, if Ms. Greer has been watching you, it's possible the Council is watching you, too. Independent of her ravens," he said. "If they've just warned you not to get involved, how lenient do you think they'll be if they catch you spying on one of their Keepers?"

I took a deep breath. He was right.

I hadn't really thought through all the possibilities. I was just looking one step ahead and assuming Ms. Greer would never know we were there.

"Okay, so what's the solution, then?" I asked. "Since you've obviously already given this some thought."

Kai studied me for a second, and then he looked around my bedroom. A warm blush blossomed on my cheeks. Thankfully, I didn't have any dirty clothes or candy wrappers on the floor, but still. What was he looking for?

His eyes landed on the mahogany spell cabinet. To anyone else, it would just look like a worn, antique cabinet, but I could tell he recognized it right away.

"Do you have any blackberry vines in there? Amaranth?"

"What kind of witch do you think I am?" I asked, tilting my head to the side.

He smiled.

"Okay, what about ashes from a cedar tree?"

I had to think about that one.

"I think so," I said.

I had a faint memory of burning several different types of wood and leaves with my mother one winter afternoon a few years ago.

"Then you can just cloak your movements," he said. "The Council won't be able to see where you go tonight, if you don't want them to."

"The Council can see through all our cloaking spells as young witches," I said. "There are several in my spell books, but I've been told they don't work against the Council."

It was his turn to look at me like I was crazy.

"You won't find this particular spell in any of your books," he said. "The Council might not teach spells that work against them to their witches, but I don't belong to your Council."

I wanted to laugh at my own stupidity.

I hadn't even thought of using magic to keep the Council out of my business. I'd always considered them a part of my magical process, and it just hadn't occurred to me that I could use magic to hide something from them.

It was still very dangerous territory, but at least it would keep them out of my hair for a little while. I hoped.

"What about Martin? I imagine he's already upset with me for ditching school," I said. "Should I tell him where we're going."

"Do you think he'd let you go?"

I closed my eyes and sighed. I didn't like hiding anything from Uncle Martin, but no. I didn't think he'd let me go spy on Blythe Greer tonight. I was putting my life and my possible future career at risk just going over there

"Are you sure you're up for this?" Kai asked. "I could just go alone."

My heart beat a little faster at the thought of going against the Council's direct orders. What if someone found out?

I didn't want Martin to be angry with me, but at the same time, he was keeping secrets from me, too.

Besides, all I could think about was Peyton's smile. What kind of horror was she going through right now? What nightmare was she trapped in?

"I'm up for it," I said. "Do you have the incantation and everything I'll need? I've never used cedar ash in a cloaking spell before."

"I can show you how," he said. "If you don't mind me watching you cast."

I swallowed. Why did that suddenly feel like such an intimate thing?

I guess because witches usually only cast in front of their most trusted allies.

Or their worst enemies.

I still didn't even know what this guy was. I should have asked him last time we were together, but I was scared to ask.

I had the feeling he wouldn't tell me, anyway. Not until he was ready.

"I don't mind," I said.

I placed a fingertip on the key hanging from my necklace and imagined the cabinet opening. It obeyed me, and the doors swung open, revealing some of the most important items I owned.

Was I crazy to trust Kai like this?

Ms. Greer had said he was breaking the rules of his own sect. What did that mean, exactly? That he'd gone rogue? Were they looking for him, whoever they were? And what had happened to his father?

I pushed back all my questions and focused, instead, on the task at hand. It was already getting to be later in the evening, and we only had a few days to investigate before Peyton and the others would die. I didn't have time to be worried about Kai's ancestry or whether he was going to be in trouble for this.

When the dust settled, we were both going to be in a lot of trouble.

If we could save Peyton and the others, though, it would be worth it.

I located all the ingredients he'd asked me to gather, but

when I went to clean out my little cauldron to mix them, Kai shook his head.

"Not in there," he said. "Here, sit with me."

He grabbed a blanket from the end of the bed and stretched it across the floor.

He motioned for me to sit down across from him, but I hesitated. If he wasn't a witch of some kind, how did he know what to do?

"Trust me," he said, warmth in his dark eyes.

I sat down across from him and set the three ingredients on the blanket between us.

"Give me your hand," he said.

I stretched my hand toward him, and he took it, turning my palm upward. His hands were twice as big as my own, and his skin was warm against mine.

He pinched off a small piece of blackberry vine and set it in the palm of my hand. Then, he sprinkled it with a tiny bit of cedar ash. Finally. He broke off a small tip from the amaranth plant and rolled it between his fingertips until the dust of it fell onto the other ingredients.

I was fascinated by what he was doing. This was a very different process from any I'd followed in the past. When he was finished, he rolled my fingertips toward me, closing my palm tightly against the ingredients.

"Bring your fist to your mouth and whisper the following incantation," he said. "*Hūnā iaʻu.*"

My eyes widened. This was definitely not a normal witch's incantation, but there was an energy that radiated from him as he said it. Not only could I feel it, I could see it shimmer in the air.

"What is that?" I whispered.

Our eyes locked, and I realized that even though I'd been worried about whether I could trust him around my things, trusting him with magic was an entirely different beast. For all I knew, he could be making me cast a spell on myself that would send me into another dimension.

"You can trust me," he said softly. "I promise I will never hurt you."

I searched his eyes and leaned in toward the energy around us. I felt for any sign of negative intention or manipulation, but all I could sense from him was goodness.

But did I trust myself to know better?

Butterflies danced in my stomach. Peyton didn't have time for me to sit here and try to figure it out.

"*Hūnā ia'u*," I whispered, not sure if I was saying it exactly right.

But Kai nodded.

"Now, open your hand."

Unsure what to expect, I uncurled my fingers and gasped as sparkling particles burst from my palm, surrounding my body for a brief, shimmering moment before disappearing.

"What just happened?" I asked.

"You just cloaked yourself from the Council's view," he said. "Good job."

"How did you know to do that?" I asked. "I've never seen that kind of magic before."

"My mother was a witch." He stood and offered his hand to me. "Come on, I'll tell you more about her when we're on our way. It's getting late."

His mother? I certainly hadn't expected that answer.

If she was a witch, she wasn't from the same coven as my

family. But now I had half the answer to the Kai puzzle. He was at least half witch of some kind. What was the other half?

"It looks like we'll be going somewhere other than that hotel, after all," he said, glancing at the map again as we both stood.

"What do you mean?" I asked, grabbing my backpack and slinging it over my shoulders.

But I could see for myself.

Ms. Greer was on the move, and if we left now, we might just be able to catch up with her before she did anything too important.

"Let's go," I said. "But not the window. We'll take the stairs, like normal people."

Kai laughed and followed me into the hallway, carefully and quietly down the steps, and out into the night.

UNPREPARED

few minutes later, we were driving west toward the outskirts of town.

This was the opposite of the way Martin and I had gone to get to the lake, and I quickly realized we were in unfamiliar territory.

"Do you know where she's going?" I asked.

Kai had been here most of the year. He definitely seemed to know the town better than I did at this point, considering I'd barely left Martin's house since I moved in.

"I'm not sure," he said, glancing at the map that I'd spread out in my lap. "There isn't much on this road for the next ten or fifteen miles. It's just a lot of woods and nothing. A few warehouses here and there."

A warehouse in the woods? That sounded promising.

The perfect kind of place to have a secret meeting. Or to hold five innocent girls hostage.

I shuddered.

What if we did find out the girls were out here? That Blythe was involved, somehow?

One step at a time, Lenny. Deep breaths.

I quickly pulled up Martin's number on my phone and checked the speed dial. If something happened, I wanted to be able to reach him fast. He'd be pissed, but I had no doubt he'd come to help me if I needed him.

What he did after that, though, was not going to be much fun.

With any luck, we'd discover a few clues and end up right back at Martin's house in an hour or so. Martin none the wiser.

I swallowed back fear and excitement as the tiny dot on the map turned left and stopped. I'd been on a lot of hunts with my parents, but I'd never had to do an investigation like this or walk into danger on my own. I was scared, but I was also hoping this would lead to a good clue.

Maybe if I went to Martin with the truth, he could reach out to the Council on Peyton's behalf. Ask for them to intervene.

I needed a place to tell them to look, though, first.

"She stopped," I said. "Turn here."

He turned down the dirt road just before the one Blythe had taken.

"Let's go," he said. "We should be able to sneak up on her through here and just watch. Maybe we'll get lucky and see a glimpse of the person she's coming out here to visit."

I situated my backpack on my shoulders and followed him into the woods, having to jog a few steps in order to keep up. Music thumped in the distance, like someone was having a party out here.

A twig snapped under my boot, and he put a finger up to his lips.

"Looks like there's a building just through these woods, but we don't want to alert anyone that we're here. We just want to look around for now," he said.

I leaned down and touched my boots.

"*Tacitus*," I whispered to silence my footsteps.

I noticed Kai didn't need to do anything like that for his footsteps to be light as air. He didn't make a sound as he walked.

Neither of us spoke as we approached the lights of the building ahead. When we got to the edge of the trees, we both crouched down and crawled forward until we had a good look at the large warehouse.

The music was obviously coming from inside, and I cringed as I realized this could be a way to hide the screams of any young women trapped inside. Had we found them?

We watched in silence as Blythe emerged from her dark car and walked toward the building.

Kai glanced at me, and we shared a look. This could be it. What if Blythe really did have something to do with the missing girls? My whole body buzzed with the possibilities.

I didn't want to believe she was crooked, though, and part of me hoped I was wrong about this place. About her.

My parents had trusted her with their lives.

I shuddered at that thought.

My parents also lost their lives, didn't they? Had Ms. Greer betrayed them? Was she evil?

Anger flared, and I tensed every muscle in my body.

"Maybe she's here to investigate this whole thing," I said as softly as I could, almost talking to myself. "Maybe the Council really is looking into this, and they just don't want to tell me. Why would they? I mean, I haven't even decided to take my test yet."

"Let's just see what happens," Kai said, leaning closer to me.

I tried to hold judgment until I'd figured out for sure what she was doing here.

Maybe she really was investigating the disappearances. Blythe was a Keeper, after all.

Unlike Slayers, who did most of the fighting on the front lines, Keepers did all the research, training, and made a lot of the judgment calls.

Still, they were usually very hands-off. They tended to do a lot of their research from the shadows. This wasn't like Blythe at all.

She knocked on the metal door of the building and waited, her arms crossed in front of her as she glanced around. She was nervous. Afraid she was being watched. That wasn't like Blythe, either. At least not the Blythe Greer I'd come to know.

"Here we go," Kai whispered as the door swung open.

The man standing on the inside of the building was smiling at first, but the second he saw Ms. Greer, the smile vanished.

I know the feeling, man.

"Do you recognize him?" I asked. It was hard to make out his features at this distance, but he didn't look familiar to me.

They were also too far away for us to hear what they were saying, but it was obvious they were arguing about something.

The guy looked behind him, said something to someone standing inside that I couldn't see, and then stepped out into the warm night air with Ms. Greer. He shut the door behind him, and if I saw correctly, he also quickly sealed it shut.

Very interesting. My heart pounded.

Was Peyton inside? Maybe Ms. Greer was here to rescue them. That didn't fully make sense, but this guy didn't act like they were friendly. I couldn't piece it together yet.

Kai gasped and shifted his weight, pulling something from his pocket.

"I know this guy," he said. "Hold on a second."

"You know him?"

Kai shuffled through the pages of a small notebook. He'd nearly filled the entire thing with very neat, precise hand-writing.

"Yeah, so after the first girl went missing, I got a job at the coffee shop. I knew it was the main place the students were hanging out, so I was hoping it would be a good way to listen in on gossip and read people's energy," he said. "And there's this one guy in particular who's been coming in almost every day to get a coffee that I've just never been able to read. His energy has been cloaked or hidden, but there have been a few instances where he leaned dark to me."

"And that's bad?" I asked.

"It can be," he said. "Like I explained to you before, I can sometimes read someone's intentions if they're pure of heart. I can't always tell what they're thinking or what they're going to do, like I did with you, but I can usually at least get a feel for their energy and whether they have good intentions or bad ones."

"Okay, so this guy has bad intentions? Or something dark about him. What does that mean?"

"Sometimes, it might mean nothing," Kai said in a whisper.

"It could be that he's got his energy cloaked the way you do now. Or it could mean that's he's into something shady that isn't exactly pure or good-hearted but also isn't murder or kidnapping."

I nodded.

"No one is ever all good or all evil," he said. "There are shades of light and darkness within all of us. This guy, Bates, though, has some dark tendencies. The truth is, he hasn't been high on my radar, because there have also been a lot of times he was just middle of the road. Nothing particularly dark about him. Just blank. I've seen people like that before, and they're usually harmless."

I wished I could actually see energy the way he did, because it might have made more sense to me, but I did my best to follow his explanation.

"To keep track of the people in town that sometimes read dark, though, I started keeping notes in a journal."

He flipped a few more pages and pointed to an entry.

"Here it is," he said. "Read this from the day before yesterday."

I glanced through his notes, surprised to see that he'd mentioned me. He said I'd come into Sir Bean with Brandy and Peyton, and I blushed when I read that he'd barely been able to keep his eyes off me. That could mean anything, right?

"I think this might be from last week," I said.

"Oh, uh, just ignore that part," he said, turning the page. "This is what I wanted you to see."

Bates: 3:45PM. Sat in the corner by the window. Watched the crowd for ten minutes, then left. Dark energy today.

"Okay, so he was there the other day with dark energy. Couldn't that just be a coincidence?" I asked.

"Sure, but turn to July 26th," he said. "Three weeks ago."

Bates: 3:45PM. Stood near the counter watching the students for fifteen minutes. His intentions are dark today.

"Do you know what happened the next day?" he asked, and I shook my head. "Marcia Valentine went missing."

Chills ran down my spine.

"Let me check something," he said.

He flipped pages very quickly, scanning them with his eyes.

"Holy crap. Look."

He pointed out a similar entry about Bates on the day before each of the other girls went missing.

"All except the first, because that happened before I started work. I can't believe I didn't see this before. That can't be a coincidence, Lenny. He's involved. He has to be."

My stomach flipped, and I felt like I might throw up.

"What else do you know about this guy? Like, does he work around town? Or is he new to the area?" I asked.

"I don't know much else about him," he said. "Like I said, I noticed his energy was dark some days, but I didn't have any other thing that drew my attention about him until tonight."

I watched as the guy Kai had called Bates stepped into the headlights of Ms. Greer's car.

This was my first good look at him, and I wasn't impressed. He was probably in his mid-thirties or so, tall and lanky with dark, chin-length hair that he kept brushing out of his eyes. He wore a pair of ripped jeans, a Rolling Stones t-shirt, and no shoes.

I tried to zero in on the guy's energy, but Kai was right. He'd cloaked himself with something, and I couldn't quite place a finger on it. He could have been a demon, but he just as easily could have been a were of some kind. Or a vampire. The guy had some definite vampire vibes going on, if you asked me.

He was obviously very upset to see Ms. Greer, but there was nothing unusual about that. Most people were upset to see her.

But what was she doing here? Maybe they were working together and this guy had done something wrong? Or maybe she was here to arrest him.

My mind was running in circles, trying to make sense of it all. I needed more information.

Ms. Greer tried to step around him and go inside the building, but he blocked her and shook his head, actually daring to put a hand on her shoulder and push her back.

Yikes. This guy was braver than most.

Or dumber.

Anger flashed around Ms. Greer in the form of a bright red pulse emanating from her eyes. Bates took two fumbling steps backward until he hit the door.

He quickly lifted his hands, throwing up a magical shield to block himself from Ms. Greer's spells. From here, I could just make out the faint shimmer of the shield in the moonlight.

It didn't last long, though, and fear grew on Bates's face as Ms. Greer calmly stepped toward him.

He tried to recast the shield, but he didn't seem to have the focus to do it. He looked like a clown, fumbling around. Magic danced on his fingertips, but he couldn't seem to get anything going.

I glanced at Kai. This guy was not some demon mastermind.

He didn't even seem all that powerful. Truth be told, he acted high on something. I wished I could get a closer look at his eyes, but as it stood right now, I wasn't convinced anymore that he was our guy.

Unless Ms. Greer was the mastermind and this guy was just her lackey. That could be it, too, no matter how much I wanted her to be innocent in this.

Ms. Greer reached into her suit pocket for something, and a second later, she was holding a fist high over her head.

Bates shouted. "Don't you dare. Stop it, now."

But she wasn't listening to him. She tossed whatever was in her hand high up into the air. Golden particles swirled above her like a galaxy of stars. She casually twirled her wrist above her head, making the particles swirl faster and faster.

Kai moved closer to me, his shoulder pressing against mine. "What's she doing?" he whispered.

"I have no idea," I said. "I've never seen this spell before."

Kai put his arm around me and moved to partially shield my body with his. If my heart was racing before, now it was practically exploding out of my chest.

Despite the fact that I was seventeen, I'd never had a boyfriend before. I'd never even been this close to a guy before. It was extremely uncomfortable and slightly intoxicating.

"What are you doing?" I asked.

"Protecting you," he said. "Just in case she's about to blow that building up."

"Well, let's hope not if the girls are inside," I said. "Surely she wouldn't hurt them."

Still, I scooted just the tiniest bit closer to him.

Part of me wanted to run up there and stop her. Confront her and find out what she was doing out here. Another part of me just couldn't believe she would blow up that building with five innocent human girls inside.

Meanwhile, the golden galaxy above Ms. Greer's head had grown massively larger. If she did plan on blowing up that building, she was going to take half the forest with her.

Bates was trying to get to her to stop the spell, but she held him back with her free hand and some kind of restraining spell.

"*Ostendo*," she shouted as she hurled the spell toward the large building.

I braced myself for impact, huddling under Kai's arm. He leaned his head down to shield me from any magic as the floor of the forest trembled.

I waited for a full-on explosion, but nothing came. Instead, I heard the tinkling laughter of several women.

Confused, I looked up to see what in the world was going on.

My jaw dropped, and it took a second for my brain to catch up with my eyes.

Ms. Greer had somehow managed to make the entire building transparent. Every wall was now invisible, meaning that we could see straight through to every single thing happening inside.

The building had been partitioned into several rooms. One space appeared to be a party hangout, which is where the loud music was coming from. On a makeshift dance floor, there were about seven moon sprites dancing together and giggling. They hadn't even noticed that their building had turned invisible, but they certainly didn't seem to be in any distress.

Another room was completely empty and dark, but there was nothing much to see there, anyway. An unmade bed on the floor and some clothes strewn everywhere.

In the very back, though, there was some kind of mechanism set up. It almost looked like a chemistry lab attached to a conveyer belt.

"What in the heck is going on in the back there?" I asked.

Kai looked as though he was in more shock than I was. He shook his head and seemed to notice the lab for the first time.

"I can't quite tell," he said. "This guy is obviously making some kind of home brew back there. See the bubbling cauldron in the very back near the wall?"

He pointed toward it, and I had to squint to see it in the very back, but he was right. There was a cauldron full of some type of glowing liquid in the very back.

"There's a glass tube siphoning liquid out of it and pulling it up to the glass beakers on the table," he said, following the progression of the liquid with his fingertip. "See those vials on the right there? The multi-colored ones?"

I nodded. There were vials in six different bright colors. Purple, pink, green, blue, yellow, and orange. We watched for a moment before Kai spoke.

"From the looks of it the golden liquid in the cauldron gets pulled up to those beakers, boiled or processed there in some way. Then, the new liquid travels up through that second set of tubes, dropping small amounts into each of the vials, where it takes on a new property. The vials then drop into small bottles before uprighting themselves to collect more liquid."

I watched the process closely. He was right. This was a factory of some kind.

"Watch the bottles," I said. "They travel down that conveyer belt, go into that small oven-looking machine, and when they come out—"

"Dust," he said, cutting me off.

"Moondust in different flavors?" I asked.

Kai closed his eyes. "This guy isn't some demon master-mind kidnapping girls," he said. "He's a glorified drug dealer."

He rolled over onto his back and ran a hand through his hair.

"I feel like an idiot," he said. "I should have seen this coming. He was probably coming into Sir Bean to distribute the drugs to someone there. I just never caught the exchange. That would explain his sometimes-dark intentions. He's doing bad things, but this is peanuts compared to kidnapping and murder. It's not like Moondust ever killed anyone."

I let my head fall into my hands.

That likely explained Ms. Greer's involvement, too. She wasn't in cahoots with some evil demon. She was following up some lead about a low-level dust dealer.

Truth be told, it seemed too small-time for someone at Ms. Greer's level, but still, it did explain why she was probably here. It had nothing to do with the missing girls or the demon.

Ms. Greer exchanged a few more nasty words with Bates, probably telling him to clean up his act or get out of town, and then climbed into her car. As she drove away, the walls of the building slowly came back into view.

Bates shook his head and sat down on the back end of his brown sedan. He pulled a cigarette out of his pocket with trembling hands, snapped his fingers to light it from a magical spark, and started to cry.

Pathetic.

"Let's get out of here," Kai said.

He stood and offered his hand to me, helping me stand.

"Well, that was a massive waste of time," he said. "I'm sorry I got your hopes up."

"It was a good lead," I said. "I still don't think it's a coincidence that Bates had dark intentions the day before each of the girls disappeared. There's something to that, if you ask me. Plus, the fact that he moved here and started this operation right before the first kidnapping. There might be a connection there that we can't see yet."

"I've never tried Moondust. Have you?" he asked as we walked back to the car.

"Once," I said. "I ate a piece of candy at a vampire's house once that had some Moondust in it. It was one of the most delicious things I'd ever tasted, but it gave me terrible dreams afterward. I never wanted to touch it again after that."

"Candy," Kai said.

He stopped walking and tapped a finger to his lips.

"What?" I asked.

"Moondust is rarely just eaten straight," he said. "I mean, you have your hardcore users who might do that, but most people put it in food, right? Candy, milkshakes—"

"Cupcakes," I said, my eyes widening.

"Exactly. I think our next mission is a trip to Olive's house to talk to her mother," Kai said. "Maybe there's still time to swing by there tonight and just take a look around. Then, we can go back to your place and come up with a plan to test those cupcakes tomorrow. It might be unrelated, but I'm not sure."

"I honestly think we can—"

My words were cut off by a blast of fire that knocked me backwards fifteen feet into a tree. My head hit, and the entire world blurred and nearly faded away, but I forced myself to stay awake and aware.

What was that?

I tried to stand, but the second I put weight on my arm to prop myself up, I screamed at the pain that ripped through me.

The entire right side of my body had been burned. I couldn't tell how badly yet, but everything hurt.

I struggled to make sense of it all, but my thinking was fuzzy.

I was pretty sure my right shoulder had been dislocated, too. I prayed it wasn't broken.

The forest around me was on fire, and I couldn't see Kai anywhere. I shouted his name, but there was no response. The flames had separated us right down the middle, so he had to be somewhere on the other side of the blaze.

Had we been attacked?

Were we still in danger?

Adrenaline surged as my brain snapped back into working order. Of course we were in danger. It wasn't like fireballs just randomly fell out of the sky.

I used my left hand to push myself up, and I moved away from the fast-spreading flames.

I thought through all of my options. I could run back to Bates's place and ask for help, but I wasn't sure that guy would help us. Or that he was any good at casting, anyway.

Ms. Greer might have been able to help, but she would be long gone by now anyway.

Unless it's her attacking us.

The thought ran through my mind, but I quickly pushed it out of my mind. I didn't have time to speculate. I needed to find help.

Kai's car was close, but the flames had come from that direction.

Then I remembered the phone in my pocket. I had to reach across my body to get it out of my right pocket with my left hand, but I somehow managed to get it done and call Martin's number as I ran away from the flames.

He was going to be so angry, and the thought of him finding out I'd gone out behind his back for the second time in one day brought tears to my eyes, but I had no choice. We needed him.

"I'm already on my way," he said when he picked up the phone. "Find a safe spot and use whatever resources you have around you to hide. Go, Lenny."

Relief flooded my body. Martin was already on his way.

Like everyone else in my life, he must have been spying on me, too.

I needed to find a safe place and stay put. I wanted to go back and look for Kai, but I was going to have to trust he was doing the same thing on the other side. Hiding.

With my arm like this, I wasn't going to be much help, anyway.

I lifted my shirt to cover my mouth, so that I could breathe through the heavy smoke that filled the air. Martin had said to use whatever resources I had around me to hide, so what resources were here?

I dropped to my knees and rummaged through scattered pine straw, twigs, and dirt.

Think, Lenny, think.

I used to consider myself a very cool-headed person. I used to pride myself at how calm I managed to stay during hunts with my parents. I was a fast-thinker who usually produced the right spell at the right time.

But now, I felt like a fledgling witch who'd never seen a day of danger in her life.

And maybe I hadn't. With my parents leading the charge,

I'd never been in any real danger. They both would have protected me with their lives.

They also never took me on the really dangerous jobs, I realized now. I used to think I was better than other witches my age. Powerful.

But look at me now.

I was burned, broken, and crying in the dirt, clueless about how to protect myself.

How had I gotten to this point? How had I become so weak?

If my parents could see me now, they'd have been so disappointed.

I took a slow breath and closed my eyes.

I needed to calm down. I needed to get centered. Someone was out here right now, hunting me down, and I wasn't ready to die.

I opened my eyes and started looking more carefully at the ground and trees around me. What could I really use here?

Blackberry vines with fresh, plump fruit grew just ten feet away. It was the perfect time of year for wild blackberries, which meant the vines out here were much more potent than the shriveled one I'd used earlier from my spell cabinet.

Blackberry vines had protection capabilities.

I crawled over and plucked two large blackberries and a six-inch stretch of vine, careful not to prick myself on the thorns.

What else?

I carefully brushed the pine needles off the forest floor and looked around. There would be something here I could use. My mom always said that the right ingredients came to a witch when she needed them most, as long as she knew how to look for them.

So I pushed back the panic growing inside me and trusted that what I needed was here somewhere.

I sucked in a breath as a dead beetle rolled out from under a twig as I pushed it aside.

I leaned back against a tree, cradling my right hand in my lap as I gathered the fresh ingredients in my awkward off-hand.

My eyes stung and my throat burned from all the smoke, but I reminded myself that Martin would be here soon. I just needed to protect myself until he got here. I could do this.

Once I had this spell in place, I could go look for Kai. It was going to be okay.

But tears of doubt streamed down my face.

I was too scared. Too unprepared. My hands were shaking.

I set the three ingredients down in a small clearing between my legs and took as deep a breath as I could manage. I quickly squished the blackberry between my fingertips and let the juice fall on the beetle's hard carapace. Next, I wrapped the blackberry vine around the beetle's body.

It was tough to do one-handed, but I managed well enough.

Now for the incantation. *"Prot—"*

Before I could get the word out of my mouth, an invisible hand seemed to lift me up like a ragdoll.

I screamed and kicked against the energy, but I couldn't get a grip on it.

I frantically searched through the woods, looking for any sign of my attacker, but the only person I saw was Kai, unconscious and wrapped in some kind of net that emanated dark, bluish-purple energy.

Seeing him squeezed what little hope I had out of my heart. There was no way Martin would get here fast enough now.

It was up to me. If I didn't save us, we were both going to die.

A SINGLE KEY

I hung in the air, my body dangling about four feet off the ground. Something invisible slithered around my neck and tightened its grip.

I struggled against it, kicking and trying to pull away, but nothing made any difference.

I scanned the woods again. I needed to see who was actually doing this to me.

Whoever they were, they were casting from a distance, and they were completely hidden by the smoke. Their magic was definitely strong, though.

Had the demon come for us?

How did he find us here? It didn't make any sense.

Not unless Blythe Greer really was involved and knew I'd followed her out here. In that case, then, Kai's cloaking spell hadn't worked.

There was no doubt the person—or creature—attacking us was powerful, though. Way beyond what my magic could handle, anyway.

What could I do? I had no idea if they were trying to kidnap me or kill me, but as the invisible rope tightened around my neck, I was leaning toward death. And I just couldn't let that happen. I was not going to go down like this to some unknown creep.

I did my best to calm my mind, despite the panic building inside me.

A lot of the magic available to me as a young witch with just a single key needed reagents, but there were a few things I knew how to do that didn't take any ingredients at all.

I longed for the dagger I brought, but I'd dropped my bag somewhere in the woods when the flames hit.

I thought back to the encounters I'd had with demons in the past. I wasn't one hundred percent sure this was demon magic attacking me now, but it was my best guess from what Kai had told me.

Demons hated salt, but I didn't have access to that right now. I made a mental note to put a handful of salt in my pockets from here on out.

I knew the command to open doors and other things without needing any spell ingredients, and what I wanted right now was for this invisible rope to open and set me free. I had no idea if it would work, but I was running out of time to figure this out. Soon, I wouldn't be able to speak.

"*Solvo*," I said with all the confidence and authority I could find.

To my complete shock, the spell released me. I fell hard to the ground below and rolled to my side, pushing up with my good arm.

I ran, wanting to put some distance between me and this demon, so that I could buy more time. I hated to leave Kai behind, but it wasn't going to do him any good if we both got caught or killed. I must have rolled my ankle when I fell, though, because each step was agony.

I stopped and ducked behind a large tree to catch my breath and try to wrap my mind around what was happening.

Since this demon was comfortable with fire, I was certain ice would help to slow it down or even harm it, but I didn't have a water source to use to create it. I'd seen my father pull moisture down from the clouds before, but my key wasn't high enough to access that magic.

I thought back to some of the jobs I'd gone on with my parents. What had I seen them do in situations like this?

I closed my eyes, pulling up a mental image of my parents at one of the last demon slayings they took me on. Once, they'd cast a circle and used it to trap a demon before banishing or containing him.

I didn't have the time or tools to cast a circle right now. I also didn't know the right incantations for it.

But then I remembered something else I'd seen them do before to push a demon back when it had us trapped in an old castle. Mom had forced it to another room with a bright light.

I remembered the incantation my mother used, too.

It was a simple spell they'd taught me when I was just a young girl afraid of the dark, but it had been effective against the demon. At least temporarily.

Each girl was taken during the night, so it was possible this demon's powers were more potent in the darkness. Light should repel it. I hoped.

I stepped out from behind the tree and pushed my left palm forward.

"*Lucerna*," I said.

A bright, focused light radiated from my palm like a flashlight.

It was one of the first spells I'd ever learned. I never dreamed I would use it on a night like this.

I rotated my arm, shining the light all around the area. It was hard to see very far, because of the smoke reflecting the light back to me, but when I turned to my left, something hissed and scurried off to my right.

I followed the movement as quickly as I could.

"*Amplio*," I said in a strong voice.

The flashlight grew stronger, illuminating a slightly larger area in front of me.

For a moment, the demon appeared in the darkness, its invisibility spell wavering in the bright, conjured light. And Kai was right. This was definitely a demon.

Most demons had the ability to appear human when they wanted to, but this demon had shed its human form, making it more powerful. My heart raced as it walked straight toward me.

In its hands, it gathered a fresh ball of flames.

The first time, I was sure the flames were meant to separate us from each other. This time, though, it aimed to kill.

I took a step backward and winced at the pain in my ankle. There was no way I could outrun its spell. I was out of options, and though the light had temporarily slowed it down, I wasn't strong enough to stop it.

This was it. I was going to join my parents in heaven.

I clasped my mother's locket, sending up one final prayer for help.

The locket trembled for a moment, the cool surface of the silver warming beneath my fingertips. Just as the demon lifted its hands to unleash its fresh flames, the locket somehow super-charged my flashlight spell, throwing a sunburst of light outward in all directions.

The sheer power of the spell flowed through me like a dam being released somewhere deep inside. It was so intense, I knew I wouldn't be able to hold it long, but since I had it now, I poured my entire soul into it.

The spell consumed the darkness completely, lighting up the forest as though the sun itself had come out.

The demon screeched and stumbled backward, dropping its focus and losing the fire spell. In the brilliant moment of light, I saw it bare its pointed teeth in a snarl.

I hoped the strong light would scare it away, but this was no lesser demon. It wasn't going to just turn and run. Whoever this was, he had great power.

My power, on the other hand, was being drained so quickly, I felt lightheaded. It was obvious to me now I was using magic that wasn't supposed to be used by a witch with only a single key.

I had no idea why or how it worked, but I was grateful for it while I had it.

I fought to keep my eyes open, but I refused to give up.

The demon stretched its hands outward and the same bluish-purple energy I'd seen pulsing around Kai now pulsed around the demon's body. With one swift motion, the demon threw the dark energy to the forest floor.

It spread out quickly, like fog, to consume my light.

I held on for as long as I could as the dark energy expanded and grew upward, quickly reaching the height of my waist. Tears streamed down my face as the light radiating from me blinked and faded.

My eyelids drooped, and I fell back against a tree. I couldn't hold it much longer.

The last of my energy cut off, and my legs gave out. Like a ragdoll, I fell to the ground. I had nothing left to give, but I'd given enough.

At that moment, Martin's face appeared in the shadows behind the demon. I saw nothing but the flash of steel as my eyes closed and everything went dark.

THAT'S WHAT MATTERS

I woke to the sound of Kai yelling my name and the feel of smoke in my lungs.

I coughed and tried to sit up, but my shoulder hurt so badly it nearly made me pass out again. I winced at the pain and lay back in the dirt.

"She's here," he yelled. "She's hurt."

My eyes fluttered open, and I smiled as Uncle Martin's face came into view.

Tears rolled down the side of my face and into my hair. "I'm so sorry," I said. "I almost died, too. I almost left you."

"You're still here, my brave girl," he said as he knelt at my side. "Everything is going to be okay."

My eyes closed again, and I drifted off to sleep.

I woke again as someone lifted me into their arms. Kai. His arms were gentle around me, and I got the sense of floating as he carried me through the woods.

Is this what it feels like to fly?

The next time I awoke, there was a faint light coming

through the window in my bedroom. I sat up with a start, wincing at the pain that covered the entire right half of my body.

Kai stood, nearly knocking over the chair he'd set beside my bed.

"You're awake," he said. He reached for my hand, as if we'd known each other all our lives.

I didn't pull away. I needed some comfort right about now.

"What happened last night?" I asked, pulling myself upright.

Kai moved to stack a few pillows behind me, never taking his hand away from mine.

"What do you remember?" he asked.

"Everything up until the attack." I closed my eyes and tried to remember what happened next. "I remember seeing you caught in some kind of netting. The demon had me. I thought we were going to die."

I touched the key and locket hanging against my chest and sucked in a breath.

"What did I do?" I asked. "How?"

Uncle Martin appeared in the doorway with a tray of his famous peanut butter chocolate chip pancakes, a large glass of water, and a rose from his garden out back.

"Somehow, you amplified a simple spell and turned it into something much more powerful," Martin said. "The how is a bit of a mystery."

"The locket," I said. "When I touched it, the spell grew so much bigger. I could hardly contain it."

"I'm so sorry I didn't get there sooner," Martin said. He set the tray down at the end of the bed and pulled up a chair on the opposite side from where Kai sat.

"I'm sorry I left without telling you," I said, guilt tightening my jaw. "I didn't realize what we were getting into out there. I still don't understand how that demon knew we were there or what Ms. Greer has to do with all of this."

"Sir, did you know about Blythe Greer and this guy Bates?" Kai asked. "Did you know what that guy was up to out in the woods?"

Uncle Martin nodded and handed me the glass of water. His eyes dipped to our clasped hands for a moment, but he was polite enough not to say anything.

I pulled my hand away from Kai's, a little embarrassed.

"I am familiar with Bates," he said. "I didn't realize he'd opened up shop here in Newcastle until Kai mentioned him last night after we got home, but he's relatively harmless. I don't believe he had anything to do with the attack, but I'll be looking into it in more detail as soon as you're feeling better."

"I take it you two properly introduced yourselves while I was passed out, then," I said.

Martin chuckled. "Kai and I have known each other for quite some time."

My eyes widened. "Are you serious?" I turned on Kai. "And you didn't think to mention that you knew my uncle?"

He shrugged. "You never asked."

I wanted to punch him. So, not only were our parents good friends, he was also friends with my great-uncle. I was going to ask him just how long they'd known each other, but Kai turned the conversation back to the attack.

"What happened out there?" he asked. "Who attacked us? Was that the demon who's taken the girls?"

"Yes. I believe it was," Martin said. "The demon ran when

I pierced it with my dagger. I'd like to go back to the area this morning and have a look around."

"I'm going with you," I said.

"No, you will stay in this bed and rest," Martin said. "I'm afraid your role in this investigation has come to an end. I will not have you risking your life for anyone else right now."

Anger flared at this news, and I shifted my weight on the bed, pulling my legs up to sit crisscross under the covers.

"What are we going to do about Peyton and the other girls?" I asked. "We have to find them. It's only two days now until the full moon. We're running out of time, and the Council doesn't even seem to care."

Uncle Martin brought the tray of pancakes toward me and set it on top of my legs. "Eat," he said. "We can discuss battle plans after breakfast. Kai, can I get you something to eat or drink?"

"I'm okay for now, but thank you for offering," Kai said.

I didn't know about him, but I was absolutely starving.

I was also really curious how my arm had mostly healed. I was in pretty bad shape last night. There were bandages across a lot of my right side, but I could tell the burns weren't nearly as bad as they had been.

"Who healed me?" I asked between bites of pancake. "I'm assuming you didn't take me to a hospital."

"I may be retired, but I'm not useless," Uncle Martin said, as if I'd offended him. "I still have many of my old Keeper supplies, which include various instruments of healing. Your shoulder wasn't too hard to put back into place, but the burns were slightly more complicated. How is your head feeling this morning?"

I shrugged and swallowed.

"I have a mild headache, but it's nothing I can't handle," I said. I touched the back of my head where I'd slammed it against the tree. It was a bit sore, but it could have been a lot worse. "I think it's okay."

"Be sure to drink all of your water," Martin said, standing. "I put a flavorless powder in it that will help your headache. I'll be downstairs in my study. Come find me when you're feeling up to it, and we'll decide what we're going to do about your friend."

"Thank you," I said. I'd expected him to be really angry with me, but he was taking this a lot better than I anticipated. "I don't know what would have happened if you hadn't shown up."

"Let's not think about that now," he said. "You're home, and that's what matters."

I touched a hand to my bandaged arm.

I was home, yes, but there were five other families out there missing someone.

"What do you think?" I asked when Kai and I were alone again. "Is he going to let me out of this room again before I'm eighteen?"

Kai smiled, and the whole room lit up.

"He cares about you a great deal," he said. "I was worried it might destroy him when your parents died, but having you here saved him, I think."

I blinked back tears. "He's been there for me every moment since the funeral. I don't know where I'd be right now without him."

"I'm glad you have each other," he said.

Sorrow darkened his eyes. It was strange how his emotions could control the mood of a space.

"Do you want to talk about it?" I asked.

"Another time," he said softly. "For now, let's just focus on getting you to a better place. There will be plenty of time to talk about my family later."

I didn't want to press the issue, so I let it go, but I really hoped he'd fill me in soon. He knew so much more about me than I knew about him.

I opened my mouth to ask him if he'd gotten a good look at the demon last night when the doorbell rang downstairs.

I glanced at the clock across the room. It was just barely after seven in the morning. Who in the world would be coming to visit at this hour?

Afraid it was Ms. Greer coming to reprimand me about last night, I pulled myself out of bed and hobbled down the hallway with Kai following closely behind.

But when I got to the stairway, it wasn't Blythe Greer at all.

A tall man in a blue suit and tie glanced up as I appeared, a strange look crossing his face as he noticed Kai at my side.

Uncle Martin, who had just answered the door, wore a look of frustration.

Looking down at my bandages, I suddenly understood why. This wasn't going to be easy to explain.

"Looks like she is here, after all," the man said, patting Uncle Martin on the shoulder and stepping inside. "You must be Lenora Thorne. I'm Detective Lancaster, and I have a few questions for you."

SECRETS OF HIS OWN

Why couldn't I have just stayed put for once?

The look Uncle Martin was giving me made me want to go back and crawl under my bed. Yes, I messed up. I should have stayed in my room and trusted him to deal with whoever was at the door, but I always felt like I needed to be in the middle of everything.

And now, I'd given myself away to this detective. I'd probably also brought Kai into this questioning session.

Not to mention the fact that my body was bruised and burned. How was I going to explain that?

Oh, no big deal officer, I just skipped school yesterday and fell into a demon's fire spell. But I swear, I have no idea what happened to Peyton.

At least I had the new girl thing going for me. It wasn't like I was here when the other girls were taken.

Which is potentially why the detective gave Kai a strange look. If this guy was worth anything, he already knew Kai had come to town just before the first disappearance. And that Kai

worked at Sir Bean, a place all the girls had visited right before
they went missing.

"I'm just going to get back to my studying," Kai said,
turning the other way.

"No, why don't you go ahead and join us down here,"
Detective Lancaster said.

Kai groaned and followed me down the stairs.

"You're here pretty early," Detective Lancaster said to Kai,
making a point to check his watch.

"So are you," Kai said with a smile.

He didn't offer any additional information, and I got the
distinct feeling these two had met before. There was definite
tension in the air between them.

"Would you like a cup of freshly brewed coffee, Detective?" Martin asked. "Why don't we all go back to the kitchen
to have a cup and sit down together?"

"I think we'll just have a seat out here," Detective
Lancaster said, motioning to the parlor.

I rolled my eyes. These couches were going to get more
use in a couple of days than they'd seen in the past hundred
years.

I sat down on the same square of navy velvet couch I'd
chosen when Ms. Greer questioned me and pulled my legs
underneath me. I wasn't exactly dressed for company, but the
loose sweats and tank top Martin must have changed me into
last night would have to do.

Kai hadn't been there when he did that, right? Surely not.

My entire body suddenly went up in fresh flames, and I
scooted down, hiding my red face behind my arm.

"What happened to you, Miss Thorne?" Detective
Lancaster asked, nodding toward my bandaged arm as he sat

down in the straight-backed chair across from me. "Those look like fresh injuries."

I didn't answer, hoping we could stall that conversation for as long as possible.

Martin opted to stand, placing an arm on the mantle of the large fireplace, while Kai took a seat next to me on the sofa. He coughed slightly as a cloud of dust rose from the fabric on that side, and I had to stifle a grin.

"Miss Thorne?" the detective asked again.

"Oh, um. Just a minor accident," I said attempting to laugh it off. "It looks worse than it is. Just a scratch, really, but my uncle tends to go overboard on the bandages."

Detective Lancaster didn't look convinced, but he apparently decided to let it go for now.

He pulled a small spiral notebook from the pocket of his jacket.

"I looked for you at school yesterday, but the office said you'd been checked out by Julie Peterson. Are you close to the Peterson family? From what I understand you've just moved to the area recently."

"Lenny moved here just before summer," Uncle Martin said, stepping in. "She had my permission to leave school yesterday, but I wasn't able to pick her up myself."

The detective narrowed his eyes.

"I'd like to hear Lenny's answers, if you don't mind," he said. "In fact, I'd love to speak to her in private."

"That's not acceptable to me," Uncle Martin said. "If you wish to continue your questions, you may only do so in my presence."

Detective Lancaster cleared his throat.

"Okay, so then Lenny. Are you good friends with the Peterson family?"

I looked to Martin, and he gave a slight shrug.

"Not really," I said. "I only just met Olive and her mom the other day."

"And what about Peyton?" he asked, leaning forward. "How long have you been friends with her?"

"About the same amount of time," I said. "I only just started school last week, so I met Peyton on Monday a week ago."

He made a few notes and seemed to chew on the inside of his cheek for a moment.

"From what some of the other girls have told me, you had an afternoon swim at Peyton's home yesterday. Is that correct?"

God, was that really just yesterday?

"Yes."

He went through all the basic questions with me. Who was there. What we did. Whether I noticed anything unusual about Peyton's behavior.

He spent a good deal of time asking various questions about my ride home, too, and what time Peyton drove off, but it all seemed pretty standard.

"And what about those bandages?" he asked, giving me a once-over. "Did you sustain your injuries before or after Peyton dropped you off at your house the other night?"

I glanced at Martin again, which I realized must look a little suspicious. I couldn't help myself, though. How was I going to explain this?

"After," I said. "After I left school yesterday."

"So, if I ask around, some of your friends from school will

verify that you had no injuries when you showed up yesterday?"

"Yes."

"What happened?" he asked. "Did someone hurt you?"

He glanced toward Kai and then back to me.

"Nothing like that," I said. "It's no big deal, really. Besides, it has nothing to do with Peyton."

"Do you feel safe, Miss Thorne?"

His question caught me a bit by surprise.

Safe? How could any girl feel safe in this town?

But I had a feeling he was talking about my present company. Did I feel safe around Kai and Uncle Martin?

"As safe as I can with what's going on in this town," I said. "But if you mean here at home, then yes. I am perfectly safe here."

He sighed, slapped his notebook shut, and stood.

"Okay, thank you very much, Miss Thorne," he said. "You've been very helpful."

He walked toward the door, so I stood and followed him out. Martin and Kai were close behind.

He may have been done with me, but I was definitely not finished with him.

"Detective, is there anything you can tell me about what happened to Peyton?" I asked. "Was there a struggle in her home? Did the kidnapper leave anything behind? Is there anything that points to who took these girls?"

He turned and tilted his head, studying me.

"I can assure you that our department is doing everything we can to find your friend."

In other words, he didn't want to tell me. But Brandy knew something about what happened. Yesterday morning, she'd said the police had told her not to talk about how they knew Peyton had been kidnapped. I wanted to know, too.

"I understand," I said. "But I'm just wondering how you know she was taken and not just visiting a boyfriend or something like that. Besides, the more I know about what happened, the more I can protect myself from having it happen to me."

That last bit must have gotten to him, because he turned around, a look of concern on his face.

"Every girl who's been taken has been alone at home when it happened." He glanced at Martin. "One of the best things you can do for yourself is to make sure you're not alone here at the house or out walking alone in the dark."

This time, he looked at Kai, and he didn't even try to conceal his feelings about him. His expression could have been categorized as a glare.

"I'd also advise you to be careful who you decide to spend time with," he said. "Not everyone who acts like a friend is a friend."

"Thanks," I said. "I'll keep that in mind."

It was obvious we weren't going to get any real answers from this detective, and I sadly had the feeling he didn't have any real answers, either.

"Thank you for stopping by, Detective," Martin said, opening the front door and ushering him outside. "If there's any other way we can be of service, please let us know. We would do anything to help find those poor girls."

Detective Lancaster turned, his brow furrowed.

"You know, there is one thing I'd like to ask you," he said. "Did Peyton ever mention anything to you about using lavender? Like keeping it in her house or receiving some as a gift from anyone? Did you notice any in her home yesterday when you were there?"

My eyes widened, and my stomach flipped with nerves.

"No, why?" I asked. "Did you find lavender in her room? Maybe under her pillow?"

He stepped closer to me, grabbing his notebook again.

"What do you know about lavender under someone's pillow?" he asked. "Does that mean something to you?"

Now, we were trading questions, but what I needed was answers.

"I know sometimes people use lavender to help them fall asleep at night," I said, trying to remain casual so he didn't start to suspect I had something to do with this. But I needed more details. This could be the kind of clue I'd been hoping for.

"There was a small bundle of dried lavender under her pillow," he said, lowering his voice as if he was afraid someone in the neighborhood might hear. "But that wasn't the strangest part."

He hesitated and glanced toward Kai and Martin, as if he just didn't trust them.

I couldn't risk him not telling me about the lavender, so I quickly slipped around Martin to join the detective on the front porch. I shut the door behind me, closing us off from the other two.

They could add it to the list of reasons to be mad at me later.

"What else was strange?" I asked.

He seemed to think it over before finally leaning in.

"The lavender was wrapped in poison ivy," he said. "Does that have any significance to you? Did Peyton ever mention being allergic to poison ivy?"

I sucked in a breath. It definitely had significance to me but nothing I was going to talk to this guy about.

"I'm sorry," I said. "She never mentioned anything like that to me. It seems like a weird thing to have in your house, though."

He looked away and nodded.

"You know, this case has really been hard on all of us," he said. "I would hate to see another girl go missing. Did you happen to see Kai the night Peyton dropped you off? Did she mention having a relationship with him? Or having any kind of run-in with him in the past?"

I wondered what this guy's past was with Kai and why he didn't trust him, but I wanted to tell him he was barking up the wrong tree. And none of us had time for following false leads right now.

"No. I don't think she really ever talked to Kai," I said.

"And how did you come to know him?" he asked. "It seems the two of you are close."

"We're old friends from a really long time ago," I said. "Our parents used to work together."

This news really threw him for a loop. "I didn't realize Kai had connections to anyone in town," he said. "Other than his grandmother, who no one seems to have heard from in a while. Have you seen her or had any interaction with her since you arrived in town?"

I had to stifle a giggle at this. I was quite certain Kai was not living in his grandmother's house, even if that was the story he'd been giving people. I would have to ask him more about that later.

"I just saw her yesterday, actually," I said, hoping to steer the detective away from his suspicions about Kai. "I think she's been travelling a lot, though, which is probably why no one's heard from her."

"Hmm," Detective Lancaster said, glancing at the door and jotting something in his notebook before putting it away. "And you're sure you feel safe at home?"

"If you're referring to Martin, everything is fine here," I said. "But thank you for being concerned about me. I'm just worried about Peyton and the others."

"We all are, Miss Thorne."

He pulled a card from his pocket and handed it to me.

"If you think of anything else, don't hesitate to call me. Night or day," he said. "That goes for anytime you don't feel safe. I hope you're having someone treat you for those injuries. You sure you won't tell me what happened there? That doesn't look like a minor accident to me."

I looked down and realized some blood had soaked through the bandage on my arm.

"It's nothing," I said quickly, pulling my arm behind my back. "Martin was a medic in the military, and he tends to go nuts when he gets the chance to use some of his old supplies. I promise, it's not as bad as it looks."

He didn't look convinced, but he seemed to realize he wasn't going to get anything else out of me today.

"Well, you take care, Miss Thorne. You know how to reach me."

He started toward his car.

"Thank you," I said. "And Detective?"

He turned back again, squinting against the harsh morning sun. "Yes?"

"Did you happen to find those same lavender and poison ivy bundles under all the girls' pillows?" I asked.

"I'm afraid that's classified information right now, but if someone does give you a gift of lavender or tries to sell you something like that as a sleep remedy, you'll give me a call?" he asked.

"Of course," I said.

He nodded and got into his car.

He hadn't verbally confirmed the lavender bundles, but I saw the answer in his eyes, which meant we had our first real clue from the crime scenes.

Any witch knew lavender was a natural sleep aid, but when it was wrapped in poison ivy, it became a dangerous drug. The moment Peyton's head hit that pillow, she would have instantly gone into a deep sleep.

Deep enough that someone could have easily kidnapped her without a fight.

I went back inside to find Martin and Kai peeking out the window. They quickly moved away, trying to pretend they hadn't been spying on me. I smiled.

It was sweet that they both seemed to care so much. It felt good to be looked after.

"What did he tell you?" Kai asked.

"He gave us our next clue," I said and then looked at Uncle Martin. "I know I can help find Peyton and the others. I understand why you don't want me to be a part of it. I know the death of my parents is still fresh for both of us. But you and me, we're a family now. And family sticks together. Besides, you know I can't just let this go. So, what do you say? Can we work together to find them?"

Uncle Martin studied me for a very long moment before finally allowing his serious expression to break into a partial smile.

"Okay, Lenora," he said. "We'll do this together. But if you're going to be ready to face a demon of this level, you're going to need some real training."

His eyes flickered toward Kai.

"Both of you," he said. "You'll also be putting yourselves in danger from the Witch's Council if you go against their orders to leave this alone. Are you sure you're up for it?"

Kai and I looked at each other, both of us holding back smiles.

"Yes," we both said at the same time.

"Well, then," Martin said, straightening his shoulders. "Lenny, get dressed and join us in the kitchen for a cup of coffee. If you're going to be a part of this now, there's a lot more you need to know about this demon."

He turned to walk back toward the kitchen, but I ran after him.

"Wait a second. Are you saying you know things about this demon that you haven't been telling us?" I asked. "After just one day of looking into it?"

Martin turned his head just enough so I could see his profile and the gleam in his ancient eyes.

"Dear girl," he said with a snicker, "I've been looking into this particular demon since before you were born."

With that, he calmly made his way to the kitchen, leaving both Kai and me standing in the foyer with matching looks of surprise frozen on our faces.

Uncle Martin, apparently, had been keeping some major secrets of his own.

THE FINAL PIECE

I had never gotten dressed so quickly in my life. I was dying to find out what Uncle Martin knew about this demon.

I winced as I pulled my loose sweatpants off and tried to wriggle into a pair of tight jeans. It just wasn't going to happen. Martin had done a great job healing what he could, but the rest was going to take some time.

Instead, I threw on a pair of stretchy black leggings and a black tank top with my black and white converse high-tops.

Perfect demon investigating clothes, but more importantly, not too painful against my fresh burns.

Nothing I couldn't handle, though, and nothing compared to what Peyton and the others were facing.

I practically ran all the way to the kitchen to find Martin casually listing the qualities of his new French press. How Kai could be this patient, I had no idea. There wasn't a calm bone in my body.

"Pour me a cup and let's do this," I said. "I can't believe

you've been looking for this demon so long. You have to tell us everything you know as quickly as possible."

Martin smiled and slowly poured a cup of coffee, fixing it up exactly the way I liked it.

I fidgeted in my seat as I waited.

"Thank you," I said when he finally sat down and pushed the steaming mug toward me. "Now, spill it. What have you been keeping from us?"

"Patience is a virtue, dear girl."

"No, right now, it's a luxury we don't have," I said. "We're running out of time."

"Yes, yes," Martin said. "So we are."

He sighed and shook his head.

"I'm not certain where to begin, so I'll just go back to the first time I met this particular demon," he said. "His name, by the way, is Algrath. That might come in handy next time you encounter him."

I nodded and quickly repeated the name in my head several times. Speaking a demon's name could give you some level of power over it under the right circumstances.

"About fifty years ago, I was working with a Slayer named Renee," he said. There was a hint of sadness as he said her name that tugged at something deep inside me. "She was very talented. Together, we hunted down a particularly nasty demon named Regmothean. He was ancient and had grown greedy over the years, taking more and more until it was impossible for the Council to ignore his actions. It took many years, but Renee and I managed to capture Regmothean and imprison him in a series of mirrors."

I shook my head. A series of mirrors? I'd never heard of something like that before.

"Why not just a single mirror? I don't understand how you would imprison a single demon in multiple mirrors," I said.

"It's true that it isn't done very often. The process is complicated and time consuming, but in this case, quite necessary," Martin said. "We essentially fragmented the demon's soul into five different pieces and imprisoned them in five separate mirrors. The Council then hid those mirrors in five different secret locations."

"Okay, so what does this demon, Regmothean, have to do with the demon here in Newcastle? I don't understand."

Kai made a strange sound and ran a hand through his hair. "I think I do," he said. "But I don't want to believe it."

"I'm afraid you're probably right," Martin said. "But I'll explain it as concisely as I can. Algrath is Regmothean's brother. I met him shortly after I helped to imprison Regmothean, and let's just say he was quite angry. He killed Renee and very nearly took my life, as well."

Martin was quiet for a long moment before he was able to continue.

"He vowed that he would someday locate his brother's five prisons and set him free."

"Oh my gosh," I said, rubbing my forehead with my hand. "That's what these rituals are all about, then? Setting Regmothean free?"

Martin nodded.

"I'm afraid so," he said. "And what's worse, the mirror here in Newcastle is the final piece of Regmothean's prison. If Algrath successfully completes his ritual tomorrow night, one of the most sadistic demons to walk the earth will go free once again."

My eyes widened. I didn't want to believe it could be true.

"Why hasn't the Council stepped in before now?" I asked, outraged. "This is the reason the Council exists in the first place. To keep the balance and exact justice. How can they just turn a blind eye to what's happening? They can't seriously want this demon to go free."

Martin touched my hand, instantly bringing a sense of calm to my heart.

"I wish I could give you an acceptable answer, but I don't have one," he said. "Making sure Regmothean was taken care of was a high priority of the Council back when I was still in service. Back then, several Slayers had also been tasked with the job of banishing or imprisoning Algrath, as well, but no one was successful."

"So what's changed?" Kai asked. "Why aren't they trying to stop this?"

I glanced over and saw there were tears in Kai's eyes, and it sent a strange feeling of protection over me. I wanted to put an end to whatever was hurting him, even if I didn't understand what it was. Was this somehow tied to his father?

"I no longer have the same privileges I once had when it comes to the Council," Martin said. "When I've inquired about the brothers, I have been shut out completely over the past several years. In fact, the Council tried to hide the recent rituals from my attention, so that I wouldn't know the first four pieces of Regmothean's mirrors had been released. This is definitely a deviation from the Council's normal behavior. As to what their motives are, however, I can only speculate."

"Do you think Blythe Greer is involved?" I swallowed back fear and anger. "Do you think this has anything to do with what happened to my parents?"

"Or my father?" Kai asked.

I looked over at him. Had his father died?

He'd never told me the full story about why he'd come here looking for his dad or what he'd discovered once he got here.

Maybe we'd both lost the most important people in our lives.

"Ms. Greer is most certainly up to something," Martin said. "Time will reveal all, I have a feeling."

"So, for now, we have to assume we can't trust her," I said. "Or the Council."

"Sadly, I have to agree with you," Martin said with a sigh. "A lifetime of service has bought me nothing with the current Council, it seems. I must admit, I hoped you wouldn't become involved in this. I'd been looking into Algrath's rituals before your parents died, and when the Council said they were sending you here, I feared the worst."

"What do you mean?" I asked.

"He means he was scared Algrath would kidnap you," Kai said. "That's why he asked me to look after you."

Of course. I should have known.

"So, no wonder you warned me to stay out of it," I said. "You were acting under orders."

I glared at Martin, but he simply shrugged and took a sip of his coffee.

"The important thing is you're okay," Kai said. "But we're both a part of this now. Like it or not."

"So, no one is coming to help us?" I asked. "The Council really won't get involved."

"It appears we're the only hope those girls have of survival," Martin said. "And if we commit to this, we'll be going against the Council's wishes. This is why I didn't want you brought into this. It's more dangerous than you could possibly understand."

Wow.

I leaned back against the chair and let Martin's words sink in.

I'd been afraid I was in over my head, but I never in a million years realized it was this serious. We were on our own, and we were running out of time.

"Okay, so how do we do this?" I asked. "How do we find Algrath and stop this ritual?"

Martin smiled, and I realized he had more secrets to tell.

"Come with me. I want to show you something."

He led us back to his study. It was a large, yet cozy, two-story office with floor-to-ceiling bookshelves framed in dark wood. His desk was an ornate antique loaded with stacks of papers and books.

Heavy, dark blue curtains covered the windows, so the brass lamp on Martin's desk was the only light as we walked in. It was the kind of room where all I wanted to do was curl up with a cozy blanket in the big, comfy leather chair in the corner and read all day.

Truth be told, that's what I'd actually done many summer days since I'd moved in.

"Have a seat," Martin said, sitting down behind his desk and putting on a pair of reading glasses with thick black rims. He motioned to the two high-backed leather chairs across from his desk.

Kai and I took our seats, both of us anxious to find out what Martin would tell us next. It was obvious he had some kind of plan.

"As unfortunate as your encounter with Algrath was last

night, it was actually the closest I've gotten to him in a very long time," Martin said. "I have tried in the past to locate him using spells, potions, and even tracking devices I placed on him at various times. None of these methods have worked effectively."

He rifled through some papers on his desk and finally pulled out a page that had a drawing of a dagger in its center.

"Ah, here we are," he said. "Over the past few years, I have been working on a new sort of tracking spell in my spare time. One that wouldn't be so easily reversed or avoided. I've used it a few times in practice with great success, but this is the first time I've used it on a powerful demon like Algrath. Time will tell if it is effective in helping us locate him."

I sat on the edge of my chair, taking the paper from him and studying it.

"This is brilliant," I said, passing the paper to Kai. "How long will it take to find him if it does work?"

Kai shook his head. "This makes absolutely no sense to me," he said. "Can you translate?"

I leaned toward him. "So, traditional tracking spells using someone's DNA can be avoided with simple cloaking spells. That's probably what this demon has used on the girls. There are also tracking spells where you can place something onto a person or creature and track that item."

"Like we did last night with Blythe's car," he said.

"Exactly. Those are also relatively simple to avoid, if you know you're being tracked," I said. "What Martin's done, if I'm reading this correctly, is he's created a special tracking potion using a drop of his own blood."

"Very good, Lenora," Martin said. "I laced the dagger I used against Algrath last night with a few drops of this potion.

The way it works is the potion slowly travels through the demon's bloodstream, essentially coating him with it from the inside. It shows no sign of its existence, because there is so little of it, and it has no side effects at all until it has been dispersed to every part of his body. In theory, the demon will have no idea he's been infected with it until it's too late. Cloaking himself will no longer work, because it won't be his energy I'm tracking."

Kai's mouth fell open as he finally understood the spell.

"So once your blood is dispersed throughout the demon's body, you simply track yourself. Your own energy," he said. "I've never seen anything like this before."

Martin smiled and nodded. "It has taken a bit of out-of-the-box thinking to come up with this method," he said. "But I'm honored you approve. The biggest downside is that it takes nearly two days for it to work."

"Two days?" I asked, slamming the paper down on the desk. He'd just gotten my hopes up, and now it felt like we were back to square one. "That's too late. We have less than two days until the full moon."

"By my calculations, we should receive the demon's accurate location just before the ritual begins," Martin said. "I'm afraid this was my best option, and we are lucky we got the chance to use it at all. The spell must travel slowly through the demon's body, or else it would be too easy for him to sense it and nullify it."

I leaned back in the chair, feeling defeated. The odds were definitely stacked against us here, and even though this might help, it also might come through too late to save the missing girls.

"What else can we do in the meantime, then?" I asked.

"For one, we can get both of you ready to face Algrath if and when it comes to that," Martin said. "There's another detail you need to understand about this demon before we face him again."

"What's that?" Kai asked.

Martin looked through his stack of books, thumbed through a few pages, and finally handed a worn book across the desk to Kai.

"Algrath and his brother are both ethologus demons," Martin said.

It was my turn to look confused. Kai seemed to recognize the word right away, because he groaned and ran a hand across his forehead.

"No wonder I haven't been able to find him by tracking the people who just came to town," he said. "This is making so much more sense right now."

"What?" I asked. "What's ethologus?"

"It means they're copycats," Kai said. "Instead of taking on their own unique human form like most demons, an ethologus demon can take on the form of any other human it chooses."

My stomach knotted.

"Wait. You're saying this demon could look like anyone? Even me? Or you?" I asked.

"Not exactly," Martin said. "In order to take someone's form, the ethologus demon must consistently feed on that human's energy. Typically, the demon will have the real human locked away somewhere in its home or den."

I closed my eyes, thinking about how horrifying that would be.

"So, in all likelihood, the first kidnapping that took place here in Newcastle wasn't a teenage girl after all. It was probably someone else in the community that no one even realizes is missing," Kai said. "This makes finding them all the more difficult. It could be anyone in town."

"Furthermore, when in its copycat form, the demon is very hard to sense or detect," Martin said. "It will have the memories, mannerisms, and even the energy of the human it is pretending to be. On the outside, everything will appear normal, even to close family members."

At the mention of the word family, I suddenly got a sick feeling in my stomach.

"What about Julie Peterson?" I asked. "Is it possible Olive's mom is really this demon? What if Olive doesn't even know her mother's been kidnapped?"

Martin slowly nodded.

"Yes, Kai filled me in on your suspicions about this woman," he said. "I have to say her potential involvement with Bates is somewhat of a concern. It could be innocent, of course. The cupcake you brought home to me the other day was delicious, but if it had any Moondust inside, it was nothing more than a trace amount to amplify the flavor or make them slightly more addictive. That's hardly more dangerous than sugar, if you ask me."

"What if some of her other cupcakes have had more Moondust, though?" I asked. "The other day at Sir Bean, Peyton had a maple bacon cupcake. The next day, she told me she'd had incredibly realistic dreams. Dreams that made her muscles ache. I experienced something similar when I had Moondust candy years ago. Also, Ms. Julie dropped off a special cupcake for Peyton to try the day she disappeared. She specifically told her not to eat it until after we'd all left. It's suspicious, if you ask me."

Martin seemed to think this over.

"There could be a connection, there," he said.

"I'm not sure what that has to do with bundles of lavender and poison ivy under her pillow, though," I said, frowning. Why drug Peyton and then also leave those bundles? "I don't know how it all comes together, but there's something to it. We just don't have all the pieces to fit it together yet."

"We need to figure out our next moves," Kai said. "So far, all we have is speculation. We need proof."

Martin stood. "I plan to go back out to the scene of last night's attack," he said. "My only concern last night was getting Lenny to safety. I didn't have a chance to look around for clues. Let's head out in the light of day and see what we can find, shall we?"

We followed him to the garage, where he kept two different cars. One was a sleek new Mercedes AMG GT 4-Door he'd bought this summer. The other was a Classic 1937 Cadillac.

Neither car was exactly the kind that would blend in, but it was one of these or the VW bug Kai had been driving. I sighed. I really needed to get a car of my own. Something less conspicuous.

"What about Julie Peterson, though?" I asked. "Shouldn't we be looking into her, too?"

"One step at a time," Martin said.

"Or we could go now," I said. "Just to have a look around. I'm not going to have any idea what you're looking for in the woods, so I'm not going to be any help out there with you. Besides, we don't have a lot of time. We should divide and conquer."

"She has a point," Kai said.

Martin seemed to think it over for a long moment before finally nodding.

"As much as I hate to let you out of my sight again, I will agree to it for the simple reason that we have a limited amount of time to find this demon," he said. "However, I want you to pack your bag with everything you might need if you get into a fight, and I want you to promise to do nothing more than observe the Peterson house at a distance. You are not, under any circumstances, to go inside. Do you hear me?"

"Of course," I said.

Martin turned his attention back to Kai.

"I'm trusting you to keep an eye on her and keep her safe," he said.

"You know I will," Kai said.

I eyed them both. I would have argued and said I could take care of myself, but after last night, that would have been a lie. I had never felt so weak and so scared in my life.

I vowed to be more careful from now on.

"I'll be right back," I said, and disappeared upstairs to pack my bag with any reagents or potions I might need while we were gone.

When I came back down, Martin had already left and Kai held up the keys to the Mercedes he'd left behind.

"Do you want to drive? Or should I?"

"Do you even have to ask?" I said with a smile as I snatched the keys from his hand.

A minute later, we were on the road, heading out to take a closer look at the house my new friend Olive shared with her mother.

CLOSE YOUR EYES

"Turn here," Kai said.

"How do you know where Olive lives?" I asked.

"I've done a little bit of reconnaissance on all of the girls who have disappeared," Kai said. "One of the missing girls lived in the same subdivision as Olive. They were apparently really good friends when they were younger. Inseparable, some said."

"What was her name?" I asked, realizing we were talking about the poor girl as if she were dead. But she wasn't. She was going to be okay. I had to believe that.

"Latasha Owings," he said. He nodded toward a grey sign up ahead. "The Oaks. This is where the Peterson's live. Turn here and just park on a side street. We can walk the rest of the way."

When I stopped, he unfastened his seatbelt and turned around, rummaging through a bag he'd thrown in the back seat. His bare arm brushed against mine, and my stomach erupted in butterflies.

Aw, man, was I falling for this guy?

I really wanted to hold back judgment until I knew more about him, but I couldn't seem to help myself. I liked him, and I felt like no matter what, he was always looking out for me.

I wanted to ask him more about why when he took a file folder out of the bag and dropped it into my lap.

"These are the notes I've kept about the missing girls," he said. "Latasha was the first girl to go missing. She lived two houses down from Olive and her mom."

I searched for her photo and the information he'd gathered on her. She was sweet and quiet, according to her school records. And she was very smart. Nearly perfect grades. President of the debate team and a few other clubs.

Her parents had gone out to dinner to celebrate their anniversary, taking Latasha's new baby brother with them. Latasha had stayed home to study. According to her parents, she'd planned to go to bed early, because she had a chemistry test the next day and wanted to be well rested for it.

They had never seen her again.

"This is so sad. Her parents must really miss her," I said, imagining what it must have been like for them to come home after a fun evening out to find their daughter gone. "We've got to bring her home."

Kai reached over and put his hand on mine.

"We will," he said.

Our eyes met for a long moment, and I realized for the first time that falling for someone didn't always have to do with how much you knew about them or even how long you'd known them.

It was in the way you felt when someone looked at you or touched your hand.

I cleared my throat and closed the file.

"So, what exactly are we looking for at Julie Peterson's house, anyway?" I asked.

"Anything suspicious, I guess," he said. "Making the cupcakes is her only source of income since she lost her job at an accounting firm last year. I've spoken to her a few times when she's dropped them off at Sir Bean. She's mentioned being divorced a few times, saying that she's had to raise Olive by herself since she was a baby. I also know that since Christmas, she almost never lets Olive near the cupcakes, anymore. She complained once that Olive always mixes flavors wrong or burns them. Apparently, they've had a lot of arguments about it."

"A likely story," I said. "She probably never lets Olive help, because she's been putting Moondust in them. She wouldn't want to have to explain that to her teenage daughter."

"You could be right about that," Kai said. "Let's go and see if there's anything going on."

"If we aren't allowed to go in, this is going to be really boring and useless," I said, my mind already working through ideas of how we could get in undetected.

I studied the neighborhood as we walked on the sidewalks several blocks to get to the Peterson house.

From the looks of it, The Oaks was an average upper-middle-class kind of neighborhood where the houses were big but they all kind of looked the same.

Nothing looked out of the ordinary or suspicious, and I wondered again what we were really hoping to find by coming out here. Olive was likely at school, so Julie Peterson was doing what? Baking?

When we got to the street where Olive lived, instead of

just walking out in the open, Kai led me back behind the houses.

I probably should have brought some kind of invisibility potion with me, but it seemed we were mostly hidden by the tall fences here. On the back side of the fences, there was a stretch of trees through which you could just barely see the backs of the next row of houses.

"What's our plan here?" I asked. "After what happened last night, I feel like winging it has not exactly served us well."

Kai smiled. "Maybe you're right," he said. "I've been looking into all of this for so long on my own that I keep forgetting I have someone else to look after now."

"Maybe I'm the one looking after you," I said. "I mean, you were the one trapped in a net last night. If it hadn't been for me—"

"I never did get a chance to properly thank you for that," he said, stopping and taking my hands in his.

Okay, if his absent touch in the car sent my heart racing, this moment with him standing so close and taking my hands was about to give me a heart attack.

"It's really no big deal," I said, pulling away. "I was just teasing you."

I left him behind, making my way into the stretch of trees behind the house. He'd said it was the fifth one down, so I made my way behind that white house and pretended to be studying the windows, looking for movement, while he walked toward me.

What was wrong with me? Why was I so afraid of getting close to him?

I didn't really want to think about it. All I knew was that I was happy being his friend for now. I had no idea if he was interested in me for more than just that, but I so did not have the capacity to handle anything else.

And still, my heart raced at the sight of him. Especially with that smirk on his face, like I'd just done exactly what he expected me to do.

I closed my eyes and groaned.

Focus, Lenny. You're being ridiculous.

I took a deep breath and looked at the house. Except that this time, I really looked at it instead of just pretending.

"Oh my God," I whispered. "Look."

Kai turned, following my eyes toward the brown sedan that pulled into Julie Peterson's driveway. A man got out and walked around to the back of the car.

"That's Bates," he said, narrowing his eyes. "What's he doing here?"

"Good question," I said. "I don't think we're going to be able to see enough from out here. I knew I should have brought an invisibility potion, but those are really tough to make if I want them to last more than two minutes. It's too bad neither one of us can just spontaneously make ourselves invisible."

I said it with a laugh, but Kai shrugged.

My eyes widened.

"Wait. You can make yourself invisible?

"Yeah, but I don't do it a lot," he said. "It takes a lot of my energy. And it kind of tickles."

My jaw fell open slightly.

"You could sneak up there and see what's going on between Bates and Ms. Julie. You could listen to their conversation," I said. "We need to figure out what their connection is to the missing girls, because I have a feeling after last night that it's about more than just cupcakes here. Plus, it would be nice to see if Julie Peterson has any injuries. Uncle Martin stabbed Algrath last night. Maybe the injury will show up somehow in his human form, too."

"Good point," Kai said. "But Martin told us not to engage. To watch from a distance."

"Oh, so now we're going to start following the rules?" I challenged.

Kai laughed and shook his head.

Meanwhile, Bates threw open the car's trunk and grabbed a large leather duffle bag.

"Moondust, maybe," I whispered.

"I'll go check it out," Kai said. "But if there seems to be any trouble, I want you to promise not to come chasing after me. Whatever happens, you run."

I shook my head.

"The only way we're leaving is together."

"I promised your uncle I'd look after you," he said. "If anything happens or it seems like I'm in any kind of trouble, just run Lenny. I won't let anything happen to you. Promise me."

I held my breath. Why did he care about me at all? Had something happened between us all those years ago when we first met?

I wanted so badly to ask him about it, but we were going to miss our window to get Kai into the house.

"Okay, I promise," I said. "But just don't let anything happen."

He smiled, sending a wave of electricity through my body.

"I'll be back in a few. Sit tight," he said. He made a face. "Oh, and uh, close your eyes and turn around for a second."

"What? Why?"

"Just do it. Please. I'll explain later."

I didn't want to waste any more time, so I did as he asked.

I only counted to three, though, before I opened my eyes.

"Can I turn around now?" I whispered.

But Kai didn't answer.

I spun around, expecting to see him still standing there giving me a look, but instead, he was gone.

I swallowed, shivers running down my spine as I stared at the space between me and the back of the Peterson's house. Kai was there, somewhere, but there wasn't a single trace of him.

I shook my head and sat down just behind one of the larger pine trees behind the house. I had some time to kill, so I pulled out my phone to make sure Martin hadn't called or texted with news about the warehouse or the attack site.

There was nothing, though, so I put my phone back in my bag and started thinking about everything that had happened so far. I still had so many questions and no real answers, unless we'd been right about Julie Peterson. That would be something, at least.

Still, how had Algrath known where to find us last night?

Had he followed us? Or tracked us in some way?

Was he tracking us right now?

What was going on inside that house? Why was he taking so long?

I needed something to keep my hands and mind occupied, or I was likely to just follow Kai inside that house.

I absently picked at the plant near my foot, tearing apart the leaves as I thought through all the questions and possibilities. There had to be some connection between Bates and the demon, and here was Bates at the Peterson house, which meant there was some tie between Ms. Julie and the demon, too.

Could it really be her? Or were we missing something important?

And if it was her, where was she keeping the others? Surely, she wasn't keeping all five girls in her house, or Olive would know about it. If Julie Peterson had the girls, she was keeping them somewhere outside of town.

I needed to talk to Olive. See if she suspected anything about her mother, or even if she was somehow working with her mother.

The thought of that made my stomach hurt. No, I couldn't believe Olive would do something like that to her friends.

But we were getting close. We had to be, or else that demon wouldn't have attacked us last night. He wanted to get us out of the way so no one would interrupt him the night of the ritual.

I pulled apart another piece of the plant before I looked down and realized just what I was doing.

I gasped and jumped to my feet, wiping my hands on my leggings. Thank God I wasn't allergic, but this was just another sign that we were moving in the right direction.

Sure, you could find this in a lot of the woods around town, but the fact that there was some right here, so conveniently located behind Julie Peterson's house, brought us one step closer to proving it.

This whole time, waiting for Kai, I'd been sitting in a huge patch of poison ivy.

NO WAY OUT

Poison ivy wound its way around the trees here behind the house. Not that unusual, but it was an awfully convenient location for Julie Peterson.

I glanced around, looking for any sign of lavender, but no one had planted any specific gardens out here or anything. It was just wild vines, weeds, and debris from the trees. I clipped off some of the poison ivy and put it in my backpack to study later. If only I had access to one of the bundles left at the girls' houses, maybe I could compare them.

I was thinking through the logistics of breaking into the evidence locker of a small-town police department when Kai suddenly appeared around the corner of the house, shaking his head.

I wiped my hands off, closed up my bag, and threw it over my shoulder as I joined him.

"What happened?" I asked. "What did they talk about?"

"Nothing happened," Kai said. "No one is in there."

"What do you mean?" I asked. "We literally just watched Bates go inside. How can no one be in there?"

He shook his head, obviously just as confused as I was.

"I searched every inch of that house, thinking maybe there was a secret entrance to a basement or a special room somewhere, but there's nothing that I can find," he said. "It's as if Bates walked in and just disappeared."

"Without a trace," I whispered. "Just like the girls. There's something going on here. Let's go."

"Where?" Kai asked, though it was obvious where I was going.

I wanted to see the inside for myself. Bates hadn't just evaporated. He was either inside somewhere we couldn't see, or he'd gone through some kind of portal in the house.

"We need to figure out where he went. Maybe that's how we find the girls," I said.

"I think we should let Martin know what we're doing," Kai said, running after me. "It's one thing to tiptoe through a house while invisible. It's something else entirely to walk in and start looking for a secret portal to a demon's lair. You're going to get yourself in trouble again. What if Martin doesn't get here fast enough next time?"

"Do you understand how close we are to the truth?" I asked, turning on him. "If there's a portal in this house, it most likely leads to wherever he's keeping Peyton and the others."

"Yes, but if we go in there now and get ourselves killed, how does that help anyone but the demon?" Kai asked.

I wanted to punch a hole in the side of the house. We didn't have time to sit here and discuss this. Bates's trail was getting cold every second we waited.

"We aren't going to get ourselves killed," I said, motioning to my backpack. "I brought some provisions this time around. I'm more prepared. The reason Algrath nearly got us last time was because we weren't prepared. Besides, we aren't going to try to fight him. We just need to see where he's hiding. If we can locate the portal, we can come back later with reinforcements. But every second we wait makes it more difficult for me to track Bates's footsteps. So, come on, already. I'm done discussing it. Stay out here alone, if you want to."

Kai's eyes widened. "You can track his footsteps?"

"Yes," I said, glancing around the neighborhood before sneaking around the front of the house and walking through the front door. I wanted to make sure no one was watching us, but it was a quiet day on this street.

We slipped into the house and shut the door behind us.

The inside was absolutely pristine, but it was still a house of secrets. Secrets I wanted the answers to.

I reached inside my backpack and took out a bag full of dirt. It was nothing fancy or magical in and of itself, but it was part of the toolkit my parents always used to pack as Slayers. Plain dirt was more useful than most people could have imagined.

"What's that for?" Kai whispered.

"Watch," I said, crouching down just inside the entrance.

I grabbed a small handful and scattered it around me in an arc.

"*Vestigia revelare.*"

I held my breath, waiting to see if it would actually work for me like I'd seen it work for my parents so many times before.

A few seconds later, a boot print appeared in the dirt directly in front of me, heading straight down the hall toward the kitchen. I followed it to the last print and repeated the process.

The footprints took us through the kitchen, into the breakfast nook, and then straight into a wall on the other side of the house.

Frowning, I studied the wall. I pushed on it, kicked it, searched for any kind of keyhole or seam in the wallpaper, but there was nothing to indicate a door or portal here at all.

"*Ostendo.*"

Nothing revealed itself, though, and I shook my head.

"*Solvo,*" I said, trying again.

Nothing happened.

"I don't know how they have it all sealed off, but at least now we know where it is," I said. "Let's take a quick look around the house and see if we can find any lavender bundles before we head out. Then, we'll go tell Martin what we found and see if we can bring him back here to help us open this portal."

Kai sighed. "I don't like this, Lenny. Something doesn't feel right," he said. "I'm getting a weird energy vibe. I think we should get out of here."

"The house is empty," I said. "This is our chance to look for proof Olive's mom is directly involved in this kidnapping and not just some Moondust dealer. If we can find that lavender, we'll know it was her."

"I think it's pretty obvious she's involved. Don't you?" Kai asked, his voice raised. "Normal people don't just have mystical portals in their home. Moondust is one thing, but this is a step too far. We need to get Martin right now. Call him. Tell him to meet us here, and we'll wait for him outside."

Wow. Kai was really serious about this. He was scared.

"Okay," I said. I pulled my phone from the front pocket of my bag and dialed Martin's number. "We'll let Martin know what's going on and see if he'll come to help. It's going to be okay."

Why wasn't it ringing?

I pulled my phone away from my ear to make sure I'd dialed correctly. Basically, since his number was programmed in, pressing the auto-dial button should have called him right away, but the phone didn't ring.

I hit cancel and tried again, but the same thing happened.

"What?" Kai asked. He'd found a broom and had been sweeping up the dirt and footprints.

I shook my head.

"No service inside the house, maybe? I don't know. I'm not used to phones, so maybe I did something wrong," I said.

Kai set the broom against the wall and grabbed my hand.

"We're leaving," he said. "Something is very wrong here. Can't you feel it?"

I couldn't feel anything but the tight grip of his hand around my wrist. He was overreacting.

I pulled my arm away and was about to try to call Martin one more time when a low-level hum grew in intensity, making the house shake slightly.

"What's that?" I asked.

It was almost like a mild earthquake at first, but then it suddenly stopped, leaving us in total silence for a long moment.

"Run," Kai said, taking my hand again. This time, he pulled me toward the door, and I followed willingly.

But when he went to open the front door, it slammed shut

and darkness descended on the entire house, blotting out all of the sun from the windows.

"Oh, no," I said, dropping to my knees and immediately getting into action, pulling items from my bag. I'd seen this before. "The Devil's Snare. This is not good."

"What is The Devil's Snare?" he asked.

"A trap," I said. "We're locked inside this house until we can kill the trap demon controlling the spell. Can you hold them off?"

"Hold who off?" Kai asked just as a window in the living room smashed, scattering glass all over the floor.

Two demons crawled in through the opening, their pointed teeth bared as they ran toward us.

Kai cursed and held his hands out straight in front of him. I had no idea what he was doing, but I didn't have time to worry about it. I had to get my things set up.

"I need two minutes," I shouted.

"I'm on it," he said.

A second window smashed, and I dropped the small bag of herbs I'd brought.

You can do this. Just focus.

With trembling hands, I picked the bag up and located the large bottle of blessed salt my mom had probably packed more than a year ago.

I opened the top and turned around, creating a ring of salt around me to keep the demons out. I would have enclosed us both inside, but it wouldn't be strong enough against so many for very long.

I just needed a couple minutes to get everything ready. I hoped he was up for it.

I glanced up just as Kai clapped his hands together.

A bright light burst forth from him, and I had to shield my eyes against it.

Apparently, so did the lesser demons pouring in through the broken windows. Several of them screeched and backed away, shading their eyes against the light of the newly conjured weapon in Kai's hands.

My jaw dropped, and I couldn't force myself to look away, even though I still had to squint to see it.

Kai had somehow managed to conjure a very big, two-handed hammer out of thin air. It looked like something I'd seen in a video game once called a great maul, but I had never seen anything like it in real life. I couldn't tell from here if it was surrounded by golden light, or if the entire hammer itself was made of pure light.

"What are you looking at?" Kai asked as he swung the hammer toward the first demon, knocking it back against the wall and shattering a painting of Olive and her mom. "Get to work doing whatever you've got to do. I can't hold this forever."

His words snapped me out of my shock, and I sat down on the floor in the center of the circle of salt. I would have to trust that whatever he was doing back there would be enough to get us through this.

It would have to be, because this time, Martin wasn't going to come to rescue us. When a Slayer was caught in The Devil's Snare, their energy was completely blocked off from the outside world. From the street, the house would have looked totally normal, but inside, we were stuck until these demons were dead.

What have I done?

I suddenly felt sick to my stomach, but I would have to be

angry with myself for getting us into this situation later. Now, I had to figure out how to get us out of it.

I rummaged through my bag and pulled out my sheathed silver dagger, a small vial of holy water, the rose Martin had given me this morning with my breakfast, and the strip of poison ivy I'd just grabbed from outside. Might as well make use of it, since an opportunity had suddenly presented itself.

I needed to get centered before I could enchant my dagger, but my heart was racing, and I was truthfully just barely holding myself together.

My eyes darted toward Kai. He kicked one demon across the room and swept his hammer in a circle, knocking four others backward. They all seemed to get right back up again. The light in his hammer flickered slightly, and I wondered just how long he could hold it together.

I still wasn't sure what his powers were, but like me, he seemed to be new to a lot of this.

I turned my back to him and took a long, deep breath to steady my nerves. I could do this. I knew what to do. I'd seen mom do this a hundred times.

Granted, I usually watched her do this in practice or long before any demon showed up, but I didn't have that kind of time. Next time, I vowed to be less impulsive and more prepared. At least I'd remembered the bag this time. That was better.

I breathed in again, shutting out the noise of the fight happening behind me and the endless chattering in my own brain. Instead, I focused on the feel of my breath entering my lungs and the flow of magic that seemed to tingle at the edge of my fingertips.

Remembering last night, I also closed my fingers around

the silver locket that had belonged to my mother. I still wasn't sure exactly what had happened, but somehow, this locket had amplified my power.

"I need you to do it again," I whispered.

"Hurry, Lenora," Kai shouted. "I'm fading."

I poured all of my intentions into the locket.

Protection of self. Destruction of evil.

The locket cooled beneath my fingers, and I let the power flow into my body. I reached for the dagger and poured the vial of holy water across the blade.

"*Viribus*," I said, repeating the mantra I'd heard my mother say so many times to strengthen the power of her own weapons.

The blade soaked up the water, as if drinking it in.

I wrapped the poison ivy vine around the blade next and repeated the word.

"*Viribus.*"

The vine grew thicker and then seemed to sink into the blade itself, which now took on a glowing, green tint.

Next, I snapped a single thorn off the fresh rose and pressed it against the blade.

"*Viribus*," I said one final time.

The silver blade grew thorns that dripped with green poison.

If I wasn't so completely terrified, I would have been really excited and impressed with myself. I just hoped it worked. Sometimes, when a young, inexperienced witch dressed their blade with spells, the spell only lasted for one or two attacks.

I prayed whatever amplification and protection this locket had inside it would be enough to make this last.

"Lenny."

Kai swung at a demon that had been lunging toward me, and between the blow of his hammer and the acidic qualities of the salt against its skin as it touched my barrier, the demon fell to the floor in agony. I stepped out of my circle and sunk my dagger in its chest.

The demon's eyes widened for a brief moment before its body exploded in a cloud of ash that fluttered to the floor.

Kai continued fighting, but I could tell the magic he'd used to summon that hammer was fading. With each blow, it flickered and dimmed.

He didn't give up, though. He just kept fighting.

I joined him and fought at his side, using every technique I could remember from the years of training at my parents' side. The other night when we'd fought Algrath himself, I had seemed to forget all of that training, wondering if I'd ever even known how to fight.

But today, my confidence was restored.

I could do this. Yes, I still had a lot to learn, but as the lesser demons fell to my enchanted blade, one-by-one, I held a sense of power I hadn't felt since my parents died.

"How do we get out of here?" Kai asked as his hammer faded almost to nothing.

"We have to kill the demon holding the trap," I said, plunging my dagger into a demon's back.

Kai lifted his foot and kicked a demon back with a quick blast of light that seemed to sear the demon's skin.

I had never seen magic like that. Not even from a fae of the summer court.

"How do we know which demon that is?" he asked.

Five more lesser demons came through the living room

windows, and my confidence faded slightly. How many more of them were there? Would they just keep coming forever?

"It won't be coming for us like these are," I said. "It will be casting. Focusing on the spell that holds the snare."

"There are too many," he said, our eyes meeting briefly. "I can't hold them. Lenny, we have to get out of here."

"There is no way out," I said quietly, my surge of confidence and power gone as three more demons ran down the hallway from the kitchen.

This was all my fault. Once again, I'd rushed into a situation thinking I was strong and could handle it. When was I going to learn that I was in way over my head? That I needed more official training before I could handle a situation like this on my own?

The enchantments on my blade had lasted way longer than they would have without the power of the locket, but now, with almost a dozen demons slain, the magic was fading. I didn't have the time or the reagents to recast the enchantments, either.

We had to find the demon holding the trap open.

I grabbed the bottle of salt from where I'd left it in the circle.

"Follow me," I said, motioning to Kai.

I ran through the downstairs of the house, fighting off demons and sprinkling salt to hold them back as I searched for the trap demon, but there was no sign of it down here.

"Upstairs," I said, leading the way as Kai watched my back.

The moment we stepped onto the second-floor landing, I saw it.

"There," I said, running toward what had to be Ms. Julie's master bedroom at the end of the hall.

Sitting on the end of her bed, a demon held the dark spell between its fingers. From here, it looked like a ball of dark thorns.

I spread the last of the blessed rock salt across the top step and ran toward the bedroom. The demon looked up suddenly, its eyes open and trained directly on me. I couldn't risk having it move or cast a new, more dangerous spell.

On impulse, I grabbed the tip of my dagger, reared back, and aimed at the center of the demon's chest. The fingers of my left hand wrapped around the locket as I threw the dagger, but I realized my mistake the moment the dagger left my hand.

This demon was a trickster. It liked traps and tricks of all kinds, and it had set up a mirror image of itself up here. I'd just thrown my dagger at an illusion. The blade passed through the image and embedded itself in the headboard.

Something behind me growled, and both Kai and I turned as the real trap demon pounced at us from behind.

"Lenora," Kai shouted, diving toward me, his arms outstretched.

A bright light flashed as Kai wrapped his arms around me. Enclosed in a shield of pure, golden light, we tumbled to the floor.

The demon slammed against the shield and screamed in agony. Its death-cries shook the house, and I clung to Kai, burying my head against his chest.

Instantly, the oppressiveness of the dark trap around us released itself. It was like a weight lifting off my shoulders, and I took a deep breath to still the racing of my heart.

Kai hovered over me, pulling back slightly to look me over.

"Are you okay?" he asked, placing a hand on my cheek.

But I couldn't answer him. All I could do was stare at the beauty of him.

Kai's tanned skin was bathed in golden light, and his eyes shone from the inside. But that wasn't the best of it.

The light he'd wrapped around me to use as a shield against the demon wasn't light at all.

It was angel's wings.

SO LITTLE TIME

I could hardly breathe as I looked at Kai. He'd been completely transformed.

Yes, of course, he'd always been a good-looking guy, but now, with his white wings extended behind him and their golden light casting the most beautiful shadows across his face, I was mesmerized.

Whatever part of me had been holding out, refusing to fall for anyone so fast, completely gave in, and I suddenly became acutely aware of his hands on my face.

"You're an angel," I managed to say, my voice barely more than a whisper.

He was like a dream, and I wondered if I'd maybe eaten a Moondust cupcake and all of this was a figment of my drugged imagination.

But when he ran a fingertip across the line of my hair at my forehead, I knew there was no way this feeling inside me was made up. It was the most real thing I'd ever felt in my life.

"Half-angel," he said with a slow smile, our eyes locked. "I was trying to keep that to myself for as long as possible, but that became impossible the second you rushed head-first into danger, yet again."

I blushed and sat up.

"I'm sorry. I didn't think we were in any real danger with them gone," I said. "How was I supposed to know the house was trapped?"

He sat back and his wings slowly faded into nothing. I missed their light and warmth immediately. He looked normal and human again, but my heart hadn't stopped racing.

"It's curious, too. Now that I think about," he said, frowning.

"What's curious?" I asked, taking my first good look around at the house.

There was a huge pile of grey ashes where the trap demon had fallen, and there were dark, burned fingerprints in some of the doorways and on the floor from the demons' touch. There was no way to really hide what had happened here.

I seriously hoped Olive wasn't going to be the first one home.

"It's curious that I didn't trigger that trap when I came in alone," Kai said. "I don't know how this particular trap works, but with most traps, they're triggered when anyone comes in contact with them. So, why didn't I trip it when I walked in?"

I stood.

"Why don't we discuss it while we walk out the door?" I asked, shuddering as I stepped over the trap demon's ashes.

It wasn't dead. Just banished. To really complete the job, we would have needed to perform an extra ritual on the ashes to either kill or contain each demon, or at least make sure it never came back from hell. But we didn't have the right tools, energy, or the time.

I quickly retrieved my dagger from the headboard in Ms. Julie's room and made my way down the stairs.

After being trapped in here with no way out, I was ready to feel the sun on my face and to see this house in the rearview mirror.

Kai apparently agreed, because he stood and followed me out the door just as quickly.

We didn't bother walking along the back fences. Instead, we made our way straight to the car and headed back toward Martin's house.

"It's possible the trap didn't trigger because you were invisible," I said. "But to be honest, I don't think that has really ever stopped a trap before, unless it was a really weak one."

"Which means someone specifically set that trap for you," Kai said.

I shook my head.

"That doesn't make any sense," I said. "If someone knows we're getting close to the truth, why wouldn't they just set a trap for both of us? We've been together every step of the way with this."

"It's something we should at least keep in mind," he said. "Maybe someone involved specifically wants you dead, Lenny. I don't want to think that could be true, but I've been investigating this for months and never had anything like this happen. You start investigating and a day later, you've already been attacked and almost killed twice. I don't think that's a coincidence."

There are no coincidences.

I could hear my father's voice in my head. He used to say

that all the time. Don't overlook anything or dismiss it as just a coincidence. Everything had meaning to some degree. Everything was potentially important.

And paying attention to those little details could mean the difference between life and death.

So, on top of everything else, I needed to think about why someone might specifically want me dead. Or want me to stay out of this whole investigation.

There was no real reason for Julie Peterson to care about me, in particular, even if Algrath was currently running around pretending to be her.

But there was one name that came to mind. Someone who would have a lot to lose if I discovered a connection between her and a powerful demon.

Ms. Greer would potentially lose everything, including her position as Keeper, if the Council found out she was involved in this, working for the other side.

Maybe she knew I'd put that bundle on her car the other night. That would explain how she'd been able to attack us in the woods yesterday, but what about the Peterson house? Had one of Ms. Greer's ravens been tracking me everywhere?

I leaned forward and looked into the sky, but I didn't see any birds. Still, it could be anywhere, watching us.

I wondered if she was still in town, and if so, if Martin knew how to get ahold of her.

When we made it back to Martin's without running into any demons, I sighed in relief. I'd been checking out every car we'd passed on the way home, and I realized my entire body had been tense the whole drive home.

We found Martin in the kitchen making paninis.

My stomach growled. I was so lucky to live with someone

who really knew how to cook. My parents had been all about quick and easy meals, so I'd grown up on fast food, canned vegetables, and ramen noodles.

I would have traded all the paninis in the world to have them back, but at least there were a few perks to my new life.

Martin narrowed his eyes at me.

"What happened to you, Lenora? You've been fighting," he said. "I told you not to engage and to watch from afar. I take it you ignored my instructions. Again."

"It wasn't exactly my fault," I said, grabbing a handful of homemade potato chips from a bowl on the counter.

Kai and I explained the entire scene that had played out at Ms. Julie's house, filling him in on everything from the back-yard poison ivy to the trap demon triggered only by me.

"You never should have gone into that house," Martin said, glaring at Kai.

"It was my decision to go in, so don't take it out on him," I said as we sat down to eat.

"Oh, I have no doubt it was your decision to go inside, but Kai here was told to keep you out of danger," Martin said. "Kai, I thought we worked this out months ago."

Kai cleared his throat.

"Yes, sir. We did," he said. "I'll do better next time."

I frowned. Months ago?

"That's not fair," I said. "I'm allowed to make my own decisions, even if they're bad ones. I don't want anyone holding me back from what I need to do."

"Yes, it would be a tragedy if someone saved your life by keeping you from rushing into things like The Devil's Snare," Martin said with a chuckle. "Don't worry, girl. No one is trying to take away your freedom, but until you develop a little more common sense and a little less jump-right-in, I'm going to continue to look out for you. It's called family."

He put his hand on mine for a brief moment, and tears sprang to my eyes. It meant a lot to have someone like Martin looking out for me.

And hey, now I also had a guardian angel. Kind of.

I smiled at the thought of it and glanced at Kai.

I still had so many questions about his heritage. Where had his mother come from? What coven did she belong to? And how, exactly, had his father fallen in love with a human witch?

There were a lot of myths about angels and some people actually doubted their existence at all, but one thing everyone seemed to agree on in the legends was the humans and angels were not allowed to be together.

Angels probably also weren't supposed to be friends with Slayers, but Kai had said his father was good friends with my parents.

I wanted to know more about that.

And more about what had happened to his father.

So many questions, so little time.

"What's next? Did you find anything at the attack site?" Kai asked, polishing off the last of his sandwich. "That was delicious, by the way. Those would be a huge hit at Sir Bean, I bet. Melvin has been thinking about adding a full menu."

Martin smiled and cleared away the dishes.

"If I ever get bored enough to need such a diversion, I will let you know," he said. "For now, though, we have quite a lot to take care of before tomorrow. I would like to go back to have a look at that portal, if there's time, but first—"

His words were interrupted by the chime of the doorbell.

That doorbell hadn't made a sound since the day I moved

in three months ago, and now it had rung twice in one day. I groaned. More bad news? I wasn't sure my heart could take it.

I wanted to rush out to the foyer to answer it myself, but after our earlier conversation, I decided to resist my jump-right-in tendencies, as Martin had called it, and wait for him to slowly make his way out there, instead.

"Aren't you going to see who's here?" Kai asked, leaning his tall frame against the kitchen counter.

"No. As a matter of fact, I'm being super mature right now and waiting to see what Martin says. I can be patient and calm if I want to be."

"I see," Kai said with a smirk. "Wonder how long that will last?"

I lifted my chin in defiance and tried to appear calm as my toes tapped inside my shoes.

What was taking Martin so long? Was it the police again? Did the detective know I'd broken into the Peterson house?

Well, that would just be a big mess I couldn't explain.

I bit my lip and frowned, checking the clock. Kai stifled a laugh.

"Lenny, come out here, please," Martin called, and my stomach flipped nervously.

Kai and I exchanged looks, and then we both practically ran into each other trying to cramp through the kitchen doorway at the same time.

I laughed as I pushed in front of him and he bumped my arm with his, but when he reached the foyer, his eyes grew wide.

Almost scared to look up, I took a deep breath and prepared myself for the worst. I expected the detective or maybe Blythe Greer, but instead, a group of five people wearing harsh expressions stood in the entryway, their eyes trained on me.

I gasped and then screamed as I ran forward. A tall woman with long, red hair in a high ponytail stepped forward, her arms wide open as she leaned forward to pull me into a huge bear hug.

"Gianna," I said, wrapping my arms around her.

My mother's best friend. I hadn't seen her since the funeral.

"What are you all doing here?" I asked, finally pulling away to look at the group of five Slayers whose presence was surely not sanctioned by the Council.

"We're here to help you banish this demon, once and for all," Gianna said. She smiled, her eyes darting from me to Kai. "But first, we're going to show you a few tricks to help you stay alive, next time you get yourself into trouble."

I smiled, excitement rushing through me like it was Christmas morning.

Five of the most powerful, deadliest Slayers in the Witch's Council were going to teach us how to fight. Our chances of saving Peyton and the others just grew exponentially.

A LOT TO LEARN

True to Martin's style, he invited everyone back to the kitchen for fresh coffee and cookies. None of the Slayers were about to say no to that, so we all made our way to the back room of the house.

After a few minutes of getting everyone situated and making introductions, everyone found a seat at the worn antique table that I'd come to think of as the coziest place on earth.

I cupped the warm mug between my hands and breathed in the earthy aroma of the coffee.

We actually had a chance now to save Peyton and the others, and I couldn't help but smile. In so many ways, I'd felt alone after the death of my parents. I had Martin, of course, but it had taken time to get comfortable with him.

Now, though, I remembered I wasn't alone at all. The people who truly loved my parents would always be there for me when I needed them.

"Does the Council know you're here?" I asked, breaking up the casual conversations going on around the table.

I was hopeful and all, but we were pressed for time here. We could talk about casual things once this demon was gone.

"Alright then. Let's get straight to the point," an old Slayer named Gowan said, winking at me before taking his seat.

Gowan's white hair and beard seemed freshly cut, and he wore a black t-shirt that stretched over his huge muscles. He was about six feet tall, and except for the color of his hair, he didn't at all look his age. Though to be honest, I wasn't exactly sure how old he was.

He'd been around for a very long time, according to my parents. Longer than Martin, even. He was the oldest, most powerful Slayer I knew, which probably put him over a hundred and fifty years old as a conservative estimate.

There weren't many Slayers his age still around, despite the slower aging of our kind.

It was a dangerous job.

"We didn't exactly advertise we were coming here," Gianna said.

She was sitting next to me on the left side. Kai sat to my right.

"I doubt our presence can stay secret for long, though," Asher said. "But as far as it stands right now, no one has expressly forbidden us from getting involved."

Unlike me.

"And if they do?" I asked.

I had my concerns about the Council. I wasn't sure why they wanted to allow this demon to free his brother, or why they didn't seem to care about the girls who'd been taken, but I had no doubt they were hiding something.

Asher shrugged.

He was the youngest Slayer in the group, besides me if I even counted yet. His long brown hair fell over his very light blue eyes. He wore a dark navy suit jacket that looked very put together and mature, but underneath the jacket was an old Metallica t-shirt and a pair of faded jeans.

I'd only first met Asher about five years ago when he first became a Slayer, officially, and had been mentored by my dad. He'd lived with us for a while when Dad had first taken him under his wing, so I kind of saw Asher like an older brother.

I hadn't seen him as much over the past year, though, because he'd been on some secret assignment in Japan. I hoped we'd get a chance to talk more while he was here. I was dying to hear what he'd been up to.

"If the Council has a problem with us coming here to stop Algrath from killing five more innocent girls with magic in their blood and releasing his brother into the world, then there's going to be a lot more to discuss than a few rogue Slayers," he said. "The entire coven will need to be contacted and told about this. The Council needs to answer for their actions in this case."

"Their inactions, you mean," Britta said, standing. She never had been one for sitting still.

Britta was a petite, dark-eyed Slayer who'd once acted as my mother's mentor decades ago. Her black hair was cut in a pixie-cut hairstyle, and she almost always wore dark red lipstick that contrasted sharply with her pale skin.

She was short and small, but she was fast and feisty.

"The Council has failed us all in this matter," she said with a slight German accent. "We all should have been alerted to Algrath's reappearance a decade ago when the seal on the first mirror was unlocked. They knew this was happening, and they've purposely done nothing to stop it."

"I think it's possible they've even been helping Algrath set his brother free."

This came from the final Slayer of the five.

Darius. He'd been my father's closest friend since they were young boys. Their fathers had fought together as Slayers, too, once upon a time, and the two families had been inseparable for a long time.

His black hair was shaved close to his head, and there was a bit of white hair that had grown into his dark beard over the past few years. He wore black pants and a white t-shirt. I couldn't help but glance again at the scars crisscrossed against the dark skin of his arms.

Darius had been through some difficult times in his life, but he was one of the strongest men I'd ever known, both mentally and physically.

He pushed his chair back from the table and crossed one leg over the other, placing his hands together in his lap.

"I've been doing some research since we got the call from Martin saying it was time to come," he said. "I've talked to a few of my friends, as well. When the mirrors were hidden, they were specifically cloaked with a powerful spell that should have been impossible to detect, even for a powerful demon like Algrath. So, how did he find them all so quickly without the help of someone who knew where they were?"

"Maybe he's grown more powerful over time, though," Gianna said. "Most powerful demons can see through illusions and invisibility spells. Maybe he'd grown strong enough to see through whatever cloaking spell was placed on them."

"Martin, you were part of the crew that first captured

Regmothean," Darius said. "What do you think? Is there any chance the cloaking spells just weren't strong enough?"

Martin stroked his chin for a moment.

"It's always possible, but it's unlikely," he said. "To gain that level of power, Algrath would have needed to increase his power exponentially over a relatively short period of time. That would have taken massive human sacrifice. Thousands of lives."

Everyone in the room grew quiet. No one wanted to believe that could be a possibility. If thousands of humans had died by the hand of this demon, the Council would have known.

I shuddered.

"Let's say that isn't the case," Gowan said. "How else could Algrath have found the mirrors, if he couldn't locate them with his own magic? Are there other options than a member of the Council telling him where to look?"

Silence again, but beside me, Kai tensed and leaned forward, letting his head fall into his hands.

"What?" I asked, placing a hand gently on his arm.

He shook his head, then cleared his throat before sitting back.

"Some angels have the ability to see the actions of the purest souls," he said, his voice strained. "The Slayers placing the mirrors had the best, purest of intentions when they did it. It wouldn't be that difficult for a powerful enough angel to see where they placed those mirrors, even if it happened a hundred years ago."

My hand rose to my mouth.

Had his father helped Algrath find the mirrors? Why would he do that?

"Zuriel would never have helped a demon," Darius said, leaning forward, his jaw tight. "Not willingly."

"I don't want to believe it, either, but I followed my father here about six months ago," Kai said. "A few weeks later, the first girl was taken. That isn't a coincidence."

Darius clenched his fists and stood. He paced the floor and muttered to himself, but I couldn't make out what he was saying.

Kai had said his father was close to my parents. He must have been close to Darius, too.

"What do you know about your father's disappearance?" Gianna asked. "You tracked him here, and then what?"

Kai closed his eyes and shook his head. "I'm not sure," he said. "I had a strong lock on his energy, so I knew he had come to this town. Knowing my father's connection to the Thorne family, I thought maybe he'd come to visit you. That's why I came to Martin when I first arrived in town."

Martin nodded.

"Kai's information is part of what led me to believe Algrath had made it to the final mirror," Martin said. "Sadly, Zuriel never made it here to visit me."

"I don't know what happened to him when he arrived in Newcastle, but before I even got here, his energy simply disappeared," Kai said. "He was here, and then...nothing. I've tried over and over to locate his energy again, but nothing has worked. For a long time, I refused to believe that he could really be gone, but what other explanation is there?"

"Can an angel really be killed?" I asked, not wanting to believe it, for Kai's sake. "There are other ways to mask energy signatures. Maybe Algrath has him locked away."

"Angels can be killed," Gowan said softly. "It isn't easy to do, but it is possible."

Kai grew very still, and he didn't say another word. I wanted to throw my arms around him. The death of my own parents was still really fresh, too, and I knew exactly how he was feeling.

Except that maybe it was harder not to have all the answers. As horrible as it was, I had seen my parents die with my own eyes. I knew what happened to them, and I would have to live with that memory for the rest of my life.

How hard must it have been for Kai over the past few months? To not know?

"We have to assume Algrath used Zuriel to locate the mirrors before killing him," Gowan said. He winced and glanced at Kai, obviously hating the words he had to say. "I hope it isn't true, but for our own safety and the safety of those missing girls, we have to assume Algrath has consumed Zuriel's power."

"What does that mean?" I asked, studying the somber faces of the rest of the people in the room.

"It means Algrath will be impossible to kill," Kai said.

"And it might mean we don't have enough firepower at this table to stop him," Britta said, sitting down.

"Who else can we call in?" Gianna asked, looking to Martin.

He slowly shook his head. "There's no one else," he said.

"Sure there is," Asher said, standing. "There's Luther and Yvonne and—"

"Sit down," Gowan said.

"I have contacted everyone I felt might be loyal to our

friendship over the Council's rule," Martin said. "You five are the only ones who agreed to come. We are alone in this."

Asher closed his eyes and sat down hard in his chair.

"How do we know, then, that no one else has already told the Council what we're planning to do? If they're working with Algrath, he could already know we're here."

"We have to trust that even though our dear friends aren't willing to risk their lives or their place in the coven for this cause, they are not so far gone that they would betray us," Martin said. "We have limited time to worry about it, I'm afraid."

"Martin's right," Gowan said. "It's useless to think about what we don't have. We need to work together to maximize the strength of those who are here now."

With that, he looked at me, a smile spreading across his face. My stomach knotted.

"Time to train?" I guessed.

"Like never before," Gowan said. "Let's get going. You both have a lot to learn before tomorrow."

I NEEDED YOU TO UNDERSTAND

For two hours, we trained in the woods alongside Gianna and Gowan. By the end of it, I was exhausted and slightly bruised. My stamina still wasn't fully restored from the encounter last night, and fighting the trap demon earlier had nearly wiped me out.

"I hate to admit it, but I need a break," I said, doubling over to catch my breath.

Gianna agreed and called for Gowan to join her by the car so they could discuss our progress in silence.

Kai slumped against a tree and slid to the ground.

"I can't believe I still have to go to work now," he said. "I'm sore all over."

We both took long drinks from our water bottles.

"Any word from Martin?" he asked.

Martin had gone back to the Peterson house with Asher to search for the portal we'd discovered earlier.

I pulled my cell phone from my back pocket and shook my

head. "Nothing yet," I said. "Do you really have to go to work? Can't you call out sick or something?"

Kai shook his head. "Martin wants me to go in and see what I can find out about Julie Peterson from Melvin," he said. "Apparently after Ms. Julie divorced her ex-husband, she and Melvin got together for a while. He even lived with her for a few years. I'm going to ask a few questions and see how much Melvin is willing to tell me."

"Will you come back out here with me tonight?" I asked. "I have a feeling they're going to keep this up long after dark."

Kai looked around. "Sure," he said. "But won't it be dangerous out here? This doesn't look so different from the area we were attacked in last night."

"No, come with me." I held my hand out to help him up. He nearly pulled me down, and I laughed as I straightened my knees and tugged harder. "Here, let me show you something."

I walked him out about fifty feet in one direction, studying the trees as I went.

"What are you looking for?" he asked, following my gaze.

"Here," I said, finally, stopping in front of a large pine tree with a symbol branded into its bark.

A circle of thorns with crossed daggers and a rose in the center.

"What is that?" he asked as I traced the burned symbol with my fingertip.

"It's the Thorne family sigil," I said.

"What does it do?" Kai asked.

"It protects this place, somehow," I said. "Martin's used this as a training ground for Slayers and even Keepers for over a century."

A twig snapped nearby, and I immediately grabbed the dagger from my back pocket.

"*Incendium.*"

In an instant, flames surrounded the blade of my dagger.

Martin appeared from behind a tree, smiling. "Impressive reflexes for someone so tired."

I released the spell with a sigh of relief. "You scared me."

"Did you find the portal?" Kai asked.

"I'm afraid not," Martin said. "There are police crawling all over that house now. We won't be getting anything from there in time."

I groaned. That meant one of two things.

Either Ms. Julie had returned from wherever she went and found the place a mess, or Olive had come home from school to that horror show.

I still didn't know for sure if Olive was involved in this whole mess, but I wanted to give her the benefit of the doubt. She'd been so nice to me.

I quickly took out my phone and sent a text to the number she'd given me the other day.

Hey, it's Lenny. Are you okay? Someone said the cops were at your house.

I waited for a second, but there was no response.

"How does your sigil protect this place?" Kai asked. "Does it keep the demon from entering or something?"

Martin smiled and started walking back toward the others. We followed.

"I wish I had the power to do something like that out here, but no. The sigil does not protect demons from crossing the barrier," Martin said. "It's a glorified warning system that's triggered when anyone magical gets too close."

He explained more about the sigil and the training ground as we made our way back to the clearing where we'd both been training earlier. As we approached, however, I saw a sixth person in the center of the circle.

A man on his knees with a black cloth over his head.

Darius knelt beside the man, whispering something in his ear that was too low for us to hear from this distance.

"Martin, what aren't you telling me?" I asked. "Who is that?"

Martin raised an eyebrow and smiled. "Don't you recognize him?" he said. "We discovered him trying to leave the neighborhood just as we arrived, only moments after the police had gotten there."

At that moment, Darius pulled the cloth from the man's head and punched him in the face. The blow turned the man's head sideways, and I gasped.

The man on his knees in the clearing was Bates.

"I assume he's refusing to cooperate," Martin said as we joined the others in the clearing.

"We're getting nowhere with this guy," Darius said. "Let me take him back to the house, Martin. I'll question him with a truth potion, if you have all of the ingredients. Then we'll have the answers we need."

"I have everything you'll need," Martin said. "But I will be returning to the house with you both. I have a few things I need to research before it gets too late. Gowan, you're in charge here. Keep Lenny's training going for as long as she can stand it. Then, come home for a nice dinner at the house."

Gowan smiled at me, his eyes full of mischief. "Will do, sir," he said. "But I won't go easy on her just because she's a Thorne."

"Of course. I would expect no less from you," Martin said.

I tried to act like I wasn't scared, but inside, I was trembling. How much more of this could I take?

"I'm going to head back into town, too," Kai said. "I have to get ready for work. I'll come back out as soon as I get a chance, though."

I was definitely sad to see him go. Could I handle this all by myself? Today had already proved just how little I really knew.

Gianna and Gowan stayed with me in the woods, drilling me on what they called the fundamentals for more than two hours, before I finally begged for a break and sat down.

My body ached, and as I sat there drinking water, I dreamed about looking through Mom's spell books for some kind of bath bomb that would cure aching muscles. I closed my eyes, daydreaming about the warmth of the bath and the comfort of my bed.

My eyes snapped open, though, when I heard Gowan scratching in the dirt at the center of the clearing. He was using a stick to draw a circle with a pentagram and other symbols inside it.

"Trying to catch a demon?" I asked, almost laughing. I had never seen anyone draw this particular symbol in the dirt, but I'd seen it in some textbooks that used to be in Dad's library.

My parents had used it once, too. But only once.

"Exactly," Gowan said.

I stood and watched him more carefully.

"I didn't think anyone used these types of Demon Circles, anymore," I said. "Mom told me they were so ancient and simple that they hardly ever worked compared to some of the more advanced techniques Slayers have now."

Gowan made a guttural sound and cursed under his breath.

"I take it you disagree?" I said, laughing.

"This is no laughing matter, Lenny. Your mom was right about this being a more ancient technique, but it was good enough for Slayers for centuries before the coven developed those so-called modern techniques," Gowan explained as he finished off the circle. "In my experience, a well-placed Demon Circle is much more effective and reliable than many of the newer approaches. A Demon Circle never fails."

"Yeah, as long as you can trick the demon into stepping into one," Gianna said, stepping out from behind a tree.

She had a small brown bunny in her hands, and I suddenly felt a bit sick to my stomach.

"What are you doing with the bunny?" I asked.

Gowan suppressed a smile as he took the rabbit from her and ran his hand across its back a couple of times.

"If you're clever enough, it's not that difficult to trick a demon into a circle trap like this," he said. "The biggest limitation is that a Slayer doesn't always have time to draw and activate it before the fight begins. Still, it's important for modern Slayers to understand why this simple magic works so effectively. Sometimes, I think the Council would rather we all turn only to modern magic, but if we abandon our old ways completely, the knowledge and understanding of the fundamentals will eventually be lost."

"And the bunny?" I asked again, chewing on my bottom lip.

"An exercise in your dedication to the cause," he said. "Since we don't have a demon handy, I want you to practice on this, instead."

I groaned. I did not want to do this.

"Lenny, you stand back about six more feet toward the trees." He turned and counted out fifteen feet back from the opposite side of the Demon Circle.

When he turned back toward me, he leaned his head toward the bunny and whispered a few words I couldn't hear. Above the rabbit's head, a small mirror image of the Demon Circle appeared, marking the bunny.

I'd never seen that particular spell cast before, but I understood immediately that it meant the circle would trap the bunny the same way it would trap a demon.

Hopefully, all he'd ask me to do was trap it. If he asked me to kill that bunny, I was going to have a serious problem.

"Okay, Lenny, see if you can trick the rabbit into the circle," Gowan said, setting the rabbit down in the pine needles. "Don't see it as a rabbit. See it as the demon you're trying to banish."

I took a deep breath. It was hard to pretend an adorable little bunny was a killer demon, but okay. I wanted to get better, and I trusted that Gowan knew what he was doing.

I tried a variety of things to convince the rabbit to cross into that circle, but if I tried to go anywhere near it, the bunny hopped away. Gowan had created some kind of barrier around the clearing so that the bunny couldn't completely hop into the woods to get away, but for about five minutes, all I'd managed to do was move it from one outer part of the clearing to another.

"If something isn't working, try something different," Gowan said. "If you want to be an effective Slayer, you have to think fast and innovate. You have to use everything around you. What else can you do here?"

I cleared my mind and tried to see past the frustration of feeling like a complete failure out here. What else could I use? If I was a bunny, what would trick me into following a human?

The image of a carrot immediately popped into my mind, and I felt a simple rush of exhilaration as I remember my training with Martin just after I'd gotten my key back.

I reached down and grabbed a handful of dirt. I knew if this was a real-life situation, I wouldn't have much time to turn this into an acceptable replica of a carrot, so I allowed my mind to forget everything else but that handful of dirt and what I wanted it to become.

Instantly, my hand began to hum with the power of my own intention. I cleared my mind and imagined a carrot. We hadn't gotten advanced enough to talk about color shifting and making things look realistic, but right now, this was the best idea I had at my disposal.

I glanced at Gianna, and she nodded.

That simple encouragement was all I needed. I poured my pure intentions into the handful of earth and smiled when it formed into a passable carrot shape with a slightly orange tint. Not perfect, but it was a good start.

But would it be enough?

I leaned down and held the carrot toward the bunny.

"Come on, little one," I said in a soft voice. "Are you hungry?"

That got its attention. The bunny sniffed along the ground and took a few hops toward me.

"That's it," I said, backing up into the circle just a couple of steps. "Come on."

As the bunny moved toward me, I kept backing up further into the circle, enticing it to keep moving. When his first little bunny foot crossed into the circle, nausea rolled through me.

Was this going to kill the poor little guy?

I glanced at Gowan, but his face was a blank slate.

I sighed and backed up again. "Come on, little bunny. That's it. Get your carrot," I said, teasing him toward me.

I kept my eyes trained on the bunny's feet, and I gasped the second he fully crossed into the circle. The area all around us pulsed with a new kind of energy, and I could just make out the faintest outline of the circle's barrier all around us.

Dang. Would I be able to step out of it now? Or was I trapped, too?

I quickly stood and took one tentative step out of the circle, then sighed in relief. Okay, I wasn't stuck at least. But what was going to happen to this little rabbit?

He tried to hop toward me, but it seemed like he was stuck in molasses. He could move, but his movements were slow and labored as he crossed the circle. When he reached the barrier near me, he pushed against it, but he couldn't cross over it.

The bunny was officially trapped and alive.

I relaxed my shoulders and smiled up at Gowan. "There," I said. "I did it."

"Very good," he said. "Not bad for your first try, although you realize if this was a real demon, you would have lost him by now. In order to use a Demon's Circle, you have to be witty. Clever. It's very different from the brute-force magic the Council trains its Slayers with now, but it works. You've also expended very little energy to get to this point."

I nodded. He was right. It was a lot more work fighting off the demons at the Peterson house this morning.

"Now, for the second part of your test," he said. "It's great that you were able to get the demon into the circle, but once it's there, you need to banish or contain it in some way. This takes quite a bit more power. Even willpower, sometimes, especially if you stop to think about what you're doing."

"What do you mean?" I asked, not sure I understood what he meant about willpower.

"Once trapped, a demon knows it has limited options, so it will often go right for your weakest spot. For a lot of Slayers, our weak point is our emotions," Gowan explained. "In my experience, most demons who get snared in a trap like this will immediately shift into the human form and begin to beg for mercy. Even though you know there's a demon inside that person, it can be very difficult to do what needs to be done."

I swallowed hard and stared at the circle. He was going to make me kill this bunny, wasn't he?

"So, now that we know you can use your wits to get the demon into the circle, we need to practice what you'll do once he's there." He took a mirror from his pocket and tossed it to me.

It was just one of those handheld compact mirrors that a lot of women carried in their purse. I opened it.

"Do you know how to use that?" he asked. "Have you ever trapped a demon inside a mirror or object before?"

I shook my head. "I've seen it done a couple of times before, but I've never done it myself."

"Well, today's your lucky day," he said. "All you have to do is point the mirror toward the demon and say the incantation. *In Quod Relego.*"

"And if I do that to the bunny, what happens?" I asked. "He's not really a demon, so it won't hurt him, right?"

"It's likely to kill it, but what's one bunny sacrificed

compared to a demon going free? Or worse, you losing your life because you didn't have the courage to go through with it?" Gowan asked, moving around the circle to stand next to me. "It's time now, Lenny. Say the incantation."

I shook my head. I couldn't do that.

I mean, I was all for practicing, but what had this bunny ever done to anyone?

"You must," Gowan said, standing so close to me now, it felt like he was practically breathing down my neck.

"I can't do it," I said, my heart racing. "Just let me practice without the bunny."

"No, you have to know that you can do it no matter who or what is inside that circle," Gowan said. "What if there really was a demon inside of that rabbit? Would you be too much of a coward to follow through because it was too cute?"

"No, of course not," I said. I wanted to just drop the mirror and walk away, but there was also a piece of me that knew he was right.

Being a Slayer was not easy, and sometimes you had to make really difficult decisions.

"Do it," he said. "Your time is running out. Do it now, Lenny."

With trembling hands, I pointed the mirror toward the bunny. Everything inside me protested, though. It just looked so cute and innocent. A few minutes ago, he was hopping through the woods, minding his own business. He didn't deserve this.

"You've got five seconds," Gowan said. "Five seconds or you fail the test and you might as well go home and forget all of this. You can't do this, maybe your friend dies."

My entire body tensed, and a tear rolled down my cheek. I didn't want to do this.

I took a deep breath, then opened my mouth and tried to force the words out. I tried to make myself say them as Gowan began counting down.

"Five. Four. Three."

I shook my head. "I can't," I shouted.

"Do it," Gianna said.

"Two..."

I looked down at the bunny. It was just staring up at me, its big brown eyes full of fear and confusion.

"One..."

I tried to imagine there was a demon hidden inside that bunny's body, but I just couldn't force myself to say the words.

Instead, I closed the mirror and handed it back to Gowan. "I can't do it," I said, trying to hold back tears. "Maybe I'm just not cut out for this."

"Fine, I'll do it," Gowan said, opening the mirror and pointing it toward the bunny.

"No, don't," I said.

"In Quod Relego."

I couldn't watch. I turned away as he said the words. I walked over to a nearby tree and leaned against it.

I didn't want to see the dead bunny, but I also knew I had failed. We were running out of time, and I was too weak to even hurt a bunny.

"Lenny, turn around," Gianna said.

"I don't want to," I said, tears coming now. Maybe I was just too tired. Too worn out after a full day of training. I couldn't force myself to turn.

Gowan placed his hand on my shoulder.

"Turn around, Lenny."

His voice was so soft and understanding, which wasn't at all what I'd been expecting. I expected him to be angry with me.

I turned, meeting his eye as I wiped the tears from my face.

Gowan stood there, the bunny in his hands. Perfectly alive and happily chewing on an actual piece of bright, orange carrot.

I wasn't sure if I wanted to laugh or punch him in the arm.

"But you said it would kill the bunny," I said. "I would have done it if I'd known it wasn't going to hurt him."

Gowan passed the bunny and the carrot to me, and I stroked its soft coat and nuzzled my nose against it.

"It's a hard lesson to learn, but I wanted to illustrate a point, Lenora. When you're up against a demon like Algrath, he could look like anyone," Gowan said. "He could look like me or even Martin. If it ever comes to that, you need to know you can do what has to be done. Do you understand me? If you want to be a Slayer and truly rid the world of evil, you have to be strong. You have to be able to make tough decisions."

He took the bunny from me and set him down on the ground. We all watched as the poor little guy hopped away.

"And sometimes," Gowan said, putting his hand on my shoulder, "you may have to kill or hurt someone you thought you loved. Or the image of someone you loved. With tricksters and mimic demons, you have to be stronger than you realize. You can't have any blind spots or weaknesses when you're a Slayer. Not if you want to survive. I'm sorry I was so harsh, but I needed you to understand what it might be like tomorrow."

I nodded, letting his words really sink in. We still didn't know who Algrath was pretending to be. He could be anyone.

As I followed them to the car to head home for an early dinner, I felt true fear deep down in my gut for the first time since all of this started. Who was Algrath? And when the time came, if he looked like someone I loved, would I be able to do what needed to be done?

All I could do the whole way home was stare out the window and pray that whatever happened, it wouldn't come to that.

WHO TO TRUST

"Pass the pasta," Britta said. "And another piece of that homemade bread. Martin, I have no idea where you find the time."

Martin smiled and passed a bowl of handmade pasta to Britta.

"When you're retired, you will understand," he said. "It's been a challenge to keep my mind and hands occupied since I left my position with the coven."

"Well, I don't ever plan on retiring, thank you very much," Gowan said as he stood and reached all the way over the table to load his plate with meatballs from the serving tray. "I still don't understand why you gave it up."

Martin didn't say a word. He simply took a sip of his pinot noir.

"He'll never tell us," Asher said with a sigh. "I've been trying to get it out of him for a while now. But we all know Martin. A man of many secrets."

I leaned back in my chair, almost too tired to eat, but so happy at the same time.

It was such a strange thing to feel so many conflicting emotions all at once. I was terrified for what might happen tomorrow and what I might have to face. Would we all survive? Would I have to fight?

But I was also sad for my new friend and the other girls whose lives were on the line. They had to be so scared. Did they know what was about to happen? Had Algrath prepared them in some way for the ritual? What conditions were they being held in?

At the same time, I was also angry at the Council for not stepping up and taking care of this a long time ago. This was their main job, and it shouldn't have taken a group of Slayers going rogue to come deal with this demon.

Finally, though, as strange as it seemed, I was also happy and grateful. Watching Slayers my parents had cared about so much, who had been part of my life for as long as I could remember, sharing stories around this cozy table made me feel warm inside.

Martin had kept me alive through my grief this past summer, but I'd also spent a lot of lonely nights crying and wondering what would become of my life now without them.

Tonight, though, I felt whole again, despite my fear.

It felt like together, we could take on anything.

"What do you say, Lenny?" Gianna asked.

I hadn't been listening, and I blushed.

"I'm sorry. What did you say?"

Asher smiled. "See, I told you she was zoning out. You exhausted her."

"I was just asking whether you wanted to head back out to

the clearing at first light for a little more training," she said. "I feel like we made really good progress today, but there's a lot more we could do with a few hours tomorrow."

I groaned. Everything ached. But I needed this. We had no idea what we might be facing tomorrow.

"I'm up for it," I said. "I just might need an extra cup of coffee first thing."

Martin nodded. "Of course," he said. "But for now, maybe it's time for you to rest, dear girl. I have left some healing balm in your bathroom for what's left of those burns. It should also help with your sore muscles."

"But there's still so much to do," I said, barely able to stifle a yawn. "We need to make potions and discuss strategy. We still haven't even found Algrath. We're running out of time."

"That's why we're here," Britta said. "Get some rest. You've been through a lot in the past few days."

I shook my head. Days? Had it really only been a handful of days since I first started at Newcastle High? Little more than a week? It felt as though I'd stepped into some kind of time warp.

I started to protest again, but even the act of opening my mouth to speak made me yawn again. Everyone at the table laughed, which then set me off, too.

"Okay. I admit it," I said, despite the fact that it was only just now six in the evening. "I'm tired. I'll head up."

Besides, that bath I thought of earlier was calling me.

"Sleep well, dear girl," Martin said. "We will see you in the morning."

"Sweet dreams," Gianna said.

"No nightmares about bunnies," Gowan said, winking.

I shuddered. "Let's hope not," I said. "I'm never going to forgive you for that, you know."

Martin tilted his head. "What's this about bunnies?"

I patted Gowan on the shoulder. "I'll let you tell him about what you did to me this afternoon."

As I left the kitchen and headed back to my room, laughter from the kitchen echoed throughout the entire first floor of the house.

When I'd first arrived here, it had felt so dark and lonely. Martin had done what he could to make me comfortable, but I had never really thought of this place as home until tonight.

I was halfway up the stairs and already dreaming of the bath when my phone vibrated in my pocket.

I'm out front. Can you talk?

I gasped as I realized it was a message from Olive. If anything, I'd been expecting to hear from Kai, but I didn't think I'd hear a word from Olive tonight.

And she was outside my front door? Why?

I stood frozen on the steps for a long moment. Was Olive involved in this somehow?

If so, I needed to be very careful how I dealt with this right now.

This could be my chance to find out the truth about her mom. At this point, after almost dying in Olive's living room, I was convinced her mom was part of this. I didn't know for sure Algrath had taken Julie Peterson's identity, but if not, she was possibly helping him or working with him.

I took a deep breath. There was nothing to do but go out there and see what Olive had to say.

I wasn't stupid, though. I'd done enough to get myself into

trouble for one twenty-four hour period, so I quickly texted Martin, too, to tell him Olive was outside.

Don't leave the property. Invite her inside, if she'll come.

I slipped the phone back in my pocket and walked out the front door. To my surprise, Olive wasn't the only one standing on my front doorstep.

Brandy was here, too.

"Oh my gosh, what are you guys doing here? Is everything okay?" I asked, finding that I was actually really happy to see them.

I wasn't used to having friends or getting close to people my age, but seeing them out there, waiting for me, put some things into perspective.

Especially seeing the tears in Olive's eyes.

These weren't demons. These were just normal teenagers who'd lost some of their friends. They were scared and confused, and they just wanted answers.

"What happened?" I asked, walking over to Olive and taking her hands in mine.

"I don't even know where to start. Have you seen my mom?"

Her question took me by surprise.

"Your mom?" I asked. "Why would I have seen her?"

Olive shook her head, tears flowing down her cheeks. "I don't know. I'm grasping at straws here," she said. "I was trying to think of anywhere she might have gone, and I keep coming up empty. I thought maybe she'd brought a cupcake over to you earlier. She was making something special for you this morning when I left for school."

Well, this was news.

"A special cupcake for me?" I asked, not missing the fact

that she'd also made a special cupcake for Peyton right before she disappeared.

"Yeah, she wouldn't tell me what flavor, but she said she wanted to do something nice for you since you'd seemed so upset about Peyton," Olive explained. "Besides, Mom bakes when she's nervous."

"And when she's happy. Or celebrating. Or when she's depressed," Brandy said.

Olive laughed through her tears, wiping her face on the sleeve of a white Sir Bean hoodie. "Okay, she bakes all the time. But she seemed excited about making this for you. I was hoping maybe you'd seen her this morning when she brought it over."

I shook my head. "I'm sorry. She didn't come by here at all."

Olive closed her eyes and sat down on the top step of Martin's porch. "I was afraid you were going to say that. I don't know where else to look. It's like she's disappeared, right along with Peyton. How is this happening? I don't understand."

Brandy sat down next to her, so I settled in on the other side. We both wrapped our arms around Olive, hugging her.

I felt terrible. What if Algrath had kidnapped her mom six months ago and had been pretending to be her all this time? Would he let her live once this was all over?

Olive would be all alone in the world, if that was true. It wasn't fair for anyone our age to lose our parents, and I didn't want that to happen to her the way it had happened to me.

If we could find Peyton and the other girls, maybe that meant we could rescue the real Julie Peterson too, if Algrath had taken her.

I was starting to feel more and more that we were right

about this, though. It made total sense that Ms. Julie would disappear after we wrecked her house and triggered that trap.

With the ritual right around the corner, Algrath wouldn't take any risks by going back to Ms. Julie's house tonight. It was too risky. He'd been discovered, which meant that he had gone back into hiding, taking the real Julie Peterson with him.

We were so close to figuring this out, but it still wasn't enough to know who Algrath had been pretending to be. We needed to find out where he had gone now that we knew the truth.

"I want to help," I said. "Tell me everything that happened from the time you got up this morning."

Olive sniffed and nodded, playing with a deteriorating tissue she held in her hands.

"Everything was mostly normal," Olive said. "Mom was up early, baking again. She said she'd had a hard time sleeping. Something about her shoulder bothering her."

My ears perked up at this. Her shoulder?

"What was that about?" I asked, trying to act casual about such a huge piece of information.

"I don't know. I guess she slept on it wrong," Olive said. "She just told me she couldn't sleep and had started baking early. She told me about the cupcake she was making for you, and she said she'd see me after school. Then Brandy showed up so we could ride to school together, and that was basically it. Nothing out of the ordinary. But the police won't even let me in the house, Lenny. It has to be bad. Someone has her, I just know it."

"They wouldn't let you in?" I asked. "I assumed you were the one who called the police."

Brandy shook her head. "No, it was a neighbor who called

the cops. That whole area's been on alert since LaTasha went missing, and I guess someone called it in. Said they'd heard screaming from inside."

Olive started crying again.

"What if she's dead?" Olive asked.

"Didn't the police tell you anything about what they found inside?" I asked.

Olive shook her head. "Only that mom wasn't in there, but that the place was a mess," she said. "And my mom was meticulous about keeping the house clean. She never left a single thing out of place, so if it was a wreck, someone else must have been there."

"I think it has something to do with her creepy boyfriend," Brandy said. "Have you met him?"

I shook my head. Technically, I hadn't met Bates. I'd only spied on him.

"He's gone, too," Olive said. "I think it's possible the cops think Mom ran off with him, but she wouldn't do that. She wouldn't just leave me here alone. I know she wouldn't."

"Of course not," Brandy said, stroking Olive's hair. "It's going to be okay."

But over the top of Olive's head, Brandy met my eyes and shook her head. She didn't believe it was going to be okay, and I wasn't so sure, either.

"Do you want to come inside?" I asked. "My uncle can make some coffee for us or something. We can talk more about where she might have gone or what might have happened."

Olive shook her head.

"No, thanks," she said. "I think I want to just change into some pj's and try to get some rest. I'm exhausted."

"Where are you staying?" I asked. "Is there anything I can do to help?"

Olive shook her head. "There's nothing anyone can do," she said. "Not unless you know where my mom is."

"Olive is staying with me and my family for a while," Brandy said. "Her dad is supposed to be coming in from Michigan in a week, but he claims he's busy with his business until then."

"I don't even really know my dad," Olive said. "I don't want to have to go live with him."

"You won't," Brandy said. "Your mom is fine. Everything is going to be fine."

I took a deep breath. This was so complicated.

The truth was here somewhere, staring me in the face, and I couldn't see it.

"I hate to ask this, but have things been going okay with your mom lately? Are you getting along?" I was skirting the line between concerned friend and inappropriate jerk, but I needed information. I was willing to be rude if it meant saving someone's life.

"What do you mean?" Olive asked. "You think she left me, too? Well, that's just great, Lenny."

She stood and walked toward Brandy's car.

I chased after her.

"No, of course not," I said. "Come on, that's not what I meant at all. I'm sorry."

Olive turned back. "Then what did you mean by that?"

"Yeah, that's not exactly the nicest thing to say right now," Brandy said.

"I'm sorry. I'm just trying to think through what might have happened. Like, if your mom was arguing with anyone or stressed out a lot. I don't know, like was she not acting like herself at all lately."

Olive looked down at her hands for a moment before she spoke.

"You know, now that you mention it, things have been stressful since Christmas," she said. "I assumed it was because Mom's cupcake business was taking off. Then, LaTasha went missing just a few doors down from us. I figured all of that was taking a toll on her."

"Everyone goes through stressful times, though," Brandy said. "That doesn't really mean anything."

"Maybe not," I said. "And you're right. Maybe it's that boyfriend you were talking about. Is it possible she just went on vacation with him somewhere? Or maybe she's staying at his place?"

Olive shook her head. "I told you. She wouldn't leave me alone like that. And she would have never left the house in such a mess."

"Maybe you could talk to him, though. See if he knows where she is."

"We tried that," Brandy said. "He's gone, too."

I didn't want to tell them I already knew Bates was gone. Or that he was actually somewhere inside Martin's house right now as we spoke.

Basically, I just wanted to see what they knew about his involvement.

"She didn't run off with him," Olive said, starting to cry again. "She wouldn't do that."

"What if he broke up with her or something? Is there anywhere else she might have gone if she was upset? Like a favorite hotel or—"

"We checked the lake house already," Brandy said. "She wasn't there, either."

Chills ran down my spine.

"Lake house?"

A secluded place out in the woods.

"Yeah, but she wasn't there," Olive said. "The whole place was locked up tight. My key didn't even work. I don't know when she changed the locks, but whatever. She wasn't there."

I was about to ask for more details about the lake house when Brandy got a text and said they had to get going.

"My mom's getting worried about us," she said.

"Are you sure you don't want to just come in for a while so we can talk about this?" I asked. "Maybe we could think through other theories. I just want to help."

Olive threw her arms around me.

"Thank you," she said. "That means a lot to me."

"If you want, you could come back to my place," Brandy said.

"That would be great," Olive said, her eyes lighting up for the first time since she got here. "Come spend the night with us. We can watch movies over there and try to get our minds off of it. It'll be fun."

It was tempting to say yes to see what else I could get out of them. Plus, I'd never had a sleepover with friends before. Under different circumstances, that could have made for a really fun night.

"I can't tonight," I said. "But maybe after Peyton comes home."

"Right," Brandy said, a strange expression crossing her features. "When Peyton comes home."

She didn't believe it was possible. I could see it in her eyes.

But I wasn't losing hope. Not yet.

I hugged Olive again and watched as they got into Brandy's car and drove off. Then, I climbed the steps and started to head inside.

Before I got through the door, though, a figure appeared out of the darkness on the side of the porch.

"What happened? Did you find out anything interesting?"

I jumped and almost cast a spell on him, but as soon as I realized it was Kai, I lowered my hands.

"You've got to stop sneaking up on me," I said. "I almost lit you on fire just now."

"Sorry, I didn't mean to scare you," he said with a laugh. "I was just coming to see how things were going, and when I saw those two here, I thought I'd hang out on the porch until they left."

I filled him in on the Slayers' conversation and what I'd learned while Olive and Brandy were here.

"Do you think the cabin might be important?" I asked.

"Anything could be important right now," he said as we walked to the door.

Standing here alone with him in the dark on the front porch suddenly brought up this nervous first-date kind of vibe that had me tapping my toes inside my shoes.

I was so stupid. He was just helping me figure this out. We weren't dating. He was probably going to leave town as soon as this was all over, anyway.

The thought hit me hard.

Dang. He probably was going to leave. It wasn't like he was really a student at Newcastle High. He could come and go as he pleased, and he had to have a life to go back to somewhere.

I still wasn't sure what had happened to his father, either.

If he didn't get the answers he needed, he'd be heading out to find them.

It would be best if I tried not to get too attached to him, but I was afraid it was way too late for that.

"Tomorrow morning, I think we're going back out to train," I said. "Are you coming?"

He nodded.

"We have to do what we can, right?" he asked. "Are you sure you're okay?"

"I just wish I knew who to trust," I said, then smiled. "I mean, you could be Algrath, right? How would I even know?"

"Two things," he said, slipping his arms around me.

My breath caught in my lungs, and my heart beat faster.

"First of all, I was there with you when Algrath attacked," he said. "And secondly, demons don't have wings."

The memory of the way he'd wrapped those beautiful wings around me earlier this morning took my breath away.

"Yeah. I doubt the demon would have bothered to save my life, either," I said with a whisper. "Thank you for that."

"You're welcome," he whispered.

"Someday, you're going to have to tell me why you even care so much," I said.

"When we're on the other side of this mess, I promise. I'll tell you everything," he said. "Goodnight, Lenny. Get some rest."

"You, too," I said, a sense of loss coming over me as he released me and stepped away.

I watched him walk away, and I wondered just what tomorrow would bring for us both.

With a sigh, I headed back inside and soon after, disappeared into a healing bath of chamomile.

MAY MY MAGIC BE QUICK AND STRONG

Despite my exhaustion, I tossed and turned all night. Images of those demons pouring in through the Petersons' windows kept terrorizing me, and I wondered how much worse it might be when we found Algrath.

How many demons would he have with him?

What kind of traps would we face tonight?

If we could find him at all.

It was just before dawn when I finally gave up on sleep and crawled down to the kitchen to make coffee. To my surprise, everyone else was already up and eating breakfast.

My long brown hair was like a bird nest from all the tangles, and I hadn't bothered to brush it or pull it back this morning. I thought I would find the kitchen empty.

Oh well. I shrugged and just rolled with it. These people were family, anyway, right?

But then I caught sight of Kai standing in one corner talking to Darius.

Oh my God.

I quickly ran a few fingers through my hair, wincing as I tried to pull a few tangles apart. This was not going to work.

"I'll, uh, be right back," I whispered, hoping no one had really noticed me yet.

Gianna grabbed my arm, though, and tugged me toward her. "Oh, no you don't," she said. "I was just about to come get you, anyway. We need to get out to the training grounds pretty soon. How did you sleep?"

I shook my head and pointed to my hair.

"I can't be here like this," I said. "I didn't think anyone would be up."

"You're fine," she said. "No one here cares what you look like."

I gave her a pointed look and moved my eyes toward Kai. "Cute angel witch guy in the corner," I said very softly. "I care what I look like right now."

She turned, and I squeezed her arm.

"Don't look. Come on," I said, hiding behind her.

Gianna laughed. "Here. I'll help."

She took my shoulders in her hands to straighten my body in front of her. Then, she took strands of my hair on either side of my head into her fingertips.

"*Bellus.*"

My tangled hair fell across my shoulders and down my back in waves as it completely untangled itself.

"Whoa. What just happened?"

I turned to stare at my reflection in the stainless steel refrigerator and gasped. My hair was the most beautiful I'd ever seen it. Thick and falling just right, with a little bit of body and wave to it that I could have never achieved on my own.

"Simple," Gianna said, tossing her own beautiful red hair back. "That will save you some time getting ready in the mornings."

"Thanks."

It didn't exactly help the fact that I was still in my pjs, but at least I wasn't wearing anything too embarrassing. Just a pair of old sweats and a tank top.

She'd helped just in time, too, because Kai and Darius had finished their conversation and had joined Asher and Gowan at the table. Everyone turned to a discussion of how the day would go.

There were potions and remedies to be made. Reagents to pack up and take with us, just in case. We still needed to have a training session for the morning, and Martin said he planned to see what he could do to speed up that location spell.

"I may not be able to determine Algrath's exact location before tonight, but I may be able to get an idea of the general area of his hiding place," Martin said.

I suddenly remembered the conversation with Olive the night before.

"Julie Peterson has a cabin," I said. "Olive didn't say where, exactly, but somewhere out near the lake."

Asher nodded. "I can find that pretty easily with a records search, I think. We might as well check it out."

"I have a few more questions for our friend Bates this morning, too," Darius said, a slight smile on his lips. "We'll see how he liked being in the basement with the—"

Martin cleared his throat, and Darius stopped abruptly, rethinking his words.

"I mean, we'll see if he has any more information for us."

"Wait, there's a basement in this house?" I asked, turning to my great-uncle. "What's down there."

He gave Darius a look, and Darius raised his hands in apology.

"We will discuss that another time," Martin said. "For now, it's none of your concern."

A man of many secrets.

That's what the Slayers had called him. This week, I was learning just how true that was.

"Okay, so we'll do what we can to locate the missing girls and figure out who Algrath is before nightfall, but if all else fails, we wait for the tracking spell to tell us exactly where he is," Gowan said. "We just need to be ready to go as soon as it comes through. There won't be a second to waste."

Nerves buzzed through me. We were cutting it close. I felt stupid for even wasting a minute caring about my hair. The morning conversation really put things into perspective for me, and I was ready to get back out to the training grounds.

By the time the sun started to rise, we were back in the clearing working on defensive spells.

Today, Gowan and Gianna both worked together to show Kai and me what to do if the fighting got too intense later.

"You've both shown that you can handle yourselves among a large group of lesser demons," Gianna said. "So, that's good work. Kai, you've obviously got your wings to use for protection if it comes to that, so part of your job tonight will be making sure Lenny never leaves your sight. Not even for a minute."

Kai nodded, and my face grew warm. I was grateful we would be together, whatever we would have to face.

"But the wings won't save you from everything, and they won't work forever," Gianna said.

"Wait, why not?" I asked. I guess I still didn't know enough about how angels worked and what his abilities were.

"The way I used my wings earlier was a type of shielding," Kai said. "It works just like any physical shield. It doesn't block every type of attack, and the power of the shield breaks down the more it's hit. Since I'm only half angel, I don't have the stamina or protection power of a full angel."

"Save that for an emergency, but let's hope it doesn't come to that," Gianna said. "Instead, I want to teach you a few defensive moves. If there's time left, we'll work on more of your attacks."

Over the next several hours, Gianna and Gowan both trained us in several types of defensive magic. We learned to manipulate air to create a temporary shield against fire spells. We also learned how to use a clump of dirt to harden a section of skin like a stoneskin effect.

When they were satisfied that we'd learned enough to protect ourselves, they moved onto new attacks.

I thought I already knew quite a bit of offensive magic, but there were a few tricks I hadn't seen before, like creating a small dagger of ice out of a single drop of holy water.

Tonight, we would all be carrying a variety of reagents and potions, so Gowan went through them all, training us in how to use them.

It was so much to remember, and I had a feeling this was just the tip of the iceberg. For all that I'd believed my parents had taught me, I knew nothing.

And still, all of this was only what was available to a witch with her first key.

"Don't get discouraged," Gowan said, patting my arm. "Most Slayers spend a full year learning what you've just learned in two days. It isn't easy, I know, but you're doing a great job. You should be proud of yourself."

"I'll be proud if we're returning those girls to their families later tonight," I said. "That's all that matters to me right now."

"I promise, we'll do everything we can to make sure that's what happens," he said. "Why don't you two take a break, and Gianna and I will talk about anything else we should go through before we head back to the house."

Kai's eyes met mine, and he smiled. "Walk with me."

I moved up beside him, and we walked deeper into the woods, away from the car and the others.

"Where are we going?" I asked.

"I want to show you something," he said. "It won't take long."

We walked in silence, and I wondered if we both were feeling the same way about tonight.

"Kai, what happened to your father?" I asked. "You really don't know at all?"

He sucked in a breath and shoved his hands in the pockets of his jeans. "I haven't really talked about this to anyone," he said. "I was sure he was here in Newcastle, but I didn't know why. I still don't know if his coming here was tied to Algrath, and no, I don't know what happened to him. But the fact that I haven't been able to connect to his energy scares the crap out of me."

"The not-knowing would be really tough," I said. "What about your mother, though? Where is she? Or is that too personal to ask?"

Kai nodded ahead, and I looked up to see a strange tree

about six feet in front of us. It was a normal pine tree, but it had grown in such a way that about three feet off the ground, it shifted to one side and created a little seat before it headed back up toward the forest's canopy.

"How odd," I said. "It's like a little tree chair."

"Isn't it cool?" he asked, taking a seat.

He patted the area next to him, and I sat down. There was just barely enough room for both of us to sit. It was more comfortable than I'd expected it to be.

"What would make a tree do this?" I asked.

"A long time ago, the Native Americans would often bend trees to mark trails or other locations," he said. "I'm guessing this tree was a way to mark the lake ahead."

"Wow," I said, leaning against him as he put an arm around me. "I've never seen anything like it."

"When I was younger, my dad would sometimes come to visit Martin and train with him here in this area," Kai said. "Mostly, dad wanted to learn about human magic and how to fight the types of creatures and beings that Slayers fought. I was too young to learn about it, so I would sometimes roam the woods. Once I found this tree, it became my little piece of the forest. I always came back here to read and play."

We sat together quietly, and I tried to imagine him as a small child, playing around here in the forest alone. After what felt like a long time, he finally spoke again.

"My mother would sometimes come with us to the training grounds back then," Kai said, his voice filled with sadness. "She was originally from Hawaii, and her coven there used a very different kind of magic than your coven, but she wanted to learn more. Sometimes, though, instead of hanging out with dad and Martin, she would come back here with me to this tree and tell me stories or teach me her family's magic. It feels like a lifetime ago now."

I slowly reached over and put my hand on top of his.

"It's easy to tell how much you love her," I said. I wanted very badly to ask him again where she was now, but his voice sounded so far away that I had a terrible feeling I already knew.

"She's actually the reason my father became friends with your parents," Kai said. "They saved her from a demon much like Algrath. He had captured her and taken on her appearance. He'd planned to kill her when he was done with his work, but your parents found her first and saved her. The demon hadn't known it, but she was pregnant with me at the time. So, really, they saved my life, too."

My heart started racing. "Wow, I had no idea," I said. "That's incredible."

"After that, my father felt he owed them everything," Kai said. "He vowed to protect them, always. That's part of what I don't understand, Lenny. Why wasn't he there when they died?"

His words hit hard. I certainly didn't have the answer to that, but I could hear the guilt in Kai's voice. I suddenly understood why he felt so strongly about protecting me.

"You feel like it's your job to keep me safe, because he didn't follow through on his promise to protect my parents," I said.

I couldn't explain why that was so disappointing to me. I was grateful he wanted to protect me, but I'd hoped it was due to some connection he felt to me, not some debt he felt he owed to my parents.

"Oh, Lenny, that's—"

"Lenny, Kai, we need to get moving," Gowan said, interrupting. "There's no more time for training now. Martin and Asher have uncovered a huge lead. They want us home right away."

The loss of the rest of that conversation was like a punch in the gut, but there would hopefully be time to discuss it later. Right now, saving the girls and finding Algrath were the most important things.

Gowan talked the entire way home, and Kai just looked out the window. I wondered if I'd upset him by bringing up his parents. Man, that was really poor timing on my part, but then again, when was it ever a good time to talk about dead or missing parents?

I hoped we would get another chance to finish our conversation, but when we got back to the house, we were immediately brought back to Martin's study. Everyone had gathered there and was talking frantically about the plan for tonight.

"What's the breakthrough?" I asked.

Martin stood up from behind his desk, and everyone got quiet.

"It turns out your investigative skills are quite impressive, Lenora. The girls might actually be at Julie Peterson's cabin near the lake, after all," Martin said.

My eyes widened. I could hardly believe it. It almost seemed too easy. Too careless.

"What makes you think that?" I asked.

"Asher located the cabin by digging through some county records. It was left to Julie Peterson by her father some years ago," Martin said. "He made a quick trip out there this morning to check it out, and there are wards set up all around it."

I glanced at Kai. More traps like the one we'd walked into yesterday.

"From my research, there doesn't seem to be any magical blood in the Peterson family, so I highly doubt Julie or her father would have the knowledge or skill to place such wards themselves. This matches up with the trap on her house, as well."

At this, Darius stepped forward.

"Bates was a little more forthcoming this morning, as I expected," he said with a sly smile. "He met Julie Peterson at a holiday expo where they were both selling cupcakes. His were made with moondust, so he sold out fast. Apparently, she struck up a conversation with him and finally convinced him to move here to Newcastle and help her build what he called a cupcake empire."

I held back a smile. This was serious stuff, but come on. A cupcake empire?

"I believe this connection with Bates may be why Algrath chose Julie Peterson as his target. As a trickster of sorts, I think it was his way of making fun of the Council. Showing his power in manipulating the brother of a Keeper."

"What?" I asked. "Brother?"

Martin nodded. "Yes, didn't you know? Bates is Ms. Greer's half-brother."

I opened my mouth in shock. No wonder Blythe had been in town visiting him. She must have been trying to convince him to stop dealing Moondust. Wow. I had not seen that one coming.

Darius paced the floor in front of the desk.

"It's my suspicion that Bates is being set up to take the fall for all of this once the girls are dead," Darius said. "Once I explained that to him, he was more than willing to rat out Julie Peterson. It turns out they'd spent some time together in that cabin over the past few months. Bates said there was a door inside that had been padlocked and warded with a strange type of magic. He said he could feel it from the moment he entered that cabin. Said it freaked him out, and he told her he didn't want to meet her out there anymore."

"I take it she didn't tell him what was locked inside?" Gowan asked.

"Apparently, she said it was her dad's fishing stuff," Darius said, snorting. "We all know that's a lie."

So, Olive's mom really was hiding something all this time. I hadn't wanted to believe it.

Except it wasn't Olive's mom at all. It was Algrath. In fact, it was probably Julie Peterson who was locked up in that closet in the cabin.

I shuddered. Was she even still alive?

Poor Olive. She would be heartbroken.

"As my tracking spell spreads through Algrath's body, his location becomes easier for me to pinpoint," Martin said. "I can't see his exact location yet, but all signs point to the same area. Julie Peterson's cabin in the woods."

"There's something else," Asher said. "When I was walking around the property, I saw a clearing about sixty feet behind the main house. I couldn't get close enough to be sure without tripping one of the wards, but I'm fairly certain it was a ritual circle."

I took several deep breaths. Could we be right? Had we really put all of this together so fast?

We knew who Algrath was. We knew where the girls were being held and where the ritual would take place.

Now, all we had to do was put a stop to it and get the girls out of there before Algrath could even get them to the circle.

We spent the next two hours going over strategy for our raid.

Everyone in the room knew Algrath was a trickster. There had been Slayers in the past who thought they knew exactly where he was and what he was doing only to storm in and find him already gone. Or standing behind them.

Slayers had died at his hands. Too many to count.

Tonight, we needed to be smarter than he was, which meant we couldn't assume we knew anything until it was confirmed with our eyes.

In the end, the plan we settled on was risky but smart.

We would surround the cabin with wards and shields of our own, designed to keep Algrath in if he tried to run. That wouldn't help us against portals, but it would at least give us some boundaries within the woods.

We couldn't put the boundaries too close, or Algrath might sense them too early. We settled on half a mile on all sides, and Martin seemed pleased with that number.

Then, we would wait for Martin's tracking spell to zero in on our target, confirming once and for all that he was inside that house. Once confirmed, we would rush in, locate the girls, and get them to safety.

That was where Kai and I came in.

Our job was to get the girls into the car and bring them back to Martin's house until Algrath was either contained or banished. Apparently, there were certain protection spells on this house that would keep Algrath from entering.

Then, everyone would join us back at the house, care for any injuries the girls may have suffered, wipe their memories of the events since their kidnappings, and return them to their families anonymously during the night.

No one could ever know who had saved them, but that wouldn't matter. As long as they were alive and safe, that was all that mattered to any of us.

After hours of prepping and talking through strategy, it was finally time to go.

I ran up to my room to grab my backpack, and I took my time carefully packing it up with everything Gowan and Gianna had said I might need.

Holy Water. My father's dagger. A large bottle full of blessed salt.

I checked off more than fifteen different reagents as I loaded them into my bag. The inside of the backpack was arranged with small straps so that I could carry lots of different vials in a somewhat organized manner.

I just worried that when the time came, I wouldn't be able to locate and use everything as quickly as I wanted.

Gianna assured me that once I graduated to my second key, I would be able to cast more magic without the use of incantations and reagents, but she also said that about a hundred more ingredients would open up to me.

A witch's key was more than just a key to a cabinet. It was a key to new magic and abilities, too.

"You'll be on your second key before you know it if you keep this up," Gowan had said to me this morning during training.

I had then asked him what level key he was on, and he'd simply given me a wink and tucked his key inside his white shirt.

But not before I had a chance to see the three ruby stones embedded in its center.

Now, as I packed up my bag, I grasped my own key and locket tightly in my hand. My witch's key had no stone or fancy inscriptions. It was just a simple, silver key, and tonight, that would have to be enough.

I knelt before my spell cabinet for a few minutes and closed my eyes. I sent up a prayer to whoever might be listening up there. It was a prayer I'd heard my parents say to each other many times before they had gone into battle.

May my magic be quick and strong.

May my aim always be true.

May the light be on my side.

So that I may return home safe to you.

I took several deep breaths before I could convince my legs to lift me up and carry me down the stairs to where the others were waiting.

The entire ride out to the cabin, I clung tightly to Kai's hand but didn't say a word. My heart had not beat so fast or so hard since the night my parents died.

Please, don't let tonight be like that night.

When we got to the cabin, the sun had disappeared behind the trees and the air had cooled off some from the heat of the day.

Everyone jumped into action, following our plan. Everything was going exactly as we'd expected, but that didn't bring me any comfort. I knew from experience that things could go wrong in an instant.

We huddled around Martin as he prepared his tracking spell again. He had to prick his own fingertip with a blade each time, but he didn't seem to mind.

He let a single drop of his blood fall onto a map he'd created of the area, and we all waited, holding our breath as we watched the blood slowly make a trail to our exact location, circling the mile or so radius around the cabin.

So, this was it.

Algrath was here. The girls had to be inside that cabin. We were going to save them. We just had to keep our heads on straight and our magic strong, and we could do this.

But just like I'd feared, something did go wrong.

It was still half an hour until we intended to storm the cabin, but Algrath had apparently decided to start early, because inside, someone screamed.

"Peyton," I said, standing. "That's her. He's hurting her."

"Lenny, wait," Kai said.

But it was too late. I was already on my feet and running toward the cabin.

AND SO IT BEGINS

I ran straight toward the cabin, my heart pumping hard as I thought about what those girls must be going through.

But before I made it even ten steps forward, something grabbed hold of my foot, and I face-planted in the grass with a thud and a groan.

At first, I didn't quite understand what happened. My mind was locked on the cabin, and I couldn't bring it back to this moment, here in the grass.

I lifted my head and gasped as I saw the glowing outline of a ward literally three inches in front of my face. In my panic, I'd almost forgotten about the wards and traps Algrath had set around this cabin. If I'd set those off all at once, we probably all would have died.

Tears sprang to my eyes.

What was wrong with me?

Gowan knelt at my side. "You've got to get yourself under control, Lenny. Do you understand how dangerous it can be if you let your emotions get the best of you?" he asked. "We're working with a powerful trickster demon here. He's going to do whatever he can to play on your emotions, make you see things that aren't there, and prey on any of your weaknesses."

He offered me a hand, and I grabbed it, letting him pull me to a standing position.

"I'm sorry," I said. "I just heard her scream and freaked out."

"If you're going to let all the training we just did fly right out the window because of a single scream, you might as well get in the car and drive home right now, do you understand?"

His words stung, but he was right.

I'd nearly killed us all at the very first sign of trouble. That entire test with the bunny suddenly made crystal clear sense to me. Tonight wasn't just about winning some battle against a demon.

It was also about mastering my own heart.

Slayers needed to be strong. I'd always known that, but I guess I just never realized how many different ways they had to be strong.

"I understand," I said. "I'm sorry."

We walked back to the group, and even though I expected Martin to be disappointed in my actions, he put his arm around me, instead.

"I have a feeling you will learn many difficult lessons tonight," Martin said. "Let's hope the first lesson is that your impulsiveness can put the entire group in danger. That spirit of yours can be your greatest weakness, or your strongest gift. Only you can decide."

I wiped a tear from my cheek. I needed to grow up fast, or I was going to get everyone killed.

But how could my impulsiveness be a gift? I didn't understand what he meant, but before I got the chance to ask him, another scream sounded from inside the cabin.

This time, it sounded like a different girl.

I resisted the urge to run and help, but I didn't want to just stand here and listen to that, either.

"What's he doing to them?" I asked. "Or is that just for our sake? Do you think he knows we're here?"

"He most definitely knows we're here," Gowan said. "This whole place has been set up as a trap for us, and he led us right in. I can promise you, we're all exactly where he wants us."

I swallowed back fear.

"I don't understand," I said. "If we're right where he wants us, aren't we doing something wrong? Aren't we just playing right into his trap?"

"Sometimes, that's the only way to face a demon like this," Gianna said. "You have to let them believe you're falling for all their little tricks, and then, when they let their guard down, you surprise them."

I frowned. That sounded extremely risky to me.

After all our planning, I'd been feeling pretty confident, but now that the actual moment of confrontation was here, I didn't know what to do.

"What if they can't be surprised? Or they anticipate our moves, too?" I asked.

"Then we improvise as we go," Gowan said. He put a hand on my arm. "Don't look so scared. We're going to get through this together."

I couldn't help but be scared. Something about this whole cabin felt off to me. Couldn't they feel that, too?

But maybe they could.

We were intentionally playing the game Algrath set up for

us. I guess I could understand why, but it still scared me. I just hoped they all knew what they were doing.

Another scream sounded from inside the cabin, and the lights inside flickered. It was a different girl, again.

"He's preparing them for the ritual, or something," I said. "Hurting them one at a time in some way."

"Perhaps," Gianna said. "Or he's intentionally setting us on edge, hoping we'll make our move before we're ready."

"And when is that going to be?" I asked. "Us being ready, I mean."

She smiled and touched my cheek. "Your mother was always so impulsive when she was a girl, too," she said. "Right now, under the light of the full moon, you look just like her at this age. It's going to be okay, Lenny. You have to trust us."

I grasped my mother's locket in my hand. My mother was impulsive?

That's not how I had known her at all. Yes, she was full of fire and spirit, but she was also very calculated, going through all the possibilities as if she could see all possible futures laid out before her.

It was hard to imagine her as a rush-right-in kind of person like me.

Maybe there was hope for me, yet.

A fourth scream from the next girl came from inside the cabin, and the lights flickered again, staying off longer this time.

What was he doing in there? It seemed like some kind of ramping up for the ritual, I guessed.

"How close are we on the tracking spell?" Asher asked.

Martin glanced at his watch. "Still twenty-two minutes."

I wanted to beat my head against a tree. Twenty-two more

minutes? It just didn't feel like we had that kind of time. Besides, who else did we think was inside that cabin hurting the girls? Santa Claus?

"I'm going to make a trip around behind the wards to check the ritual circle," Asher said.

He sprinkled something over his head that looked like glitter and ashes.

"*Abscondo.*"

Asher disappeared completely, and I got chills all over my arms. I hadn't seen that invisibility spell before.

"Why not just use something like *obscuro*?" I asked.

"Demons at this level can see through those types of lower-level invisibility spells. The one Asher just used is a much higher level and not available to a witch like you just yet," Gianna said. "So please don't go getting ideas into your head about sneaking around this cabin to find the girls. Besides, the wards and traps will still trigger, even if you're invisible."

A few minutes later, Asher reappeared beside Martin, nearly scaring me to death. I actually started to pull my dagger on him, and then I laughed nervously. Talk about being on edge. I was losing it.

Couldn't we just please raid this place, already?

"It's already been activated," he whispered. "I think he's going to start earlier than we expected."

I kept my mouth shut. I wanted to trust the experts here. They'd done this before, and I basically had no idea what I was doing.

But still, I was ready to go. Anything but stand here and wait while my friend might be dying.

An hour seemed to pass before Martin turned to Gowan.

"I defer to you in this," he said. "Do we wait?"

Gowan ran a hand across his white beard.

"I think we wait until we have confirmation of one of the girls being brought out to that circle," he said. "Right now, we don't know for sure that any of them are inside. It could all be a trick of our ears. If we trigger any one of those wards or traps he set up, we might be too overrun to change locations if we're wrong."

Martin nodded, but I wanted to scream.

Kai, who had barely even looked at me since our conversation earlier about his parents, seemed to sense my frustration. He touched my arm and motioned for me to join him a few steps away from the group.

"Sit down," he said. "Face me."

"Why?" I asked, snapping harsher than I'd intended. I immediately wanted to take it back. "I'm sorry. I'm struggling."

He sat down first, cross-legged with his hands on his knees. I joined him reluctantly. I was ready to go inside. Get this thing done. Not sit out here and sing campfire songs.

"You're going to be fine," he said. "You just need to find your center. Your heart. It's where your intuition and your deep knowing come from. This is what you need to find and trust right now, more so than your eyes and ears. Close your eyes and take a deep breath."

"I don't think I can," I said.

I was sitting just like him, but I couldn't seem to get my toes to stop tapping or my hands to relax.

"Just try," he said. His voice was so calm and cool. How was he doing that? "For me?"

I sighed.

"Okay, I'll try it. If nothing else, it will help pass the time, right?"

I closed my eyes, and Kai directed our breaths, telling me when to breathe in or out.

Soon, I was able to focus only on the sound of his voice and the feel of the air filling my lungs. For the first time, I noticed it was a breezy night. I had my long hair pulled back, but some little wisps must have pulled free, because they were tickling my cheeks and the back of my neck with each gust of wind.

"When your heart is calm, you can listen to the voice inside you, instead of listening to fear," he said.

I smiled. "You sound like my parents. They were always telling me to listen to my heart."

"It's something my mother always said, too. Feel any better?" he asked.

I opened my eyes. "I do. Thank you for that."

"If things get difficult tonight or scary, just come back to this," he said. "Before you act, come back to yourself. To your heart. Forget your fear."

"Sounds easy," I said, sarcasm coating my tone.

"It will be good practice for you."

"You say that like you've had a lot of experience with battles yourself, even though I know you haven't."

He shrugged. "Not battles, but I've had other demons to fight," he said. "This is one of the only things that helps when I'm feeling scared."

It was hard to think of an angel feeling scared, but maybe it was his humanity that allowed him to feel so much. Realizing that about him also made me see that he was beautiful, even without his wings.

Kai started to reach for my hand, but before either of us could express how we were feeling, the fifth girl screamed and all the lights in the cabin went out, as though someone had blown out a candle.

Kai and I stood, staring at the house, waiting for the lights to flicker back on.

Only, this time, they stayed off.

"What's happening?" I asked.

No one answered. We all just stared at the cabin, waiting. The breeze I'd noticed a moment ago ramped up, increasing steadily until the trees around us bent over from the force of it.

Lightning and thunder cracked together, lighting up the sky with a loud boom that shook the ground beneath our feet. At the same moment, the sky darkened as clouds moved to cover up the light of the full moon.

Cool rain poured down on us, and because of the wind, the drops stung my cheeks.

Darius reached into his satchel and crushed a vial of something in his hands as he shouted, "*Protectio.*"

The rain stopped instantly, and I wiped my eyes, shocked. But then I realized the rain hadn't stopped at all. Rather, a protective shelter had appeared over our heads. It looked like glass above us as the rain hit it and slid down each side.

"And so it begins," Martin said. He stood holding his map and staring at a new droplet of blood. "Algrath is near. Keep your wits about you, and we will prevail. Asher, bring the first ward down and trigger the first trap."

"We still have fifteen minutes before that spell is accurate," Asher said. "We're jumping the gun here."

"We no longer have the luxury of waiting," Gowan said, nodding toward the cabin.

An eerie bluish-purple glow emanated from inside, and the front door suddenly flew open. Dark smoke billowed out of the house. At the same time, the windows exploded, oozing the same dark purple smoke.

I wanted to run straight inside and grab the girls, but I held myself back. There were still wards and traps up everywhere. We wouldn't save anyone if we were killed or overrun. I had to find a way to trust the experts around me.

"What do we do?" I asked.

"Wait for Asher. Whatever comes at us, we fight," Gianna said. "Then, we trigger the next trap until we've made our way up to the house. This is it. Everyone ready."

Beside me, Martin placed a hand on Kai's shoulder.

"Young man, no matter what else happens, you do not let Lenora leave your sight. Do you hear me?"

"Yes, sir. I promise."

Okay, so I did have a guardian angel.

In the past, I might have been upset that no one trusted me to get things done on my own, but if I'd learned anything over the past week, it was that pride was not doing me any favors. I needed help, and there was no shame in having someone there to look out for me.

I would be looking out for him, too.

Sparks flew as Asher cast a spell off to our left, but I couldn't quite see what he was doing through the downpour.

It soon became apparent what was happening, though, because a dark mass of hellhounds surrounded our small shelter, their teeth bared and dripping with poison. They scratched at the glass-like spell, and after just a moment, something inside it cracked, letting a single paw through.

"It won't hold much longer. Prepare yourselves," Darius said as he leaned down and grabbed a handful of mud. He slathered it across his arms, and it turned to what looked like leather armor.

Seeing him threw me into action, too. I repeated his motions, using the spell Gianna had given me.

"*Saxum*," I said, and the mud on my arm turned to stone. It was a bit tight and uncomfortable against my skin, but if it worked, I was okay with being uncomfortable.

I had prepared my dagger's blade ahead of time, coating it with salt and poison. I pulled it from its leather sheath now, my hands trembling.

Darius's shelter shattered under the weight of the hellhounds, and they rushed toward us in a pack.

I knew from my reading that hellhounds were extremely dangerous. They weren't so hard to kill, but if they broke skin with their teeth, you were done for. A hellhound rushed toward me and immediately tried to sink its teeth into my calf.

It didn't get far, though, because Gianna had put a protective spell on my jeans that made them the much lighter equivalent of chainmail armor. Sending up a prayer of thanks to her, I buried my blade into the hound's skull.

It exploded into a pile of smoke and ash, and I turned to the next one and the next, slashing and sinking my blade into each one in turn.

As a group, we made quick work of the hellhounds, but that didn't mean we had any time to rest.

Somewhere in the darkness, more screams rang out through the trees.

"Help me," someone screamed.

My stomach turned, and for a second, I thought I was going to be sick. It sounded like Peyton. I told myself it was just a trick, though. Algrath was trying to mix us up. Cause us to make a mistake.

We just had to hold steady and stick together.

Asher appeared in front of us, rain sliding down his face. His light blue eyes practically glowed in the dark, and it made me wonder if he'd cast some kind of spell to help him see out here.

"Someone is leading the girls to the back," he shouted. "I don't know what he's playing at, but this isn't what we expected. We can't let him start this ritual. If we get locked out of the circle, we'll end up just watching it all happen and not being able to do a damn thing about it."

Now, I really was going to be sick.

This was already a mess, and my heart was pounding so fast, it was messing with my vision.

If Kai hadn't helped me center my energy before this fight began, I might have already lost my mind.

"Keep the traps coming," Gowan said, needing to shout over the sound of the storm growing around us. "As soon as one is half-down, we trigger the next one. No matter what, though, we stick together."

As they spoke, I removed a packet of reagents from my bag. Even though my hands were shaking, and my body shivered from the cold rain, I managed to keep my wits about me as I dressed the sword with more salt, poison ivy, and thorns.

I clasped my locket as I finished off the spell, praying that it would last.

I had five more packets like this in my bag, too, so that I could quickly reapply the spell once its power had faded.

The more experienced Slayers with much higher-level keys still had swords, daggers, and other weapons that glowed with the light of their initial spells, but as a relatively new witch, I didn't have access to their power.

Any uncertainty I'd had about joining up with the Slayers when I turned eighteen faded to nothing. I wanted this. I wanted the kind of power they had. I wanted to be able to save people and banish evil.

I let that determination and will flow through me as the next trap was triggered.

As lightning illuminated the sky, I screamed in horror at the shadowy figures that rose from the ground. Wraiths of some kind. They weren't made of flesh and bone, like the hellhounds.

Instead, these types of creatures were made of air and shadow.

My dagger would be no use against these things.

I sheathed it, so as not to let the spell fade away, and instead, reached into my bag to grab a vial of trapped sunlight.

To any normal eye, it just looked like an empty vial, but I had captured this bit of sunlight myself on the beach a few years ago with my parents in France. To me, that made it stronger than normal sunlight, since it was captured at the height of my joy and infused with laughter.

Mom had told me to save it for a special occasion when I needed to lift myself from a dark place, and I couldn't think of a better time for it than right now.

I carefully uncorked the vial and tipped it over, letting a single drop of sunshine fall toward my palm.

"*Conlumino*," I said, squinting as a bright ball of sunshine appeared in my hand.

Even some of the more experienced Slayers looked over, respect shining in their eyes.

I was just relieved I'd remembered the right word for the incantation. After our quick training, they were all starting to run together a bit.

I took a deep breath and grasped my locket, allowing the power of it to flow through me and amplify the sunlight in my hand.

I could have sworn I heard my mother's laughter trickle from the sunlight as it grew stronger, lighting up the entire forest and the clearing ahead.

The wraiths that remained screeched and tried to fall back to the shadows.

My heart raced as I tried to remember the right word to scatter the sunlight. There was no time for doubt. I had to think fast and be strong.

"*Dispergat,*" I said.

The ball of sunshine in my hand seemed to explode outward, sparkling as it shot out in a radius around me, its light slicing through the shadowy wraiths until there were no more.

Gowan winked at me, even as he drew his sword and pushed it through the heart of a demon about twice his height. The next wave was here, already.

As we fought, there was no time for second-guessing or doubt. We couldn't worry about the rain pouring down on us or the lightning that seemed to flash closer and closer to the cabin. I couldn't even let the sound of screams break my focus.

The only way through to them was to kill everything in our path. That was what mattered, and I was surprised how quickly I focused on the creatures that surrounded us, wave after wave in the darkness of the night.

Through it all, Kai was right there at my side.

"We did it," he said, out of breath as we joined the other Slayers near the steps to the cabin.

"Is that all of them?" I asked, scared to hope.

Asher nodded. "That's all the traps I was able to detect," he said. "And I just checked out back. No activity, anymore. It seems they've all gone back inside."

"That means, we're all on our guard the second we walk into this place. Consider everything a trap from this point forward," Gowan said.

"Where's Darius?" I asked, panic filling my heart as I counted and saw that one of us was missing.

"He's getting the car," Gianna said, placing a hand on my arm. "As soon as we have the girls, you and Kai will get into Gowan's SUV and head back to Martin's."

I nodded, relief filling me as Darius pulled up in the black SUV.

This was the plan we'd discussed, and even though things had not gone exactly like we originally thought, we seemed to be back on track.

"The car is cloaked?" Kai asked.

"With everything we've got," Gowan said. "There's not a soul in the world that can find this car now without physically laying eyes on it. You'll be safe all the way home, and we'll deal with Algrath here."

Nervous energy flowed through me as my heart pounded.

We just had to get to the girls, and everything was going to be okay. Asher and Gianna ran around to the back to guard that door and the ritual circle, while the rest of us waited to go inside.

Darius handed me the keys to the SUV. "You've got this."

"Thanks," I said, putting them in my pocket.

"Let's go," Gowan said, leading the charge up the steps.

With a flash of something from his hand, he blew the door off its hinges to keep it from closing us in later. The dark smoke that had billowed from the place earlier smelled of sulfur, and a black goo covered the floor of the main room.

There was no sign of the girls there.

"Kai and Lenny, you both stay here," Gowan said. "Everyone else, find those girls."

The cabin was small, but I was still nervous when they left us in the room alone. Kai guarded the main doorway, while Gianna stood guarding the back door just through the other side of the main room.

Gowan and Martin split to the left side of the cabin, while Britta and Darius took the right side of the cabin.

I didn't know what else to do, so I reapplied the poison spell to my blade and looked around the smoke-filled room for any kind of clue. Footsteps, weapons, anything.

That's when I noticed the door Bates must have been talking about before. A plain brown door in the back of the room with a large lock on it.

He was right, there was magic holding that lock closed. Something so powerful it put a strange taste in my mouth.

"Nothing back there," Darius said, coming back into the room.

"Here," I said. "The door Bates was talking about."

"Stand back," he said. "It's likely to be cursed."

He pulled something sticky and red from his bag and placed it on the lock. "*Abstergo*," he said.

A black goo oozed from the lock, and everyone in the room instantly covered our mouths and noses.

"What the heck is that?" Gianna asked. "That's vile."

"And deadly," Darius said. "It's demon's blood mixed with nightshade grown in the underworld. Don't let it touch your skin."

He took a glass tube covered in black paint out of his satchel and carefully scooped the black liquid up from its puddle on the floor. Quickly, he corked it and sealed it with a strong spell that would prevent it from opening back up.

"Stand back and expect another trap," he said.

Darius also took several steps backward before holding one palm flat toward the door and closing his eyes. "*Solvo*," he said.

The air wavered as the intention of his spell flowed from his palm to the lock on the door, which instantly popped open.

My heart pounded against my ribs as he stepped forward and opened the door.

I don't know what I was expecting, but I certainly wasn't expecting the end of the battle. I thought that behind that door, we'd find another trap or the demon himself.

Instead, lying on the floor, wrapped in a dark netting that pulsed with dark light and shadows, was Julie Peterson.

I gasped and nearly fell to my knees. She was here. We were right.

Algrath had been pretending to be Julie Peterson all along.

Darius quickly dispelled the netting around her and lifted her into his arms. "She's unconscious, but she's alive."

He set her down on the couch in the center of the room as a commotion broke out in the back bedrooms on the other side of the house.

Everyone in the room turned to fight, but Martin held up his hand as he emerged from the bedroom.

"It's alright," he said. "We've got them. It's going to be alright."

I gasped as the five kidnapped girls stepped out of the bedroom, one at a time. I recognized the first girl, LaTasha, from her photograph. She was the first taken, but she was here now, alive.

Her body was trembling, and she kept rubbing her arm where it looked like some kind of strange symbol had been burned into her skin, but she was alive.

"What's happening?" she asked as she led the group into the main part of the cabin.

"I know it doesn't all make sense yet," Gianna said, placing a blanket around the girl's shoulders. "But you're okay now. You're safe."

One by one, each of the girls came out of the room. Each one had been marked for the ritual, but it seemed we had gotten to them in time.

When Peyton stepped forward, her eyes widened at the sight of me, and she ran forward, crying.

"Oh, my God, Lenny. What are you doing here?" she asked as I threw my arms around her. "I thought we were going to die. Who are all these people?"

"They're my friends," I said, hardly controlling my own tears. I couldn't believe we'd actually found her. "Are you hurt?"

I held her at arm's length for a moment, checking for any other injuries, but the mark on her arm seemed to be the only one. She was still wearing pajamas that looked like they'd seen better days, and she obviously hadn't showered for a while, but she seemed to be okay.

When her eyes landed on Julie Peterson, though, she screamed and backed away.

"She's the one who did this," she said. "Don't trust her.

She's got something wrong with her. I know it's going to sound crazy, but you have to believe me. She's dangerous."

"Peyton, it's okay," I said. "She can't hurt you now."

I turned to Martin.

"Where is he?" I asked. "We need to get them out of here."

"He wants us to think he's just left them here and run away," Gowan said. "But he's still got a trick or two up his sleeve, I think."

"Take the girls and go," Martin said. "The car is cloaked, but don't let your guard down."

"I'm going with them," Gianna said. "This doesn't feel right."

Martin nodded. "Yes. Keep them safe and wait for us at the house."

There were a lot of questions as we led the girls to the SUV outside. I didn't even know for sure what to tell them. I wanted to say this whole thing was over, but until we knew for sure where Algrath had gone, no one was safe.

I felt better with Gianna in the car as Kai took the wheel and drove us away from the cabin.

I sent up a prayer that Martin and the others would be okay when they faced Algrath. His ritual may have been disrupted, but I didn't believe he would just give up without a fight. Not if he truly wanted to set his brother free.

Which meant we needed to get home as quickly as possible.

Kai was doing better than I would have, taking it easy in the storm. I wanted to tell him to step on it, but we couldn't afford to get into an accident. Not until we were through those wards.

It was only half a mile until we hit the wards that Algrath

couldn't pass through, but as we approached the barrier, the car's engine switched off and the brake engaged.

Panic filled me as the car stopped just fifty yards shy of the barrier.

"No, no, no, no," I muttered. "The barrier is right there. What's happening?"

Kai tried to restart the engine, but it was completely dead.

"Get out," Gianna said, her tone urgent. "Get everyone across the barrier. Now."

She threw open the door and started pulling the girls out, urging them to run.

At the same time, my phone buzzed in my pocket.

I answered as we ran.

"Martin, something's wrong with the car," I shouted. "We're running for the barrier, but I don't know—"

"Lenny, this is Gowan, listen to me," he said. "We've just found another girl hidden underneath the house. She had to have been the first girl taken. Not the last."

"Another girl?" I said, a funny feeling in the pit of my stomach as a dark purple shadow suddenly spread across the pavement in front of me.

"Who?" I asked, my entire body trembling. This couldn't be real.

Everyone up ahead fell to the ground. All except one person.

She turned on me, then, her eyes sparkling as her form shifted.

"Lenny, Algrath is with you," he said. "The girl under the house is Peyton."

That was the last thing I heard before the phone slipped from my hand and everything went dark.

THE RITUAL

I woke to the sound of my body being dragged through the dirt and pine needles on the forest floor.

Peyton—or rather the demon who had stolen her appearance—had wrapped me in the same kind of netting I'd seen around Kai a few nights ago and was pulling me by my ankles. I struggled against the restraints, but it was no use. My arms were pinned to my side, and the more I struggled, the tighter the net became.

I also no longer had access to my backpack. That meant I had no weapon, no reagents, no hope.

I glanced around, trying to get my bearings. We were definitely still in the forest. I had no way of knowing if it was the same forest near the cabin, though, or not. Asher had said the wards wouldn't work to keep Algrath from going through a portal, so we could be anywhere by now.

Martin's tracking spell would lead him straight to Algrath as soon as it was fully activated, but would he make it here in time?

I had no way of knowing how long I'd been unconscious, but it couldn't have been long. Algrath had to cast this entire, complex ritual by midnight. It was all happening so fast.

Up ahead, voices spoke in hushed tones. It sounded like they were arguing, but I couldn't quite make out what they were saying.

I craned my neck to try and see what was going on and where Algrath was taking me, but my vision remained slightly blurred from whatever smoke had knocked me out earlier. My body and mind were both slow to react, as if I'd been drugged with something.

"Don't worry, Lenny. We'll be there soon," Algrath said, but he still had Peyton's face. Her voice.

It broke my heart to even think about it.

My first real friend, and she had turned out to be a demon in disguise.

I'd never even met the real Peyton. How could I have fallen for her friendship act? Was I really so desperate that I was blind to people's true nature?

At least the real Peyton was safe, for now. That was one girl who would make it home to her parents tonight. But where were the other four? And what had Algrath done with Kai and Gianna?

I didn't have to wonder long, though, because Algrath only pulled me about fifteen more feet before dropping my legs and bending down near my face.

He still wore Peyton's face, but I had to force myself to see beyond that. No doubt he was only keeping up the charade to mess with my emotions, just like Gowan had said he would.

"Oh, Lenny, you can't imagine how long I've dreamed of this moment," Algrath said, smiling. "Ever since Martin helped to put my brother in those mirrors, I have dreamed of someday using the sacrifice of someone he loved to bring my brother back again. When he finds you here...The balance of it all is just so deliciously beautiful. Martin, of course, will be devastated. It will be so much fun to watch. At least until we kill him, too."

I struggled harder against the shadowy netting, but it only grew tighter around my body.

Algrath laughed. "This is every bit as much fun as I'd hoped it would be."

"Ouch," someone said. "This stupid broken mirror cut my finger again. I'm so tired of this. When are we going to get started, already?"

I recognized that voice.

Confused, I turned my head toward the girl who'd just walked up behind Algrath, and I gasped.

Brandy stood there, one hand on her hip, holding a bloody finger toward the demon.

"Do you see what that mirror did to my finger? You promised me immortality and eternal youth," she said. "I didn't sign up to drag girls through the woods and draw pentagrams in the dirt. Seriously, Peyton, I don't know what kind of game you're playing here, but if you ask me to do one more ridiculous thing, I'm giving up on you."

Algrath made Peyton's eyes sparkle with mischief, but it made my stomach turn.

How long had Brandy been caught up in all of this? And how could she seriously believe that was still Peyton in there? Didn't she realize what was happening?

I wanted to warn her that she was making deals with a demon, but I didn't want to interrupt their conversation. For now, I needed to just listen and observe. Brandy had gotten herself into this mess, so she could deal with the consequences.

"I don't want to be here anymore, either," Olive said, stepping forward. She had her arms wrapped tightly around her body, and she was shivering.

I wanted to scream at both of them. Had they been part of this the entire time? Were none of my new friendships real?

"Shut up, Olive," Brandy said sharply. "You seemed more than happy to do this when we talked about it a few weeks ago."

Olive frowned and looked at me, shaking her head.

"I didn't know we were going to have to do this," she said. "I thought we were just setting my mom and that Bates guy up for drug dealing. I just wanted to teach her a lesson. If you'd told me this had anything to do with our friends going missing, you know I wouldn't have been a part of this."

"Well, it's too late to back out now," Algrath said, but it was obvious Olive still believed that was her friend Peyton.

I had no idea what story they'd fed her about why Peyton had only pretended to go missing, but poor Olive was in this just as much as I was now. We were probably both going to die before all of this was over.

Algrath pulled Brandy's finger to his lips and kissed it. Brandy made a face, but when she looked down, she smiled and clapped her hands.

"There we go," she said. "That's the kind of magic I want to be able to do. Olive, did you see that? I told you Peyton was a witch. She's going to give us some of that power tonight. That and more. I'm going to have flawless skin for the rest of my life. I'm going to become a famous model. We just have to get through this one ritual, and we'll have everything we ever wanted."

Olive didn't look impressed by the magic. Instead, she turned away, leaning her head against a tree, her shoulders shaking.

Brandy shrugged and pulled a small mirror from her pocket. She applied a thick layer of lip balm and stared at herself for a long moment before scrunching her nose in disapproval and snapping the mirror shut.

She put it back in her pocket, and turned to Algrath.

"When is our magic going to kick in, by the way?" she asked, a look of disgust on her face as she glanced at something on the ground at her feet.

If I was reading her right, there was also sheer terror locked away somewhere in her eyes, but she seemed to be willing to face that terror in order to gain eternal beauty.

I was going to be sick.

"Don't tell me you're losing your stomach for this, already?" Algrath asked with Peyton's voice. "We're just getting started, Brandy. But don't worry. You'll get your magic soon enough, and I promise you, once you do, you'll hardly remember what it was like to be so plain."

A hurt look flashed in Brandy's eyes, but she quickly shrugged it off and pulled her shoulders back.

"Good, because I've done everything you asked me to," Brandy said. "I made those little bundles of lavender and poison ivy you asked me for, making sure to use vines from Olive's backyard. I put that black vase in Olive's house the other day before school for you, for whatever good that seemed to do, except tearing that house to shreds."

Algrath met my eyes and smiled again.

The Devil's Snare. He'd had Brandy plant the trap in the Peterson's house before Kai and I got there.

"I tried my best to get Lenny to come stay at my place last night. And now, I've even drawn this design you gave me and put these broken mirrors beside each of the girls and their symbols," Brandy said. "I'm not doing one more thing until you give me a taste of that beauty and power you promised. I've had to betray a lot of people I cared about to get here, and I just want to make sure we're still in this together, Peyton."

Algrath, apparently, had already gotten tired of Brandy's non-stop talking, because when he turned, his face flashed from Peyton's to his true, demonic form.

Even though I'd half been expecting it, I still had to look away. To see something so pure and beautiful instantly turn into something so grotesque was unsettling, to say the least.

Brandy screamed and fell back on her butt in the dirt.

I gasped as the mirror she'd used to put her lipstick on slipped from her pocket.

I had no idea how I might be able to use it, but right about now, I was looking for anything that might help me get out of this situation. Now, I just needed to get out of this netting and get my hands on it.

Brandy dug her heels into the dirt to push herself backward, but Algrath simply pointed a bony finger toward her, sending a dark rope around her waist and pulling her back toward him.

"You will not make demands of me, human. And you won't threaten me, either," Algrath said. His face settled back to Peyton's. "You'll do whatever I tell you to do, or you will die with the rest of these worthless girls. Now, finish the preparations. I want you to double check each symbol and make sure each girl is exactly where she needs to be placed for this to work."

"Of course," Brandy said, her hands visibly shaking. Tears glistened in her eyes.

Well, that answered my questions about whether or not Brandy knew what was really going on out here.

It blew my mind that someone who seemed so sweet and genuine had come out here willingly to help her friend kill five girls.

And not just us.

About fifteen feet away, Kai hung suspended about halfway up a tree. I prayed to see his eyes flutter open or his body move in a way that would let me know he was even still alive, but he didn't move at all.

I looked for Gianna, too, but I didn't see her anywhere.

From what I could tell between the conversation and what little visibility I had around here, the four girls who had been kidnapped after Peyton all lay on the ground in a clearing just ahead.

LaTasha Owings, Marcia Valentine, Samantha Anderson, and April Green.

I'd never officially met any of them, but as Algrath grabbed my ankles again and began pulling me toward the clearing, I realized that I shared something in common with those girls.

Peyton had never really been the fifth girl intended for the sacrifice.

It was me Algrath intended to kill tonight.

"Why me?" I asked. "Why not just use the real Peyton for the fifth sacrifice? Why do you need me? Or is this really just about getting back at Martin after all this time? That's a long time to hold a grudge, don't you think? Besides, I never did anything to you. I don't deserve this."

"What I feel is not a grudge," Algrath said, sucking air through his teeth. His anger made Peyton's eyes turn black for a moment. "This is so much more than a grudge. It's hatred that runs so deep, it crosses the boundaries of time and blood. You are a Thorne, and in my mind, that makes you guilty of crossing my family."

He laughed and then glanced at Brandy, who was leaning over something on the ground a few feet away.

"Besides," he said softly, "to restore my brother to full strength, there are three things I must do. One, release each piece of the mirror into which he was banished. As you no doubt already know, tonight's ritual will release the final piece."

I couldn't quite see what Algrath was doing with his hands, but it was no use straining myself to look. The shadowy netting was already so tight, I could hardly move at all.

I had no idea how much preparation this ritual required, but one mistake we'd all made was assuming Algrath was working alone. We never even discussed the possibility that someone else might be setting up a second location for the ritual.

That first circle by the cabin had been nothing more than a decoy to throw us off.

"Second, of course, I must sacrifice young, magical blood. The more innocent and powerful, the better," Algrath said, a smile slowly spreading across his lips as he looked directly into my eyes. "Imagine my joy when I was able to convince the Council to send you here. I held Peyton as an insurance policy, just in case I couldn't capture you, but when you showed up at the cabin tonight, you made all my dreams come true."

"You convinced the Council to send me here?" I asked, chills going through me.

Algrath giggled.

"Don't tell me you haven't put that piece of the puzzle together yet," he said, clicking his tongue with disapproval. "And I thought you were supposed to be smart."

I didn't take the bait. Obviously, part of Algrath's game was that he used insults to get you riled up. I didn't care if he thought I was smart or not. What really bothered me was the idea of the Council sending me to Newcastle High like a lamb to the slaughter.

"What's the third thing?" Brandy asked.

"I didn't realize you were listening to our conversation," Algrath said. He stood and ran a hand down Brandy's curls. She instantly seemed to forget her question.

Did he have some kind of coercion powers, too?

"What was I saying?" Brandy asked with a shake of her head.

"Nothing important," Algrath said. "Let's take Lenora out of her net and wake everyone up. It's almost time."

That seemed to cheer Brandy up a bit. Her eyes lit up, and she bounced on her toes.

"I was hoping you would say that. I can't wait."

I honestly couldn't tell if Brandy was under some kind of spell, or if she really thought sacrificing five girls was a reasonable price to pay for eternal beauty. Still, the fact that she seriously believed this demon would follow through was a little heartbreaking.

Algrath hadn't gotten a chance to say what the third thing

was that he needed in order to help restore his brother's power, but I was pretty sure I knew what it was.

He needed a vessel.

When Regmothean was first released from the mirrors, he would be weak from having been split into pieces for so long. The ritual itself would give him his body back, but he would need to rest.

I knew from my reading that the best place for a demon to rest and regain power was inside a host. In this case, a non-magical human who would not interfere with the fact that Regmothean intended to consume her entire life force in order to restore his former power.

Plus, Martin and the others would be looking for them. Regmothean needed a place to hide for a while. At least until his host died.

If Brandy hadn't looked so happy about the prospect of killing all of us to get what she wanted, I might have felt sorry for her.

Algrath bent down next to me again, and despite Peyton's lovely face, he stank of sulphur and ash.

"Now, listen here, Lenny Thorne, you be a good girl, you hear me?" he said. "I'm going to let you out of this net, but if you make so much as a single attempt to get away from me, I will kill your little boyfriend over there and your red-headed Slayer friend. Do you promise to be a good girl?"

I nodded, feeling powerless as Algrath finally dissolved the purple, shadowy netting around my body. He left my hands bound behind my back, though, and moved me into place in the circle, propping me up on my knees.

Gowan had said our emotions were our greatest weakness, and he had been absolutely right. How could I do anything now when Algrath had control over people I loved? I had no choice but to do as I was told.

Even though I knew Algrath intended to kill us all. I still hoped I would be able to find a way to save my friends.

Now that I was upright, I did a quick scan of the clearing.

Gianna lay on the ground about twenty feet away. She was wrapped in the kind of netting that had held me, but she didn't seem to be conscious at all. I glanced up at Kai, and for a second, I thought I saw his head roll to one side slightly, but when he went still again, I wasn't sure if I had imagined it or not.

The four other girls intended for the sacrifice were all kneeling in the dirt around the ritual circle, just like me, spaced out at each point of the pentagram. They seemed to be awake but under some kind of trance or spell that made them unaware of what they were doing.

At least I hoped they were unaware. That, at least, would have been merciful.

Each girl had a symbol burned into her forearm, work Algrath had done back at the cabin. A matching symbol had been drawn in the dirt in front of each girl.

I had been moved to the fifth point of the pentagram, and the symbol there, I realized as I focused in on a sore feeling on my own forearm, had likely already been burned into my skin, as well.

Panic threatened to overwhelm me, and I wanted to just run. But I thought of Kai and Gianna. I couldn't put their lives at risk.

Besides, where would I go? We were deep in the woods somewhere, and I had no idea which way to go to find the road or the cabin. It was also possible this was all some kind of trick

SARRA CANNON

and Algrath had taken us through a portal to another town while I was passed out.

Where exactly were we?

I couldn't act on impulse without thinking it through, but if I was going to do something, I had better do it fast. I had a feeling that as soon as I was locked into that circle on my knees, it was already too late to stop this thing.

"That was a clever trick with Julie Peterson," I said, wanting to get Algrath talking so I could at least give Martin a chance at finding us.

The last I'd heard, we were only fifteen minutes or so away from the location spell being dead accurate. How much time had passed since then? It had to have been at least ten minutes. He could be here any minute.

"Even Martin really fell for it, as you saw. Seeing her there in the closet made it seem like she'd been there the whole time, but you really only abducted her yesterday when she went through that portal with Bates. Is that right?"

"It's always so much fun to come up with ways to trick Slayers and Keepers," Algrath said. "It was relatively easy to make it seem that Julie and Bates were working together to kidnap innocent girls. Once all of this is over, that local detective who thinks he's so smart is going to be blaming this entire thing on the two of them. Such a local tragedy, but our heroes in blue have it all figured out."

"How are they going to explain her motive, though?" I asked. I needed to keep him talking. "Why would Ms. Julie want anyone dead? Especially her daughter's friends. It's not like the police know about the moondust in the cupcakes."

"No, but they'll find poor Olive's diaries," Algrath said. "She was always so jealous of her more popular friends. Even the new girl in town seemed to catch the eye of the hard-to-get bad boy. The diaries, combined with the scene they'll find out here, will be enough to convince them."

I shook my head. "But why even bother? Why do you care if the police wrap this up or not?"

Algrath had been using some kind of wand or stick with a few crystals encrusted at the tip to draw in the dirt, but he suddenly stopped and gave me a curious look.

"You know the Council doesn't want the human world to find out about our kind. This is part of my agreement with them," he said. "As long as I promised to make sure to keep our world concealed in all of this and provide a somewhat logical explanation for the normal world to swallow, the Council promised to send me you."

I didn't really want to believe him, but it made sense. Was this real, or another one of his tricks to manipulate me?

"Of course, that meant they had to let two of their most powerful Slayers die, but that didn't bother them too much," he said. "Your parents were getting in the way of their progress, anyway. Doubting the coven's power over their abilities. It was only a matter of time before they needed to be put down."

Tears welled in my eyes, and I shook my head.

"That's not true," I said. "The Council had nothing to do with my parents' death."

Algrath raised an eyebrow and stopped moving for a moment.

"Didn't they?" he asked. "Not that it matters now. Once you're gone, there are only a handful of people who will know the truth, and they'll never admit to it. With any luck, I'll be able to take out a few more of their insubordinate Slayers before this is all over. Then they'll really owe me."

"I don't believe you," I said. "The Council would never work with a demon like you. You're lying to get under my skin."

Algrath laughed, throwing his head back.

"I love how incredibly naive you are," he said. "You're so innocent and trusting, just like your mother, really. You believe that just because the Thorne family has been loyal to them for centuries, the Council must have pure intentions. But the truth is, there are many within the coven and even the Council itself who believe it's time for a new way of doing things. This new group of leaders understands that the only way to gain the true power they desire for the coven is to work with demons. Not against them."

I didn't want to believe a word he said, but there had to be some reason the Council had refused to get involved in such a high-profile case. And they had, in fact, commanded me to go to school here in Newcastle.

As for the death of my parents, many of us had been confused about how that whole thing went down. I had blamed myself, but maybe it really hadn't been my fault at all.

A tear fell down my cheek.

My parents had dedicated their lives to the Witch's Council, and this is how they'd been repaid?

I was so glad they weren't here to see this. I was glad they had died not knowing how badly they'd been betrayed.

And if I somehow managed to survive this night, I vowed to find every last person who'd had anything to do with that betrayal and put an end to them myself.

"It's fun to see the fire spark in your eyes," Algrath said. "It will be even more fun to watch that spark go out."

From what I could tell, he was almost done drawing those extra symbols in the dirt. Olive and Brandy had their backs to me, so I couldn't exactly make out what they were doing, but it looked like maybe they were tying some bundles of herbs together.

How much longer until I got locked into this circle, though?

How much longer until Martin found us?

I knew I should just stay put. Wait for the others to rescue us and not do anything impulsive that could get everyone here killed, but I couldn't help but think through all the possibilities.

Earlier at the cabin, Asher had said something about how once the ritual had begun, the circle would be locked or protected somehow, and no one would be able to do anything but sit back and watch.

Once the ritual was over, they would be able to fight Algrath and his brother, but the five of us girls would all be dead. That wasn't exactly giving me good vibes right now.

Especially since Algrath seemed to be anointing the circle with some type of oil. That seemed like one of those last-step kinds of things. I was starting to feel antsy. All I needed was a single opening. One opportunity to get the upper hand.

I needed a sign.

And what better person to give it to me than an angel from above.

Kai's head did roll slightly to the side. He was coming to.

I glanced at Algrath to make sure he wouldn't see what

was happening, but he wasn't paying attention at all. Instead, he was yelling at Brandy for moving too slowly.

I moved my eyes back to Kai, willing him to open his and see me here. To do something.

Come on, I begged. *Please help me.*

I sent it up like a prayer, and he heard me. By some miracle, he actually opened his eyes and lifted them to mine.

At that moment, I wished so hard for the ability to read minds or communicate telepathically, but facial expressions would have to do for now.

I nodded very slightly toward Algrath, Brandy, and Olive off to Kai's left. Then, I turned my body slightly to show that my hands were bound behind my back.

Kai did a good job taking it all in without actually moving too much or drawing anyone's attention. I wanted to cry in relief. Even though we were both bound and basically powerless, it just felt so good to know I wasn't alone in this.

Just meeting his eyes and knowing that someone here cared about me made all the difference.

I was not going to let Algrath bring us down. If he was right and my parents died just so he could get me here, I was going to make him regret that choice for a thousand years to come.

I needed a plan.

Yes, I had been told over and over again to stop rushing into things or being impulsive, but what else could you do when your back was against the wall? I had no idea if Martin was actually coming for us.

What if they'd all gotten caught in some kind of trap back at the cabin? Or what if Algrath had put more wards and traps here in the woods? It might take Martin and the others too long to get to us.

Questions rushed through my mind, and I lost focus to the panic building inside me.

So, instead of letting it take over, I closed my cyes. I remembered just how focused I'd been back at the cabin when the fight had started. That was all because Kai had convinced me to sit down for a moment and just breathe. Recenter.

Maybe if I could just do that now, something would come to me.

I took several deep breaths, listening to Kai's voice in my memory. I let go of everything else around me and just focused on that breath. I focused on connecting to my own true center. My heart.

And I knew the moment I had really done it, because I could suddenly feel the wind on my cheek and hear the rustling of the leaves above our heads.

I opened my eyes and looked around again, seeing from a new, calmer perspective.

A strange feeling in my gut told me it was now or never as Algrath turned to place some kind of woven crown of vines and dark flowers on LaTasha's head.

The ritual would begin soon. There was no more time to wait, and there was no time to doubt myself. Impulsive or not, I was our best hope.

I glanced from Algrath to Kai to the circle, looking for an answer.

And suddenly, there it was.

My mother had always insisted the right answers came to a witch when she needed them most, as long as she knew how to look for them.

I just hadn't been looking in the right place.

The truth had been right there in front of me this entire time. Algrath spoke of balance, so of course he had brought me here.

Heart pounding, I worked through all the calculations. Could this really work?

But I knew that it could. And if anything went wrong, the only one who would die tonight would be me.

I wasn't ready to leave this world just yet, but if I could save the rest of them, what other choice did I have?

I was done thinking it through. Martin or Gowan might be angry with me for being impulsive, but if they had a chance to yell at me, that would mean I'd won, so that was a risk I was willing to take.

I waited for Algrath to turn around as he grabbed another of the strange, dark crowns before I made my move. Kai seemed to sense my intentions, and he shook his head, but it was too late. My plan was already in motion.

I turned around and picked up a piece of the broken mirror that had been set on the ground in front of my chosen symbol. It was so sharp, it sliced through the skin on several of my fingers, but I simply gritted my teeth and focused on the task at hand. Cutting through the magical rope that bound my hands together.

To my relief, it worked, and my arms were instantly freed.

Algrath sensed my movement, though, and turned, throwing a poison spell toward me. I deflected the spell with the mirror, sending it back toward Algrath. Brandy screamed and fell to the ground, her hands covering her head like the coward she was.

But I didn't have time to worry about her.

Without hesitation, I positioned the mirror shard in my right hand, reared back, and threw it straight at Kai. At the same time, I reached down and grabbed the small compact mirror Brandy had dropped before, slipping it into my pocket.

My mouth went dry with nerves as the mirror flew through the air. It was either going to free him or stab him, but luckily, my dad had spent enough time practicing dagger throws with me that my aim was true.

The shadowy ropes that held Kai's body were severed as the mirror sliced through them and then embedded into the tree's bark.

Algrath hissed, his form shifting again from Peyton to his true self as he threw a massive ball of hot flames toward me. This time, I had no mirror to deflect it, and since Algrath had taken my key, I had no magic to shield with, either.

I braced myself for impact as I dove toward the ground, but just as the flames should have hit me, a bright light flashed all around us. Kai knelt above me, his beautiful, golden wings shielding us both from the flames.

"How are we going to fight him?" he asked. "I can't keep this up for long. We need more help."

I shook my head and nodded toward the tree where the mirror had landed.

Kai's eyes widened, and he understood immediately. "I'll do it," he said.

"It has to be me," I said. "He left Peyton back at the house, and those other two girls don't have magic in their blood. He needs me to make this ritual happen. He doesn't need you."

Kai waited a long moment before he finally nodded.

"Run," he said. "Now."

With him as my temporary shield, I stood and ran.

Algrath couldn't release his brother from that last mirror without a full sacrifice. If he didn't get it done tonight, he'd have to wait until the next full moon, and he knew as well as I did that Martin and the others weren't going to give him another chance.

Every step I took was followed by the pounding of foot-steps right behind me. I pushed my body harder, sliding once on a pile of pine needles and somehow managing to straighten up and keep running.

Spells exploded all around me, but nothing too deadly and nothing I couldn't dodge. Algrath couldn't risk killing me here. He needed me to die inside the circle.

My heart pounded, and I opened my mouth to breathe. I had never run so fast in my life, but still, it didn't seem to be enough. Algrath was right behind me, practically breathing down my neck.

Once, I even felt what I imagined to be claws scrape down my back, and I shuddered.

To gain more power, he must have shifted back to his demon form, which was fine with me. I was so tired of seeing him wear Peyton's face.

"You won't escape me," Algrath said. "You're just wasting everyone's time."

Time.

I just needed a little more time.

My lungs burned as I pushed harder. Faster. I just needed to get a little bit further into the woods, and everything would be okay.

But I couldn't take another step. Exhausted and spent, I fell to my knees, tears streaming down my face as I struggled to catch my breath.

Algrath laughed, and I spun around, skittering backward like a spider.

"You aren't going to win," I said. "Martin's on his way as we speak. He'll save me, and he'll send you to the same kind of prison you're brother's been rotting in for decades."

"Martin can't save you now," he said. "You've been cloaked from his sight with one of the most powerful cloaking spells ever cast. I was even able to disarm the family sigil here in the training grounds. I've sent him down a different path, but when he gets there, he'll realize he's too late. By the time he finds you, you'll be dead and gone. Can't you see that I've already won?"

"You're wrong," I said, scooting backward another foot or so. I couldn't let him catch me and drag me back there. "Martin is tracking you right now. That night you attacked us in the woods by Bates's factory, he injured you with a dagger laced with his own blood. That blood is now pumping through your veins. An untraceable tracking spell that will lead him and the other Slayers straight to you."

Algrath tilted his head strangely to one side.

"You're lying," he said, stepping toward me. "Martin's not that clever. No one tricks me."

"It's true," I said, showing absolute terror on my face as I backed up again, two more feet toward the tree behind me.

Algrath lashed out with his shadowy ropes, but I was ready for him. I pulled Brandy's mirror from my pocket and deflected his spell with it. I just needed to pull him a little bit closer.

"Martin will be here any minute. I won't let you hurt me. I won't let you take me back there to that ritual. I'll run all night, if I have to."

I scrambled to my feet and turned as if to run again. Algrath followed me, anger and hatred in his eyes as he reached for me.

Only, as soon as he stepped over the line drawn in the dirt, his movements turned to molasses.

"What is this?" he asked, obviously slower to catch on than I'd expected.

Slowly, I turned back toward him, my chest rising with each labored breath as my heart pumped so hard.

Had I really done it?

"It doesn't feel good, does it?" I asked, stepping right up to the outer line of the Demon's Circle Gowan had drawn for me in training yesterday. "To be trapped with no way out?"

Algrath shook his head in confusion and, for the first time, looked down.

Terror and disbelief blossomed on his face like a series of fireworks.

"This is impossible," he said, attempting to run toward the barrier. His movements were slow and labored, and despite his determination and energy, he hit the invisible barrier and fell back. "No. No one tricks me. You couldn't have had time to set this up. No one even uses these, anymore. There's no way you knew how to draw this."

"I didn't," I said. "I have an old friend to thank for that, but it's really you I should be thanking."

Algrath growled at me.

"You're disgusting," he said, spitting at the ground. Acid sizzled in the dirt at his feet.

"You're the one who chose this location in the woods, of all places," I said. "Martin's training grounds? That was your decision, wasn't it?"

Algrath pushed against the invisible barrier of the circle, testing his boundaries, but each time the barrier repelled him, the reality of his situation seemed to deepen.

Finally, he screamed so loud it shook the ground.

"I wanted Martin to find you here on his own property, where he trained the Slayer who captured my brother," Algrath said, dropping to his knees. "I wanted him to know that it was his own actions that took you from him. How did you know where we were?"

"There are symbols burned into the trees at the edge of the training grounds," I said. "The moment I saw one, I knew what had to be done. It's over, Algrath."

He took several ragged breaths before looking up at me, his teeth bared.

"It's not over yet," he said. "You may have me trapped, but you can't hurt me. Surely you didn't think that small mirror could hold me. You couldn't even banish me if you wanted to. I took your key, remember?"

I reached for the familiar key and locket at my neck and shook my head.

"You really don't think much of me, do you?" I said. "What kind of witch wears her real key in plain sight of a demon?"

This was a trick Gianna had told me about. Just before the battle began, she'd had me take a handful of dirt and transform it into a passable replica of my key. Apparently, it had fooled even Algrath.

When all of this was over, I would have to thank both her and Gowan for everything they'd taught me. They'd saved my life.

I reached down into my boot and tugged on the silver chain tucked inside.

Algrath screamed again as I secured the locket and key around my neck.

"You aren't strong enough," he growled. "You aren't even a real Slayer."

"Maybe not," I said, real tears falling down my cheeks as a set of familiar faces appeared on the other side of the circle. "But they are."

Algrath's eyes got so big, I thought they would burst, and he let his head fall back in a loud roar that shook the trees around us.

Martin nodded to me from across the circle as the others spread out around Algrath.

"You," Algrath said, turning to stare at Martin with pure hatred in his eyes. "I will make you pay for this. Someday, you will burn in agony for eternity, my plaything in hell."

Martin raised an eyebrow.

"Will I?" he asked. "Because I seem to remember your brother making a similar statement right before I sentenced him to eternity inside a mirror filled with flames and terror. I believe he's still there, isn't he?"

Algrath hissed and beat his fists against the circle's barrier, but he was ours now.

Martin nodded to Darius, who then pulled a much larger mirror than mine from his satchel and pointed it straight at Algrath.

"Don't do this," Algrath said, turning to me as he shifted one final time into the girl I thought I'd grown so close to on that first day of school.

To me, Peyton appeared on her knees in the circle, tears streaming down her face.

"Don't let them do this to me, Lenny," she said, her voice

sounding so real and sincere, it tugged at my heart. "No one will ever be your friend if you live this kind of life. Have mercy on me. I'm begging you."

I shook my head, amazed at how the manipulative powers of a demon like this could still make me feel anything even though I knew who was really inside.

It hurt to let go of the idea of having a friend like Peyton. I wanted so badly to feel like I was part of something. Like I mattered to someone.

But as Kai stepped out of the shadows with Gianna and the other girls, I looked around the circle at the Slayers who had been willing to go against the Council to stand at my side. I did matter to a lot of people, actually. I had all the friends I needed, right here.

"Wait," I said, wanting to get answers before we banished him to a fate worse than hell. "You had an angel with you. Zuriel. Where is he?"

Kai and I shared a look of hope and fear.

"Zuriel, yes," Algrath said, turning to look at Kai. "I threatened to kill his child if he refused to help me find the mirrors, so he did as I told him. I planned to feed him to my brother when he went free, but sadly, heaven took him from me when we reached Newcastle."

"Heaven?" I asked.

"Yes, he was summoned," he said. "By God himself, for all I know. I decided his half-breed son would work as a good substitute, and I was so close to making it happen. I promise you, you won't get away with this. When I find a way out, I will hunt each one of you down and make sure you and everyone you've ever loved suffers for eternity."

I took a deep breath and turned to Darius, my eyes questioning as I held my hands out. I wanted a piece of this guy.

Darius looked to Martin, who tried to suppress a small smile before he nodded.

Darius handed the mirror to me, and with a deep breath, I pointed it straight toward Peyton. A friend I'd never had.

A demon who had taken so much from me, it was going to feel good to put him where he really belonged.

"Don't," he screamed, attempting to shift and stand up, but as he did, Martin took something from his pocket.

"Just like your brother, you deserve to burn inside that mirror," he said, calmly throwing a handful of some kind of dust toward Algrath. "*Incendium.*"

Algrath's body went up in white flame that brought him back down to his knees.

"Now," Gowan said.

I took several deep, nervous breaths and held the mirror straight with one hand. I closed my other hand around the cool silver case of my mother's locket, drawing power from her memory and her love.

"*In Quod Relego,*" I said.

Algrath's image wavered before us, and a thin line of smoke and flame formed from the mirror to his body, pulling him forward.

Gowan and Darius stepped toward me, placing their hands on the edges of the mirror.

"*In Quod Relego,*" they repeated.

The wind around us kicked up and rain began to fall again in sheets all around us. Lightning flashed and a moment later, thunder boomed in the distance. In my hands, the mirror vibrated and warmed.

"More," Gowan shouted over the storm.

Britta and Asher ran toward us, placing their hands over ours as we huddled together.

As a group, we all repeated the incantation one more time, pooling our power together. Standing as one.

"In Quod Relego."

With that, Algrath's body was pulled into the mirror and the storm around us stopped instantly.

Drained and exhausted, I released the mirror and fell to my knees just outside the Demon's Circle.

It was over.

Algrath had finally been defeated.

A WITCH'S DOOR

As it turned out, trapping a powerful demon in a mirror, even when you had a lot of help, could take a lot out of a girl.

The last thing I remembered from the night we banished Algrath was passing out beside the Demon's Circle. Well, that and the feel of Kai's arms under me before I hit the ground.

I spent the rest of the weekend fading in and out of consciousness.

Every once in a while, I woke up in a panic from a dream about being chased through the woods, but every single time I awoke, someone was there at my side to comfort me and give me something to eat or drink before I fell asleep again.

Martin. Kai. Asher. They were the ones I saw most often, but it seemed everyone, even Gianna, had taken turns watching out for me.

I remembered waking up once and asking about the other girls and being assured they were all safe. Even Brandy and Olive had been allowed to go home after it was determined their actions were greatly influenced by the demon's manipulations.

Everyone's memories had been wiped clean of what happened to them and another, more believable story about a serial killer, was given in its place.

Satisfied that everyone was okay and I wasn't needed, I allowed myself to sleep again, getting lost in dreams for longer than I realized.

Then, late one afternoon when the light coming in through the window was already beginning to fade into evening, I woke to the distinct feeling that it was really done. Whatever side effects I'd suffered from Algrath's banishment had worked their way through my system, and I had somehow managed to find myself on the other side.

This time, it was Kai watching over me, except he was actually sitting on the roof outside my window, watching the beginning of the sunset.

I stood on shaky legs and joined him, placing a hand on his arm and leaning against him for support.

"My own personal guardian angel," I whispered.

In some ways, it still stung to think he was only looking out for me because of the promise his father made to my parents, but no matter why he was here, I was grateful for him.

"Half-angel," he whispered, turning his head slightly and pressing his lips to my forehead.

I closed my eyes and focused on the feeling of warmth and safety that radiated through me.

"Half is good enough for me," I said softly. "How long have I been asleep?"

"A few days, off and on," he said. "Martin said someone your age with only a single key has never taken part in such a powerful ritual before. He doesn't expect you to really wake up for another day or two."

He smiled and put his arm around me.

"Overachiever," he whispered.

"Yeah, that's me," I said with a gentle laugh. "The only person to ever simultaneously be a constant disappointment and an overachiever."

I was only partly joking about the first part, but Kai's expression grew serious and he shook his head.

"You saved everyone," he said. "If you hadn't acted when you did, it would have been too late. Martin and the others got there as fast as they could, but Algrath had set up all kinds of traps in the woods. It took them too long to get through it all. If Algrath had started the ritual, they would have been too late to stop him, and we all probably would have died."

I shivered, thinking of just how close we were to death.

"And your father?" I asked. "Any news on where he is? Was Algrath telling the truth about him being summoned back to heaven?"

Kai swallowed and looked back out to the sunset that colored the sky outside my window.

"I'm not sure," he said. "But Algrath didn't have my father's powers. I could at least tell that much."

I squeezed his arm.

"Then he's still alive," I said.

"I hope so," Kai said. "I've been searching for him for so long. I just want answers."

A wave of sadness washed over me, and I clung to him a little tighter.

"What will you do now, then?" I asked, unable to stop my

voice from trembling. "I guess you'll be heading out to look for him again."

I held my breath as I waited for him to speak. I understood why he needed to keep looking for answers, but at the same time, I wasn't ready to say goodbye.

"Do you really think I'd leave? Just like that?" he asked.

I turned, looking into his eyes, my heart pounding nervously.

"I don't know," I said. "I know how badly you want to find him. I wouldn't blame you if you felt you needed to go."

Kai's dark eyes searched mine, and then he pulled his arm away and began to fidget.

My mouth suddenly went dry. We'd never really had a chance to say how we felt about each other, but I was so scared I'd imagined it to be more than it really was.

What if he only cared out of obligation?

I wasn't sure my heart could take more disappointment after finding out the truth about my new friends. Two of them had been willing to murder me for beauty, and the other, well. The other had been a demon.

My track record for friendships in Newcastle wasn't exactly looking good right now.

"I never got a chance to tell you about that time we first met in Romania," he said. He kept his eyes toward the sunset, and his golden skin seemed to glow in the half-light. "My mother had just recently passed away, and even though I had my father, I'd never been as close to him as I had been to her. He was always busy, and even though you might think angels are always loving and caring, he was difficult to get close to when I was young. I always got the feeling he didn't quite know what to do with me or how to care for me."

I blinked back tears, imagining a young Kai feeling so alone. Losing his mother so young.

I wanted to pull him close, but he seemed to need his space.

"Back then, I remember feeling so alone," he said, looking into the distance. "I honestly wasn't sure if I would ever be able to open my heart up to anyone ever again. I just felt empty. Hopeless, in a lot of ways."

I closed my eyes, my heart breaking for him.

He turned to me, then, his eyes full of tears.

"When we went to visit your parents, I had just gotten into an argument with my father. I went into an empty room in your house to cry, and you found me," he said. "I thought for sure you were going to make fun of me or go tell my dad where I was, but you didn't. Do you remember what you did?"

I shook my head. Locked somewhere inside, I had a small memory of a beautiful boy crying in a small room, all alone, but I hadn't ever put it together until just now that it was him.

The corners of his mouth twitched into a smile, and he brushed the back of his fingers across my cheek.

"You walked in and sat down next to me on the floor," he said, taking my hand in his. "You slipped your hand in mine and told me it was okay to cry. That sometimes even the strongest people in the world needed to cry."

A tear slipped down his cheek, but he didn't move to brush it away. He simply pulled me closer.

"It was such a simple moment," he said. "But it was an act of kindness that changed me forever. I had been spending all of my time with an angel, expecting him to teach me about unconditional love, but in the end, it was a human child that reminded me of my own strength. You may not remember it now, but you helped me hold onto my own humanity, and because of that, I have also held onto my mother and who she really was. I can't ever repay you for that."

I gripped his hand tightly.

"You don't have to repay me," I said. "And you don't have to stay because of your father's promise to my parents, either."

He shook his head.

"I'm not going anywhere, Lenny. But I'm not staying because I feel obligated to. I'm staying because I think I'm falling in love with you," he said, his voice hitching slightly on the words.

I always imagined my first real kiss would be awkward and strange, or that I would be full of doubt when the time came.

But when Kai spoke those words, I felt nothing but absolute certainty inside.

I slid my arms around his neck and pressed my lips against his. There was nothing awkward about it at all. Instead, I felt a rush of joy and love and warmth that buzzed through me from head to toe.

When I realized what I'd done, though, I pulled away, my face flushed.

"Still impulsive, I see," Kai said, trying to hide his smile and failing miserably.

Nerves knotted my stomach.

"I'm sorry," I said. "I don't know why—"

But before I could say another word, he pulled me into another kiss.

I sighed and leaned against him, definitely awake now and happier than I'd been in a very long time.

We sat together watching the last of the sun's light disappear behind the nearby houses.

"Everyone is waiting to see you," he said. "And I know Martin will want to talk to you."

I nodded. "We should get downstairs, then."

I was anxious to know how the girls were doing and what we were expected to do from here, but I was also sad to leave our little private perch outside the window.

When we got downstairs, though, I was so happy to see everyone gathered together in the kitchen, eating dinner. They were all so relieved to see me awake and feeling better.

"I told you she'd recover fast," Darius said. "She's a warrior just like her father."

"You mean a fighter just like her mom," Gianna said with a smile.

"She's a natural, just like generations of Thornes before her," Martin said, pulling me into a hug. "I am so proud of you, my dear girl. When I learned we'd been tricked, I was so scared I might lose you. But it turns out I shouldn't have been scared at all. You were very brave and clever, Lenora, and I am proud of you."

"Lenny?"

A woman walked into the room, her face showing signs of vulnerability like I'd never seen before.

"Ms. Greer?" I looked to Martin. "What's she doing here?"

Had she come to tell us that the Council was bringing us in?

"Just hear her out," Martin said, pulling a chair out for me.

I sat down, my heart racing. I had no idea what she could say that would make all of this okay.

"You were right to question the Council," Ms. Greer said. "I couldn't tell you at the time, but I'd been petitioning for them to look into the Algrath situation for a very long time.

Being a Keeper is complicated, as Martin can confirm. I answer to the Council, so the decision of whether or not to intervene was not mine to make."

I picked at the napkin on the table. I heard what she was saying, but I wasn't sure if I could forgive her for not standing up to the Council. Plus, I still wasn't sure if Algrath had been telling the truth about my parents' death or not. Had the Council been involved? Had my parents been killed just to get me here?

"I know you have a lot of questions," Ms. Greer said. "I have those same questions, but finding the answers is not going to be as easy as simply asking the Council for the truth. Martin and I have been working together on this in secret for months, but we thought it for the best if it appears I had no involvement. That way, we could still have someone on the inside with access to information."

I looked to Martin, and he nodded. She was telling the truth.

"For now, the Council seems to be looking the other way when it comes to the actions of the Slayers in this room, but I have a feeling that's more to protect themselves than all of you," Ms. Greer said. "If we want real answers, we have to be smart about how we go looking for them. Do you understand?"

I shook my head.

"Not really. I just want to know what happened," I said. "And if the Council really offered me up as a sacrifice to gain favor with demons, what are we going to do about it? Am I just supposed to pretend it didn't happen and go about my life as a good little Slayer? Because I don't know if I can do that."

"There's no doubt in my mind some of the Council was

involved," Blythe Greer said, her jaw tight. "Our job now is to figure out who is on our side and who betrayed us."

"And once we find them?" I asked, looking at Martin.

"They will wish they'd never heard the name Thorne," Martin said, sipping his coffee. "Of that, I can assure you."

I sat back in my chair, relieved.

The Council wasn't coming after us, at least for now. And if there really was a split in the coven and some of our members were working with demons, I had a feeling the people in this room were just as determined to find out the truth as I was.

"There is one thing the Council wanted me to bring to you, though," Ms. Greer said, setting a small package down in front of me before she walked around to the other side of the table to take her seat. "Congratulations, Lenny."

Eyes wide, I tore open the package and gasped.

I ran my fingertips across the smooth silver of the key inside.

This one was slightly more ornate than my first key, and it had a tiny emerald embedded in its center.

"But I haven't even taken my test yet."

"The Council has decided that considering your role in capturing a demon of Algrath's power, you have already passed the first test," she said. "That is, if you're willing to accept your place as a Slayer in the coven."

I took a deep breath. It was a big decision, but I knew now I could never turn my back on magic. It was a part of who I was, and even if there were problems with the coven and its leadership, the best place for me to fight back and protect the lives of the innocent was from the inside.

"I am," I said.

"Then, it's a celebration dinner," Gowan said, giving me a wink.

Laughter and congratulations rang out as we all gathered together. A team, now bound together by an experience we would never forget and sworn to find out the truth about the Council.

A family.

When dinner was over and our guests had either left or retired for the night, Martin pulled me aside and studied the key with admiration. I was sure he'd seen many second keys in his day, but it just went to show how much he loved me that he was still proud of me for getting mine.

"Not many Slayers get a second key without taking their test," he said. "You should be very proud of yourself, Lenny. I have no doubt your parents would have been very proud of you and the witch you have become."

"I still have a long way to go," I said. "But I'm willing to learn."

"And that's what matters," Martin said, placing an arm around my shoulders as he led me back toward his study. "And speaking of learning, you do have to go back to school tomorrow."

I groaned.

"You've gotta be kidding me," I said. "Why can't I just stay home? If I'm going to be a Slayer, why do I even need high school?"

"I know how difficult it was to feel so betrayed," Martin said. "But there is a lot normal human life can teach you about being a better witch and a better Slayer. Trust me."

I nodded, not happy about it. But I knew from the tone of his voice that I wasn't going to talk him out of it.

To my surprise, he stopped several feet shy of his study and turned toward the wall.

"After school, of course, your real education will begin," he said, tapping on the wall to reveal a large mahogany door with more than a dozen keyholes. "This is a Witch's Door, and tomorrow, I will show you how it works and what treasures lie inside. But for now, get some rest. Tomorrow is a big day."

I stared, astonished, at the large door and then at Martin.

How many secrets were still locked away inside him? And inside this house?

I went up on my tiptoes and kissed his weathered cheek.

"I love you," I said. "Thank you for everything."

He smiled, and I could have sworn tears sparkled in his ancient eyes for just a moment before he pulled himself together again.

"I love you, too," he said.

And I knew that he did.

EPILOGUE

The next day, I shook my head as I fumbled with the stupid lock on my locker. I could trap a demon in a mirror, but I couldn't even open a simple lock.

It was too bad I couldn't use my magic out here in the open. It would have really come in handy about now.

I turned to search for Kai, but he was taking the rest of the week off to tie up some loose ends and follow one final lead about his dad. He promised he'd be back at school with me on Monday, but for now, I was on my own.

I had never felt so lonely.

Frustrated, I pushed away from the locker to head toward homeroom, but as I did, I backed into someone and my books fell and scattered across the floor.

I dropped down, hurrying to gather my things.

A girl knelt down on the floor with me, her blonde hair pulled back in a ponytail and her eyes sparkling.

"I'm so sorry. I'm such a clutz," she said, laughing. "Let's just say it's been a long couple of weeks."

I took a deep breath, trying my best to hold back tears.

I had expected the girls to all be out of school for a while, despite the fact that they were all safe and no one had been seriously injured. Martin refused to explain to me how their memories had been wiped, insisting those were secrets I didn't need to know about just yet, but I still hadn't expected to see her so soon.

If I'd known I was going to run into her, I would have prepared myself emotionally. Now, though, my heart overflowed.

"You're the new girl, right?" she asked with a smile that made me wonder if we really could be friends, after all. "I heard about you. What's your name again?"

"Lenora," I said. "But my friends call me Lenny."

"Well, Lenny, it's very nice to meet you," she said, holding her hand out to me. "My name is Peyton."

Chocolate Peanut butter Pretzel Cupcakes

Level: beginners

Yield: 14 cupcakes

INGREDIENTS

- Chocolate cupcakes
  - Peanut butter frosting
  - Pretzels or chocolate covered pretzels
  - Ganache (optional)

Chocolate cupcakes
Yield: 14 cupcakes

Ingredients:
  1 cup all-purpose flour
  1 cup sugar
  7 Tablespoons cocoa powder
  1 teaspoon baking soda
  1 teaspoon baking powder
  1 egg
  ½ cup sour cream (buttermilk or milk are good substitutions)
  ½ cup oil
  1 teaspoon vanilla extract
  ½ hot coffee (or hot water)

Procedure:
  1. In a mixing bowl combine flour, sugar, cocoa powder, baking soda and baking powder. Set aside.
  2. In a separate mixing bowl combine with a whisk egg, sour cream, oil and vanilla extract.
  3. Add the egg and sour cream mixture to the flour mixture and mix until well combined.
  4. Add hot coffee or water a little at a time and mix until batter is smooth.

5. Line cupcake pan with liners. Spoon the batter equally into 14 or a little more than half way.

6. Pre-heat the oven to 350F or 180C.

7. Bake them for 12-17 minutes until they feel spongy to the touch or when a tooth pick is inserted in the center comes out clean.

8. Remove from the oven and let them cool completely before decorating. If you decorate them when they are warm the frosting will melt.

Peanut Butter Frosting

Ingredients:
    1 stick butter, soft
    ½ cup peanut butter (if you are going to pipe the frosting use smooth peanut butter)
    1 ½ cups powdered sugar (confectioners' sugar)
    2 Tablespoons of milk (if needed)

Procedure:
    1. Place in a mixing bowl butter, peanut butter and half of the powdered sugar.

    2. Using the paddle attachment of the mixer, combine until smooth. Add remaining powdered sugar and milk if the frosting is to stiff.

Note: if you don't have a mixer you can use a spoon or spatula. Just make sure the butter is soft.

Ganache (optional)

Ingredients:

> 6 oz semi-sweet chocolate (bittersweet is fine)
>
> ½ cup heavy cream

Procedure:

1. Chop the chocolate into small pieces and place it in a bowl.

2. Heat the cream either in a small sauce pan or in the microwave and add it to the chocolate.

3. Still the mixture until all the chocolate is melted and the mixture is smooth. You can use a whip if necessary.

To finish the cupcakes

1. Place peanut butter frosting on pastry bag with a star tip and pipe on the cooled cupcakes. If you don't have a pastry bag or pastry tip you can use a spoon or knife and spoon some frosting on top of the cupcake.

2. Decorate the cupcakes with either chocolate covered pretzels, plain pretzels or crushed pretzels and drizzle some ganache on top.

THANK YOU to Pamela Batalla for creating this amazing Moondust Cupcake Recipe. For others like a S'Mores cupcake and Lemon Meringue, join my Facebook Group!

ABOUT THE AUTHOR

Sarra Cannon is the author of several series featuring young adult and college-aged characters, including the bestselling Shadow Demons Saga. Her novels often stem from her own experiences growing up in the small town of Hawkinsville, Georgia, where she learned that being popular always comes at a price and relationships are rarely as simple as they seem.

Sarra owns her own publishing company and has sold three-quarters of a million copies of her books. She currently lives in Charleston, South Carolina with her programmer husband, her adorable redheaded son, and her brand new baby girl.

Love Sarra's books? Join Sarra's Mailing List to be notified of new releases and giveaways!

Also, please come hang out with me in my Facebook Fan Group: Sarra Cannon's Coven. We have a lot of fun in there, and I often share exclusive short stories and teasers in the group. Join now.

Want more? Come join us LIVE three times a week on my YouTube channel.

Connect With Sarra Online:

www.sarracannon.com